A GABRIEL HUNT NOVEL

HUNT AT WORLD'S END

NICHOLAS KAUFMANN

A GABRIEL HUNT NOVEL

HUNT AT WORLD'S END

TITAN BOOKS

Hunt at World's End
Print edition ISBN: 9781781169926
E-book edition ISBN: 9781781169933

Published by Titan Books
A division of Titan Publishing Group Ltd
144 Southwark Street, London SE1 0UP

First edition: May 2014
12345678910

A CIP catalogue record for this title is available from the British Library.

Printed and bound in the United States.

www.huntforadventure.com

Did you enjoy this book?
We love to hear from our readers. Please email us at readerfeedback@
titanemail.com or write to us at Reader Feedback at the above address.

To receive advance information, news, competitions, and exclusive
offers online, please sign up for the Titan newsletter on our website
www.titanbooks.com

A GABRIEL HUNT NOVEL

HUNT
AT WORLD'S
END

1

GABRIEL HUNT HAD TAKEN A LOT OF PUNCHES TO THE face over the years. He'd come to think of it as an occupational hazard, dealing as he often did with criminals, pirates, gangsters, brawlers and all kinds of thugs who let their fists do the talking, and he usually gave as good as he got. But this time was different. This was the first time the guy throwing the punches was wearing a big, sharp silver ring in the shape of a horned stag's head.

The punch stunned him, knocked him back into one of the large elephant tusks flanking the fireplace of the Discoverers League lounge. The tusk wobbled on its base, and Gabriel, feeling wobbly himself, dropped to his knees. Blood trickled along his cheek where the stag's horns had cut him. He looked up at the slender blond man standing over him in a gray houndstooth blazer and gray slacks. He was wearing a crooked sneer. Glancing at his hand, he wiped a spot of blood off his ring.

"We can continue this as long as you wish, Mr. Hunt," he said. "I have nowhere else I need to be. But you see my friends back there? They don't have as much patience as I do."

Behind the blond man, three men clad all in black stood with guns in their hands. One revolver was trained on Wade Boland, the weekend bartender, where he stood behind the bar. The second was pointed at Clyde Harris, a retired cartographer in his seventies who came to the League every Saturday to partake of his two favorite pastimes, drinking and swapping tall tales. He sat on his usual barstool at the end of the counter and stared at the gun unblinking. Neither Wade nor Clyde looked particular frightened by this turn of events, though they kept their hands dutifully raised above their heads.

But the third revolver was leveled at Katherine Dunlap, and she was a different story. The willowy redhead sat trembling at the table she'd been sharing with Gabriel before the blond man and his cohorts had stormed in and started waving their guns around. Her fingernails dug into the plush arms of the red leather chair, and her pale green eyes were as wide as soup bowls. It was obvious she'd never had a gun pointed at her before. Gabriel had only met her that morning, on his flight back from Brazil to New York City. Seated next to her in first class, he'd passed the hours answering her questions about his just-completed expedition along the banks of the Amazon, and once they'd landed he'd invited her back to the Discoverers League for a drink. She clearly hadn't expected their date to end in violence. Of course, neither had he.

The blond man reached into the inside pocket of his blazer, pulled out a large, well-polished chrome handgun and leveled it at Gabriel. Gabriel eyed the gun unhappily. The three bouncer types he figured he could take even though they were armed. But this man was another matter. Compared to the other three he looked almost scrawny, but he punched like someone had taught him how, and he was holding his gun with a professional's grip.

"I don't have what you're looking for," Gabriel said, rubbing his jaw.

"I want you to think very carefully about what you do next, Mr. Hunt. I'd hate to have to tell my men to start shooting." The man gestured around the lounge at the bookshelves filled with antique volumes and the display cases of artifacts, many of them fragile, all of them irreplaceable. "These beautiful things might get damaged. Bloodstains, you know. So difficult to wash off."

"Gabriel," Katherine pleaded, her voice shaking.

The man smiled. "You see? Your friend has a good head on her shoulders. I'm sure she would like it to remain there."

Gabriel rose slowly to his feet.

"No more heroics, Mr. Hunt," the man cautioned. "And no more lies. I know you were in the Amazon until this morning, and I know you brought the Death's Head Key back with you. Just hand it over and we'll go quietly." He smiled slightly. "Its name notwithstanding, no one has to die over the thing."

"Why should I give it to you?" Gabriel asked.

The blond man cocked his head and knit his brow. "Why? Because I am the man with the gun, Mr. Hunt."

"Why do you *want* it?" Gabriel said. "It's not that valuable. It'll fetch maybe five, six grand on the black market, if you're lucky. It hardly seems worth your time."

The blond man stepped nearer. This close, Gabriel got a good look at the man's eyes and could see the brutality he concealed beneath his veneer of civility. The man opened his mouth to answer, then changed his mind and swung his Magnum, slamming the heavy butt into Gabriel's jaw. Gabriel's head snapped back. At least this time he managed to stay on his feet.

"The key," the blond man repeated.

Gabriel narrowed his eyes. He tasted blood and spat red-tinged saliva onto the carpet. "You better hope I never see you again."

The man cocked the Magnum. "You will never see *anyone* again, Mr. Hunt, if you don't hand over the key." And when Gabriel failed to do so: "For heaven's sake, Hunt, what difference does it make to you? What were you planning to do with it, stick it in one of these cases? Photograph it for *National Geographic*? Give it to the Metropolitan? What a colossal waste. You don't even know what the key unlocks."

"And you do?"

The blond man leveled the barrel of the Magnum at Gabriel's forehead and said, "Five."

"Tell me," Gabriel said. "Tell me what the key opens."

"Four."

"Gabriel, for God's sake," Clyde muttered from his barstool. "My ice is melting. Just give the man whatever he's looking for, and I'll buy you and the lady a round."

"Three."

The blond man swung the gun to point it at Katherine. Her hands shot up as though they might be able to deflect a bullet. "Two."

"*Gabriel!*"

"One—"

"All right," Gabriel said. "All right. Just... put that thing away."

The blond man took the gun off of Katherine and swung it to face Gabriel instead.

Gabriel unbuttoned his shirt. The Death's Head Key hung on a leather strap around his neck. He lifted it over his head. The blond man snatched the heavy bronze key with his free hand and held it up, eyeing it with satisfaction.

No one knew how old the Death's Head Key was. It had been given its name in 1581 when the explorer Vincenzo de Montoya found it on a trip through Asia and noticed its bow was shaped like a skull, with concavities where the eye sockets might have been and a diamond-shaped groove between them. No one, not even de Montoya, knew what it unlocked—but whatever it was, Gabriel could guess from the look of the thing that it was no simple door. Most keys had a single blade that fit into the keyway of a lock, but the Death's Head Key had three, one straight and the other two flanking it at forty-five degree angles. De Montoya had reportedly worn it around his neck as a good luck charm, but it hadn't kept up its end of the bargain. His luck ran out when he disappeared during an Amazon expedition a few years later, and the Death's Head Key had been lost with him.

Lost, until Gabriel found it, still dangling from the broken neck of de Montoya's skeleton at the bottom of a deep pit in the rain forest.

Now, watching the blond man stuff the Death's Head Key in his pocket, Gabriel couldn't help feeling it was about to become lost once again.

"Very thoughtful, Mr. Hunt," the blond man said.

"You've saved the custodians of this establishment quite a bit of mopping." He backed slowly toward the lounge door, keeping his gun leveled at Gabriel. "Let's go," he said, and the three thugs holstered their revolvers and exited before him. The blond man gave Gabriel a final nod and disappeared through the doorway.

When he heard the front door open, Gabriel followed at a run, passing Hank, the League's elderly doorman where he lay slumped unconscious on the floor.

In the street outside, a pair of doors slammed on a gunmetal gray Cadillac and it peeled off, tires squealing against the asphalt. Gabriel raced out into the street and ran half a block after them, but they shot through a red light and vanished in the distance.

Gabriel walked back to the League building and into the lounge, where Wade was already dialing the police from the phone behind the bar. "Button up, young man," he said, aiming a finger at Gabriel's chest. "There are women pres—oh, hello, yes, I'd like to report an incident."

There was only one woman present, and Gabriel lowered himself into the chair beside her, fuming. For weeks he'd meticulously traced de Montoya's path through the Amazon, sweating through the jungle heat and all the days of false starts and backtracking, and for what? So the artifact he'd worked so hard to recover could be stolen by some skinny blond thug with bad taste in jewelry?

He looked up and noticed Katherine was still trembling. "Are you okay?" he asked her.

She stood slowly and walked to the bar, grabbed the scotch glass out of Clyde's hand and downed it in a single gulp. Then she returned to the table where Gabriel sat. She put a hand on his arm.

"So," she said, and Gabriel could tell she was trying to keep her voice steady. "Does this happen every time you take a girl out for drinks?"

Gabriel touched the cut on his cheek and winced. "Not every time."

Katherine patted his arm. "Don't call me," she said. Then she turned and walked out. A moment later they all heard the front door shut.

"The police are on their way," Wade said, handing Clyde another scotch. Then he reached into his pocket, pulled out two twenty-dollar bills and handed them to Clyde as well. When he saw Gabriel watching the transaction, he said, "We had a bet."

Gabriel frowned. "What kind of bet?"

"I bet Clyde twenty bucks you never lose a fight."

"I could have told you otherwise," Gabriel said. "What's the other twenty for?"

"I also bet him that you always get the girl." Gabriel rubbed his sore jaw. "Sorry to disappoint," he said. "And sorry about..." He waved his hand in a circle, indicating the room's two overturned chairs, the painting that had been knocked askew, the shattered decanter still in fragments on the floor.

"How long have we known you, Gabriel?" Clyde asked, sipping his scotch. "We're used to it by now."

2

GABRIEL SAT ON THE TABLE IN AN EXAMINING ROOM at Lenox Hill Hospital with the noise from the emergency room seeping in through the closed door. He fidgeted, the stiff paper that covered the table crinkling under his weight. The police officer standing by the door fidgeted too. He tapped his pencil against his notepad like he was marking time.

"This is ridiculous," Gabriel said. "I told you I'm fine."

"It's standard procedure following an assault," the officer said. He was a few inches shorter than Gabriel, maybe five-nine, with curly, close-cropped hair and a thin mustache. The nametag above his badge read JACKSON. "Most people appreciate being taken to the hospital after they've been beaten, slashed and pistol-whipped."

Gabriel hated hospitals, especially the strong, antiseptic smell of ammonia that seemed to permeate every square inch of them. It was the same smell he remembered from the hospital in Gibraltar when he'd gone there in the early weeks of 2000 in the hopes of identifying his parents' remains. Ambrose and Cordelia Hunt had been on a millennium-themed speaking tour of the Mediterranean when their ship disappeared. No visuals, nothing on the radar, just gone. Three days later it had appeared again out of nowhere, not a living soul on board, only the dead bodies of three crew members. Soon after, more bodies began washing ashore—crewmen, passengers, more than three hundred in all—but a dozen or so never did. It had been a bad few weeks, looking at corpse after corpse and not knowing each time whether to hope he wouldn't recognize it or that he would. In any event, he never did. And nearly a decade later, the smell still got to him, still gave him an uncomfortable feeling of bad news and unfinished business.

"So this man," Officer Jackson said, looking at his notes. "About your height, six feet, blond hair, slim build, gray blazer and slacks. And you say he was in charge of the others, the three other men?"

"That's right. He gave the orders. The others didn't talk at all."

"Have you ever seen him before?"

Gabriel shook his head. "No. Never."

"Are you sure? It's easy to forget a face."

"I tend to remember the men who hit me."

"Have there been a lot?"

Gabriel rubbed his sore jaw. "One or two."

"Well, you say this one knew your name, knew where to find you and knew you were in possession of this... this *key* he took from you."

"That's right."

"So you think he's been following you, or what?"

"I've been out of the country for the past several weeks. I doubt he could have followed me where I was. But someone must have gotten word to him about what I brought back—one of the locals, possibly, or someone on the expedition."

Jackson nodded and scribbled in his notepad, though that answer put it well out of his jurisdiction. "There anybody you can think of who might have it in for you?"

Gabriel sighed. "How much time do you have?"

The officer flipped his book shut, capped his pen. "Not enough," he said. "You ever think of changing professions, Mr. Hunt? Maybe something a little safer, like firefighter or undercover narcotics officer?"

"I'd miss the flexible hours," Gabriel said.

The door opened then, and a woman in green scrubs stepped in. She had straight black hair tied back in a ponytail, deep brown eyes and smooth skin the color of caramel. She clutched a clipboard to her chest and nodded at Officer Jackson. "Can you give us some privacy?"

Jackson said, "All right. Mr. Hunt, we're going to put your assailant's description out there and try to get a lead on him." He didn't sound too optimistic. "If you think of anything that might help, call the precinct, okay?"

"Of course," Gabriel said.

Officer Jackson left, closing the door behind him. "I'm Dr. Barrow." The woman scanned the papers on her clipboard. "Gabriel Hunt, is it? Okay, Mr. Hunt, let's take a look at you. Would you mind taking off your shirt?"

Gabriel frowned. "Really, doc, I'm fine. This isn't necessary."

"That's what they all say. Then one day they collapse in a grocery store and it's our fault. So. Your shirt."

Gabriel unbuttoned his shirt, pulled it off and tossed it onto the empty chair by the door. "I got hit in the face, nowhere else," he said.

"You think that can't put stress on your neck, your windpipe, your heart?" Dr. Barrow took the stethoscope from around her neck, put the buds in her ears and placed the metal disk against his chest. "Breathe for me."

Gabriel breathed.

"Again." She moved to his other side and he felt the cold metal press against his back. "Once more."

He kept breathing and she kept shifting the stethoscope around. Then the metal went away and he felt her finger tracing a line along his shoulder blade. "This looks like a scar from a knife wound," she said.

"Yes, well, there's a reason for that," Gabriel said.

"And is this—" she probed a little lower "—from a bullet?"

"Grapeshot."

"And this?" Her finger pressed lightly at the base of his spine.

"Spear," Gabriel said.

"Good lord," Dr. Barrow said. "I'd say the cut on your cheek is the least of your worries."

"You should see the mark a saw-toothed Aztec dagger left on my thigh. It's a beauty."

"Maybe some other time," she said.

"Yeah," Gabriel sighed. "I'm getting a lot of that today."

WHEN GABRIEL LEFT THE HOSPITAL, HIS BROTHER Michael was waiting for him outside, pacing on the sidewalk, his straight, sandy hair blowing in the breeze. He pushed his round, wire-rimmed glasses up his nose. "Well, well, well. I guess I am my brother's keeper after all."

"You didn't have to pick me up," Gabriel said. He touched the bandage on his cheek. It protected the four stitches Dr. Barrow had given him. She'd told him he was lucky his jaw hadn't fractured. Then she'd recommended rest, aspirin for the soreness and, if possible, significantly fewer gun butts to the face.

"Come on," Michael said. He put a hand on Gabriel's back and led him to the shiny black town car waiting at the curb. He opened the door for Gabriel, then slid into the back seat next to him.

Up front, an older man with a salt and pepper mustache looked at Michael in the rearview mirror and asked, "Home?"

"Yes. Thanks, Stefan." The driver nodded and pulled out into traffic. "I hope you don't mind coming back with me," Michael said, turning to Gabriel. "It's just that I feel better about our security at the Foundation than what they've got at the Discoverers League. Those men might come back for you."

"They already have what they came for," Gabriel said. "I'm sure they're long gone by now. Back to whatever hole they crawled out of."

"Maybe you're right," Michael said, "but better safe than sorry." He looked out the window. "You know I really wish you'd stop all this and just come work with me at the Foundation."

"Doing what?" Gabriel asked. "Answering mail? Reading grant applications? I'd go stir crazy within a week."

"You'd get fewer guns pointed at you. Not the worst tradeoff, Gabriel."

"That's a matter of opinion," Gabriel said.

The car pulled up in front of the marble entryway of the Hunt Foundation's five-story brownstone on 55th Street and York Avenue, in the heart of Sutton Place. They got out, and as Stefan drove the car off, Michael fished his keys out of the pocket of his tweed jacket and opened the door. Inside, he pressed a code into an alarm panel on the wall, which beeped in response. Satisfied, he led the way up the stairs, past the offices on the first two floors of the building and up to his triplex apartment.

He turned on the lights, big hanging chandeliers that illuminated an enormous library lined with bookcase after bookcase. Beginning with the numerous volumes their parents had amassed, Michael had compiled the largest collection of obscure and ancient texts since the Library of Alexandria, a collection Gabriel himself had made use of many times. A red leather couch sat in the middle of the room, with a wrought iron, granite-topped coffee table in front of it and a long polished oak desk off to one side. The pages of a manuscript lay stacked on the table: the *Oedipodea* of Homer, translated by Sheba McCoy. *Good for her*, Gabriel thought, remembering how close they'd both come to getting themselves killed after discovering the lost epic in Greece. *Have to read it one of these days, find out how it ends.*

At the far end of the library, an enormous stuffed polar bear, rearing with its mouth open and its teeth bared, towered above a small breakfront bar. "Would you like a drink?" Michael asked, opening the breakfront and pulling out a bottle of Glenfiddich.

"Definitely."

Gabriel sat on the couch. Beside Sheba's manuscript,

there was an open cardboard box with the Hunt Foundation's address written on one of the flaps in black marker. He reached inside and dug through shredded paper until he felt something dry and brittle. He pulled the object out. It was a shrunken, mummified human hand. With six fingers.

"Gloves, gloves, gloves!" Michael yelled. He nodded anxiously toward the box of disposable latex gloves sitting on his desk. "You know better."

Gabriel dropped the hand back in the box. "Sorry."

Michael carried over a glass, handed it to him.

"None for you?" Gabriel said, sipping.

"In a moment." Michael went over to his desk and opened his laptop. "I just need to check on something." He clicked the mouse a few times, and then a cloud of disappointment darkened his features.

"What is it?"

Michael slumped in his chair and rubbed his face with both hands. "I was hoping I'd have an email from Joyce Wingard. We gave her a grant for a research trip to Borneo and she's been there since August. She was checking in with me every day, and then three days ago the emails stopped."

"How well do you know her? Maybe she just ran off with the grant money."

Michael stared at him. "You don't recognize the name? Joyce Wingard. Gabriel, she's Daniel Wingard's niece."

Daniel Wingard. There was a name he hadn't heard in years. Wingard had been a professor of archeology and cultural anthropology at the University of Maryland and a good friend of their parents. And Joyce Wingard... now it came back to him. The last time he'd seen Joyce he'd been fifteen, and she'd been, what, seven? Their parents had taken them to spend the weekend with the professor and his niece at Wingard's home on the shore of the Potomac. Gabriel remembered an impatient little girl with blonde pigtails. During dinner, she'd called him stupid and dumped a bowl of potato salad in his lap.

"Joyce Wingard," Gabriel said. "What the hell is that little girl doing in Borneo?"

"Working toward her Ph.D., Gabriel. She's thirty years old."

"I guess she would be, at that," he said. *Thirty years old and probably still a terror.* "Does she have any field experience?"

"She didn't need any. This was just supposed to be a research trip."

"What was she researching?"

Michael got up and walked to a bookcase. He scanned the spines, pulled a weathered tome off the shelf, and brought it back to the couch. He sat next to Gabriel and opened the book. The title page said ANATOLIAN RELIGION AND CULTURE.

"Have you heard of the Three Eyes of Teshub?" Michael asked.

"I've heard of Teshub. Storm god of the Hittites, right?"

Michael turned the pages until he found the photograph he was looking for: a stone carving of a bearded man with a conical headdress standing on an ox's back. Beneath the photo was the caption TESHUB IDOL, 15TH–13TH CENTURY B.C.E. "According to legend, Teshub gave the Hittites a powerful weapon called the Spearhead to protect them from their enemies. But the Spearhead was so powerful that Teshub had second thoughts. He came to believe that even his beloved

Hittites lacked the wisdom to use such a weapon responsibly, so he took it away from them and hid it until some unspecified future date when three armies would meet in battle to decide its fate." He flipped the page and handed the book to Gabriel.

On the next page was an illustration of three enormous jewels. "Looks like an ad for DeBeers," Gabriel said.

Michael shook his head. "Those are the Three Eyes of Teshub. Supposedly, they were three gemstones that together were the key to using the Spearhead—or possibly to locating it, or perhaps to retrieving it from where it was hidden, the stories varied."

"Don't they always," Gabriel said. He downed the rest of his scotch.

"Documents from the period say that when Teshub hid the Spearhead away, he called up three winds to blow the gemstones in three different directions, scattering them as far apart as possible, so that they would never be found. People have looked for them, of course. No one has found any evidence that the Three Eyes of Teshub actually existed."

"But Joyce…?"

"Joyce discovered incomplete rubbings from a pair of tablets she thought might shed some light on the legend. The original tablets are buried away in the archives of Borneo University. She applied to us for a grant to cover the cost of her trip." Michael returned the book to its spot on the shelf. "Her application might not have leapt to the top of the stack otherwise, but…" He went back to his desk, checked for new e-mail once more. Nothing. "But how could I say no to Daniel Wingard's niece? And it wasn't much money. I figured no harm could come of it, a trip to a university library." He dropped into his chair. "And now she's missing. I've tried calling her, I've called our man down there, I've asked people at the university if they've seen her—nothing. Who knows what sort of trouble she might have gotten herself into? I couldn't live with myself if I thought anything had happened to her because of me."

Gabriel set his glass down on the table, pushed the box containing the mummy's hand to one side. "If you're really worried about her, Michael, I can go down there and look around a bit. Shouldn't be too hard to find her."

Michael shook his head firmly. "No. Bad enough that she's missing, think how I'd feel putting you in danger as well."

"Putting me in danger? You're kidding, right?" Gabriel said. "I don't think a week's gone by since Joyce Wingard was in pigtails when I wasn't in danger. It's what I do."

"And you know I've never been comfortable with it," Michael said. "I certainly wouldn't want to be the cause of it."

"You wouldn't be the cause," Gabriel said. "Joyce Wingard would. Besides, I haven't been to Borneo in ages. About time for a trip back."

"You might not recognize it," Michael said in a quiet voice. "Half the rainforest's gone."

"All the more reason to go now, before they cut down the other half."

"Gabriel…"

"She's probably fine, Michael. I'll probably find her in the museum archives, elbow deep in notes and files, with her phone turned off and no idea how long it's been since she last e-mailed you."

"But what if you don't?" Michael said.

Gabriel thought of the headstrong, impish, pigtailed girl chasing him around her uncle's picnic table, squealing with laughter as she tried to catch him. He remembered her showing him her toys, how she took special pride in one in particular, a Barbie dressed in safari gear and an explorer's pith helmet. He remembered her playing tag in the woods with Michael, who'd been only a couple years older than her. Joyce had fallen, skinned her knee on a rock, and wouldn't let anyone pick her up and carry her back to the house. She'd insisted on walking, even with blood trickling down her leg, and shouting that she could do it herself, didn't need anyone's help.

But this time maybe she did.

"Then you'll be glad I went," Gabriel said. "How soon can you have the plane ready?"

3

IT WAS MONDAY AFTERNOON LOCAL TIME WHEN THE
Hunt Foundation's jet touched down at Sepinggan
International Airport in Balikpapan, on the southern
coast of Borneo. In the airport's waiting area, small
suitcase in hand, he scanned the crowd. Michael had
arranged for a man named Noboru to meet him here.
Formerly Japanese Intelligence, now employed by the
Hunt Foundation, he'd been Joyce's contact on the
tropical island. If anyone was in a position to turn up
any clues as to what had happened to her, it would
be Noboru—though he hadn't found any yet when
Michael had spoken to him from New York.

The waiting area was crowded with people
holding signs written in Indonesian and Malaysian
Bahasa, Kadazandusun, Iban, Bidayuh, Arabic and a
dozen other scripts. Despite the air conditioning, the
room smelled of sweat and spices. Small vendor huts
were set up along the walls, selling dumplings, pork

buns and bowls of noodles.

A hand fell on Gabriel's shoulder. "Mr. Hunt?"

He turned. A man of about fifty stood behind him. He had long, shaggy black hair, Asian features, a jawline spotted with dark stubble, and a face deeply wrinkled from the sun.

"Mr. Noboru?"

The man nodded and shook Gabriel's hand. "Your brother told me you were coming. Welcome to Borneo. I just wish your visit were under better circumstances. Here, let me get that for you." He took Gabriel's suitcase and led the way outside. The moment Gabriel passed through the sliding glass doors into the open air, an oppressive humidity pressed down on him like a heavy, moist blanket. He followed Noboru to the parking lot, where hundreds of cars gleamed in the sweltering sun. Noboru threw the suitcase into the back seat of a mud-spattered, topless jeep and climbed into the driver's seat.

Gabriel joined him up front. "Where are we headed?"

"Inland, toward Central Kalamitan," Noboru said. "Where I dropped Joyce when she first arrived. It's a long drive, but we ought to be there before nightfall, Mr. Hunt."

"Mr. Hunt was my father," he said. "And these days it's my brother. I just go by Gabriel."

Noboru nodded. "Make yourself comfortable." He started the engine, stepped on the gas, and the jeep lurched out of the parking lot with a great roar and a plume of black exhaust. Gabriel grabbed the roll bar as Noboru sped through a series of hairpin turns to get them onto the highway.

The farther they got from Balikpapan, the more

it felt like they were traveling back in time. The highway devolved into an unpaved dirt road and the tall apartment buildings of the city were replaced by wooden shacks surrounded by dense jungle. They passed a line of women walking alongside the road, dressed in the brightly dyed linens of the indigenous Dayaks and balancing water jugs and baskets of rice on their shoulders. A few minutes later, Gabriel saw another woman kneeling beside the road and hammering something into the ground. As they drove past, he saw it was a wooden post with the skull of a goat lashed to the top.

"What was that?" he asked.

Without slowing down, Noboru took both hands off the wheel to light a cigarette. "She's warding off evil spirits," he explained. He took a deep drag and gripped the wheel again. "The farther out you get from the cities, the more superstitious the people become. It's beautiful here, loveliest place on earth—when I came here after I retired from the service, I never considered going anyplace else. But you wouldn't believe how much people here cling to the old ways. They don't trust anything new. Or anyone. It's taken five years for them to start trusting me. Most of them think outsiders bring bad luck."

"Joyce was an outsider," Gabriel said. "Did anyone give her any trouble?"

"I don't know," Noboru said. "I only saw her the one time, when I picked her up at the airport and dropped her off at the guesthouse we're going to. It's strange. I was supposed to drive her to the hotel your brother arranged for her, but she said she'd made her own arrangements to stay in this local hostel. She said she wanted to be closer to the jungle."

"Why?" Gabriel asked. "She was here to study some materials at the university."

"I know—that's what was strange. I told her your brother had put me at her disposal, that I was supposed to take her wherever she needed to go, do whatever I could to help with her research, but after I dropped her off, she never called me. Not once. I guess she didn't need any help."

Gabriel thought back to the incident with the skinned knee. "Or thought she didn't," he said.

"Don't get me wrong, Mr… Gabriel. She was a nice girl, very friendly, easy to get along with. Reminded me a lot of my daughter, actually. She's in university in Singapore now—my daughter, I mean. I don't get to see her very often; it was nice to see a girl her age, with the same sort of personality…" He fell silent for a moment. "I was upset when your brother told me that Joyce was missing. I hope you'll be able to find her."

"Any idea what might have happened?"

Noboru weighed his words carefully before speaking. "As beautiful as it is here, the country has a dark side. People get kidnapped all the time by bandits and held for ransom, especially out in the jungle."

"As far as we know, there hasn't been any ransom demand," Gabriel said.

"That's not necessarily a good thing," Noboru said. "If they get someone they think no one will pay for, they kill them. Or worse, for women. It would be better if she'd broken her leg somewhere in the jungle—then at least she would die of starvation, or exposure. Much better than what the bandits would do to her."

Gabriel knew Noboru was right about the country's bandits—but he couldn't bring himself to hope she was lost in the jungle. Borneo was the third largest island in the world. He wouldn't even know where to begin looking. "Michael told me he called the university to see if she showed up, and they said they never saw her. Did she tell you if she was planning to go anywhere else? Any particular part of the island?"

"No, we only talked in general terms. She was very interested in the island's history. She had a lot of questions."

Gabriel could picture her putting Noboru through the third degree, squeezing every bit of information out of him that a budding cultural anthropologist would find interesting.

"The only thing she asked that was about a specific place," Noboru continued, "was right before I dropped her off, she wanted to know if anyone had ever found an ancient cemetery in the jungle. I asked her if she was thinking of the Bukit Raya nature preserve—they have a cemetery nearby that's fairly old. But she said no, she meant in the jungle itself. I told her unless the orangutans had started burying their dead, there weren't any." Noboru shook his head. "She didn't look happy with the answer, but what could I say? There aren't any cemeteries in the jungle. Not that I know of, anyway."

Gabriel reached into his pocket and unfolded a sheet of paper Michael had given him, a grainy color blow-up of Joyce Wingard's passport photo. She'd come a long way from the seven-year-old girl Gabriel had met in Maryland. The blonde pigtails were gone, replaced with shoulder-length hair she wore pulled back in a tight ponytail. She still had the same wide smile, but a little more jaded, a little more cynical. Her eyes were crystal blue, her chin and cheeks slender. She'd become a beautiful woman.

What have you gotten yourself into? he thought.

* * *

THE SUN WAS A HAZY RED BALL SINKING TOWARD the horizon when Noboru turned off the road onto a narrow dirt lane. Thick, leafy branches crowded the path on either side, pressing inward as if the foliage were trying to reclaim the road. Birds shrieked and cried, and unseen animals shook the branches above them. Half a mile in, the road widened and they found themselves entering a small village. Wooden houses with rusty corrugated metal roofs were arranged roughly in a circle around an open central area marked by a single, small pagoda. The villagers stopped what they were doing and stared at the jeep as it passed. A man filling a water bucket from a hand pump stiffened when he saw them, then spat and touched his forehead twice, once above each eye. It reminded Gabriel of someone protecting himself with the sign of the cross.

Noboru brought the jeep to a halt in front a ramshackle two-story building. Most of the paint had peeled off long ago, leaving small patches of coppery red stuck to the flat concrete walls. Gabriel reached into the jeep's back seat and pulled two items out of his suitcase. The first was a holster, which he strapped around his waist. The second was a Colt .45 Peacemaker, fully loaded. He slipped the revolver into the holster.

As they stepped out of the vehicle, the front door burst open and an old woman ran out shouting and waving a dirt-smeared shovel. Gabriel tensed, but Noboru stepped in front of him.

The old woman stopped running but continued gesturing with the shovel and shouting.

Gabriel had picked up many languages in his journeys around the world, but Bidayuh wasn't one of them. It was close enough to Indonesian Bahasa that he was able to make out a word or two, but that was all. He leaned over to Noboru. "What's she saying?"

"Her name is Merpati," he said. "This is her guesthouse. She wants us to leave. She says your presence here as an outsider is bad luck and will bring evil spirits."

Gabriel frowned. It didn't make sense. If Joyce had made arrangements to stay here, if it was a guesthouse used by visitors to the island, why would this Merpati react so negatively to their arrival? This wasn't a matter of bad luck or evil spirits, Gabriel decided—something had happened, something that had changed this old woman's mind about letting foreigners through her door.

Gabriel held up the passport photo. "Ask her when she saw Joyce last." Noboru spoke, and Merpati lowered the shovel, answering in a quick and anxious voice. She passed her hand over her face, from forehead to chin. Though Gabriel didn't recognize the words, the fear in her expression was unmistakable.

Noboru nodded, then turned to Gabriel. "You're going to love this. She says ghosts came in the night and took her."

Upon hearing the word 'ghost' in English, Merpati nodded and passed her hand over her face again.

"Ghosts without faces," Noboru went on. "She says they took Joyce into the jungle. This was a few nights ago."

The old woman pointed toward the far end of the village, where the houses thinned and the jungle rose in a thick green wall beyond them.

"Does she know where these… these ghosts would have taken her?" Gabriel said.

Noboru asked, and in response Merpati said something curt, biting her words off fiercely.

"She says," Noboru translated, "the girl is dead now, trapped among the ghosts in the land of the dead. If you go after her, you will be trapped too. Become a ghost yourself."

Gabriel put the picture of Joyce away in his jacket pocket. "I'll take my chances. Will she at least let us see Joyce's room?"

Noboru asked and Merpati chewed her lip. When she finally replied, Noboru said, "For fifty Ringgit she'll let us up—that's about ten dollars. It's a lot here."

"Hell," Gabriel said, digging in his pocket, "I can do better than that." He pulled out a hundred dollar bill, unfolded it and held it out to the old woman. She eyed him warily, then snatched it out of his hand. She stared at it briefly, crumpled it in her palm and hid it away in a pocket in her torn shift. She muttered something out of the side of her mouth.

"She says we can't stay long. It's a full moon tonight, and apparently that's when the spirits are at their strongest. She doesn't want you hanging around and bringing the ghosts back."

"No, we definitely wouldn't want that. Listen," Gabriel said, "you should go. It's getting dark, and you've got a long drive back. I can take it from here."

"You kidding?" Noboru said. "I like my job. Nice hours, good benefits. How long do you think your brother would let me keep it if I left you in the middle of the jungle by yourself?"

"I'm not a Ph.D. student on her own in Borneo for the first time," Gabriel said. "I can handle myself."

"Against ghosts?" Noboru asked with a grin. "Two's better than one against ghosts."

"Against practically anything," Gabriel acknowledged. "All right. Just stay close and don't wander off. One missing person is enough."

"You don't have to worry about me. Didn't I just tell you I'm not going anywhere?"

"You armed?"

Noboru lifted his pants leg to reveal a long knife strapped to his calf.

Gabriel nodded. "I guess that counts."

Merpati led them to the door of the guesthouse. Gabriel noticed a short wooden post had been hammered into the ground by the door, and atop it was a goat's skull, like the one they'd seen on the road. Merpati's attempt to protect the house from the evil spirits that took Joyce, presumably. The old woman took them inside, past a kitchen that smelled like spicy stew and steamed pork, and up a wooden staircase to the second floor. The warped steps creaked loudly under their weight. Barring the culprits actually having been ghosts, which Gabriel was inclined to doubt, there was no way they could have sneaked up these stairs to take Joyce without being heard. Which suggested that whoever had taken her must have found another way in.

On the second floor, a long corridor ran the length of the building, five doors lined up along one side. Each door they passed was open, each room empty but for a neatly made bed with a short dresser beside it. Nothing on any of the beds, nothing on any of the dressers.

"The other boarders must have left after Joyce was taken," Noboru said.

"Can you blame them?" Gabriel said.

Merpati stopped in front of the last door, which was the only one that was closed. She pulled a ring of long, heavy keys out of her pocket, unlocked the door and pushed it open for them. Gabriel and Noboru walked past her into the room. The old woman hung back, reluctant to set foot inside. She shouted something at Noboru. Gabriel didn't need him to translate that time. Merpati wanted them to finish quickly and go.

Looking at the state of Joyce's room, Gabriel could understand Merpati's reaction. Everything was in a shambles. The dresser's drawers had been dumped, the bed stripped, the mattress slashed. Clothing, books and personal items were scattered everywhere—Gabriel nudged a hairbrush with his foot. On the far wall, the window was shattered, the broken glass taped over with a bedsheet. He crossed to the window, pulled the sheet aside, and stuck his head through, taking care to avoid the jagged edges. This must have been how they'd gotten in. It was probably the way they'd taken her out, too, maybe with a ladder or a rope, after tossing the room and its contents.

"What do you think they were looking for?" Noboru said.

"I don't know," Gabriel said. "But it's clear they weren't here just for Joyce. You don't have to slash open the mattress if you just want her."

Noboru squatted to sort through the books on the floor. Gabriel did the same to search the items that had been dumped from the drawers. It was mostly clothing, but under a crumpled pair of pants he found Joyce's passport and beside it an old-style analog wristwatch, similar to the one Gabriel himself wore. Its face was cracked, the hands stopped at 3:10. "Well, now we know what time it happened," Gabriel said, showing Noboru the broken watch. Then he lifted the passport. "And we can rule out one possibility. If it had been bandits, they would never have left a U.S. passport behind."

"No," Noboru said. "You can get more on the black market for one of those than you can for most hostages."

"So if not bandits, who?"

"You ruling out the 'faceless ghosts' theory?" Noboru said, then before Gabriel could answer he raised one hand. "Hang on. This looks promising." He pulled a composition notebook out of the pile. "It's her expedition journal." He began flipping through the pages. "Let's see, arrived in Borneo, met Mr. Noboru at the airport. Oh look, she says I seemed 'interesting'." He kept going, scanning lines of cribbed handwriting quickly. "Looks like she spent most of her time exploring the fringes of the jungle. And look at that." He tapped the bottom of one page with his forefinger. "She writes here that she thinks she's being followed."

"Let me see."

Noboru passed Gabriel the journal. The entry in question was dated one week back.

Probably imagining it, but… I think someone was following me at the Malawi River today. Not someone I'd ever seen before. But everywhere I went in the marketplace, this guy was there. Kept turning away and pretending to look at pottery or whatever when I caught him staring in my direction. Didn't look Bornean, which made it kind of hard for him to disappear in the crowd. One of those bandits N warned about? But he didn't look like that at all. Merpati's opinion when I told her about it was just that "it's dangerous for single women to wander around without a man." Well there's a newsflash. But I'm damned if I'm going to hide in my room.

The Malawi River? What was she doing there? What was she doing *anywhere* but the university archives?

Gabriel flipped ahead, scanning the pages for any more mentions of being followed, but didn't find anything until the final entry. It was dated Wednesday, the same day Michael had gotten his last e-mail from her. Joyce's handwriting was noticeably different, more uneven and hurried: *Another guy following me today at the marketplace in Tarakan. Definitely not the same man, though same type—white guy, maybe five-eight, five-nine, and too damn interested in everything else around him anytime I turned to look at him. This one had curly hair and a beard. White shirt, brown pants. He followed me for a good ten minutes, before I finally lost him in the crowd. Damn it. Could this have something to do with SOA?*

Gabriel looked up from the page. "SOA. Any idea what that might be?"

"School of the Arts? Society of Actuaries? State of Alert?"

Gabriel walked back to where Merpati stood wringing her hands in the doorway and showed her the page in the book. He pointed to the letters 'SOA.' She shook her head and started talking loudly, gesturing back toward the stairs.

"She wants us out," Noboru said, unnecessarily.

Taking Joyce's passport and journal, Gabriel followed Noboru out of the room. Merpati escorted them downstairs and all the way back outside, as if she didn't trust them to leave on their own. She loudly locked the door behind them.

Night had settled over the village, barely cooling the sticky, humid air. A full moon glowed over the treetops, its round face covered briefly by a passing cloud. All around them, light seeped out of the windows of the village houses, bright and steady from those with generators, dim and flickering from the ones that used oil lamps. As Gabriel walked to the jeep, a man across the way finished hammering a post topped with a goat skull into the ground in front of his house, then spat, touched his forehead twice and went inside. The door slammed, and Gabriel heard a heavy bolt slide into place. He glanced around and noticed goat skulls had been posted in front of every house he could see. Not a great place to be a goat.

Gabriel reached into the jeep's back seat, unzipped his suitcase and slid Joyce's passport and journal inside.

"So now what?" Noboru asked, coming up behind him.

"They took Joyce into the jungle," Gabriel replied. "So that's where we're going."

"It'd be safer to wait until morning."

Gabriel reached into the suitcase again and pulled out a flashlight. "For us. Not for Joyce."

Noboru puffed out his cheeks and blew air. Then he nodded.

Gabriel reached into the suitcase again. "That knife of yours looks handy, but…" He pulled out a second revolver and passed it to Noboru. "Maybe you'd better carry one of these, too."

4

NOBORU HAD HIS OWN FLASHLIGHT IN THE GLOVE compartment of the jeep, and together they entered the jungle at the edge of the village, twin beams of light bouncing in front of them. Moonlight filtered through the trees and glistened on the thick leaves all around. They moved forward, the blanket of undergrowth on the jungle floor clinging to their feet as they went. Where the foliage was too thickly knotted to pass, Noboru cut away the vines and creepers with his knife, swinging the keen blade machete-style, the revolver jammed in his belt.

The high whine of insects filled the night air, and the rustling of leaves; the beam of Gabriel's flashlight revealed tree frogs and geckos clinging to the trunks and branches in their path. Mouse deer whose heads didn't reach higher than the tops of Gabriel's boots fled before them through the underbrush. Clicking beetles scurried away into tiny holes amid the twisted roots.

"Tell me if you see any tarantulas," Noboru muttered.

"Why?" Gabriel asked.

"So I can get the hell away from them. I hate those damn things. Always have."

Gabriel tilted his flashlight down to shine it along the ground. No tarantulas in sight. "Remind me sometime to tell you what happened to me in Chile."

"Not if it involves a tarantula."

"Not *a* tarantula," Gabriel said. "A whole nest of them. Chilean flame tarantulas."

Noboru shivered. "I never, ever want to hear that story." He stopped suddenly and bent down, shining his flashlight at some thin branches poking out from a tree at knee level. "Hold on. Look at this."

Gabriel came over, adding his light to Noboru's. "What have you got?"

The branches were snapped, their bent tips all pointing in the same direction. Something heavy had passed—or been dragged—through them.

"It's too big to be from squirrels, too high for mouse deer," Noboru said.

"Monkeys?"

"Too low. This was done by people."

Gabriel straightened and shone his flashlight in the direction the snapped branches pointed. The jungle seemed to stretch on forever, tree after tree, vine after vine, forming an impenetrable net of vegetation. After five days, the signs remaining of Joyce's passage through the jungle would be few; that was more than enough time for rain and wildlife activity to erase the trail. But there should still be some signs. It just meant they'd have to be that much more vigilant to spot them.

Gabriel started walking again, following the direction of the broken branches. Several yards farther on, his flashlight beam located something at the mossy base of a thick tree.

"There." He hurried to the tree. More branches were snapped and bent like before, but this time there was also a piece of torn fabric stuck on the sharp end of a twig. Gabriel brushed aside a long-horned beetle that had made the cloth its bed and plucked it off the branch. It was filthy, covered in mud, but under the dirt he saw a tight weave and a blue and white pattern. It felt like cotton. "It's clothing," he said. "Piece of a shirt or a dress, maybe."

"Well, I can tell you we're definitely not the first people to pass through here," Noboru said, his voice low. He pointed his flashlight at the ground ahead of them. Past the tree, the vegetation had been trampled flat.

They followed the trail deeper into the jungle. They passed whole tree trunks covered with swarms of ants and termites. Stick insects clung to nearby leaves and waited patiently for their chance to snatch up prey. Above their heads, an enormous tropical centipede with red mandibles and spiky legs sprouting like daggers from its segmented body crawled along a thick branch. Gabriel saw Noboru look away, disgusted, as they passed beneath it. It wasn't just tarantulas, then. Gabriel was beginning to think the jungle was no place for him.

Ahead, Gabriel could just make out a dim orange light flickering between the leaves, growing brighter as they moved along the trail. They proceeded cautiously. The path, he saw, came to an end at the edge of a wide clearing. Just shy of the edge, while they were still hidden by a screen of trees, Gabriel dropped to the jungle floor and pulled Noboru with him. They switched off their flashlights, hid behind a low barricade of fallen branches and took in the sight before them.

Six tall wooden posts jutted from the ground around the perimeter of the clearing, forming a rough hexagon. Each post was topped with a shallow stone bowl of burning oil. These were the source of the flickering orange light they'd seen through the trees.

At the far end of the clearing was a crude but fairly large hut constructed of wood and what appeared to be scavenged pieces of metal. There were no windows in the one wall of the hut they could see, only a single door, which was currently closed.

And at the center of the clearing, directly in front of the hut, were two massive, bent tree trunks bowed in a double arch over a ten-foot-wide circular stone that rested on the ground like a giant manhole cover. He'd seen a stone cover like that once before, in the rain forest of Guatemala; there it had protected the waters of a sacred well. He wondered what this one was protecting.

But that wasn't the main question on his mind, because of what he saw hanging above the stone, suspended from the bent tree trunks by a pair of heavy metal chains: a wooden cage.

And it looked like there was a figure lying across the bottom of the cage.

Just as he was about to stand up, movement by the side of the hut caught Gabriel's eye. A man emerged from the shadows. As he walked out into the light from the bowls of flame, Gabriel saw he was wearing a white robe and carrying a tall metal pole. A curved sword hung from his belt. He had the robe's hood pulled over his head and over his face he wore what looked like a clay mask in the shape of a skull.

One of Merpati's faceless ghosts. Gabriel and Noboru exchanged glances.

The man walked under the cage and struck the end of the pole against the wooden slats. The figure inside the cage didn't move. Gabriel couldn't help wondering if it was Joyce—and if so, whether she was alive or dead, merely asleep or too sick or weak to move. Stopping at the edge of the circular stone slab on the ground, the man slid one end of the pole into a socket beside the slab and turned it until it audibly locked in place.

Noboru clutched suddenly at Gabriel's arm. Gabriel turned—and saw a fist-sized tarantula creeping across the branches directly in front of Noboru's face. Noboru's eyes widened and even in the dim light Gabriel could see the blood drain from his face. His jaw dropped open.

Gabriel clamped a hand over Noboru's mouth before he could make a sound.

The tarantula continued picking its way along the branch and disappeared into the underbrush. Gabriel glared at Noboru, who nodded, and then he let go. Noboru swallowed hard and took a few deep breaths.

When Gabriel looked up again, the man in the robe and the skull mask was standing under the cage with his back to them. He'd picked up a long stick from the ground and was poking it up between the wooden slats at the person inside the cage, who stirred and moaned quietly. *Whoever it was, she or he was still alive.* Gabriel signaled to Noboru to stay put, then pointed to himself and the man in the clearing. Noboru nodded to show he understood, which was more than Gabriel could say for himself. He feared his gestures may have conveyed the impression that he had more of a plan than he actually had.

Gabriel rose quietly to his feet. The skull-faced man still had his back to them. Gabriel crept toward him, one hand on the butt of his Colt in case the man turned too soon. Luckily he was too intent on waking the person in the cage to notice Gabriel coming up behind him. Gabriel wrapped one arm around the man's neck. He meant to put him in a sleeper hold but the man spun quickly, slipped out of Gabriel's grasp, and went for his sword. Moving fast, Gabriel threw a punch, connecting with the mask, which shattered. The face below was pale, with bushy eyebrows and a scraggly beard—definitely not Bornean. It looked like it could be the man Joyce had described in her last journal entry. He opened his mouth to shout for help, but Gabriel dropped him with a second punch to the face.

Gabriel dragged the man's body into the trees where it wouldn't be seen, then returned to the cage. Up close, he saw that the chains it was hanging from were attached to gears mounted at the top of the arched tree trunks. He peered up through the mossy slats along the bottom of the cage. Lying inside was a woman in a torn blue-and-white shirt and dirt-smeared khaki shorts. She'd been gagged with a cloth tied around the back of her head, and had ropes tying her hands behind her back and binding her ankles together. She was facing away from him.

"Joyce?" he whispered.

She started. She struggled to sit up, then realized the voice was coming from below her and turned to lie on her stomach. Even with her face smeared with dirt, her hair tangled and matted, Gabriel recognized her and his heart leaped with relief.

Joyce squinted down at him, studying his face, then her eyes spread wide. "Ayiel Unn?" she said around the gag.

That took him by surprise. He hadn't expected her to recognize him after so many years. He certainly wouldn't have recognized her without the passport photo.

"Yes," Gabriel whispered. He glanced at the hut. No one seemed to have heard them. Not yet, anyway. "Noboru's here, too. We're going to get you out of here."

"Obo-oo eeyah?" *Noboru's here?*

Gabriel looked around for some way to lower the cage. "Are you okay? Will you be able to walk?"

She nodded. "Uh-ee. Ay'll ee ere oon." *Hurry. They'll be here soon.*

A wooden door was set in the side of the cage, locked with a heavy metal padlock. Maybe he could bash it open, or find a way to pick it, but first he had to figure out how the hell to get up there. He'd have to climb one of the trees and make his way down the chains…

Voices sounded from the hut, a sudden clamor that sounded like the "Hear, hear!" at the end of a convocation. He looked toward the door and saw a crack of light spill out as it slowly swung open. "Hang tight," he whispered. "I'll come back for you."

Joyce's eyes widened again and she shook her head vehemently, tried to say something, but Gabriel put a finger to his lips and ran for the shadows at the edge of the jungle. He slid behind a tree as a procession of robed men emerged from the hut. He counted twelve in total, then quickly amended it to thirteen when a man who was clearly their leader or high priest or something appeared behind them. Unlike the others, he didn't wear a skull mask or a white robe. His face was bare and he wore a red tunic with curling gold designs sewn into the fabric. A rectangular headdress of the same colors perched atop his head and in one hand he held a staff tipped with a bronze blade that gleamed in the reflected light of the flames.

The men gathered in a semicircle around the stone on the ground and the metal pole planted upright beside it. They started chanting in a language Gabriel didn't recognize. Not Bidayuh, which he simply didn't speak—this was a language he had never heard before.

He tried to catch a glimpse of Noboru, but from where he was now it was too dark to see the spot where they'd been hidden.

The chanting grew louder, more insistent. One of the masked men stepped up to the metal pole and pulled it toward him like a lever. Gabriel heard a grinding of gears underground and the circular stone began to slide sideways, revealing a hole beneath. No, it wasn't a well this time. The bright orange flames of a roaring fire licked up out of the darkness.

Gabriel's eyes went from the fiery pit to the cage hanging on chains directly above it. Not good. He drew his Colt.

The men in the skull masks looked up at the cage. Gabriel noticed a change in their chanting. He may not have spoken the language, but he knew the sound of a climax approaching when he heard it.

He needed to stop this before either the cage or its contents got dropped into the flaming pit. But how? There were too many men for him to take on at once. What he needed was a diversion, something to distract them before they could start lowering the cage…

A gunshot rang out. Gabriel saw a muzzle flash in the darkness and the skull-faced man who'd pulled the lever cried out, clutching his stomach where a red stain had blossomed on the white robe. He fell—but as he fell, he caught the lever in the crook of his arm, yanking it the rest of the way.

The cage began slowly lowering, chain link by chain link, toward the fire pit.

Gabriel's heart slammed into his throat. Not good. Not good at all.

The men in skull masks were shouting angrily, drawing their swords, pointing toward the area where the gunshot had come from. Where Noboru was hiding.

And from inside the cage came the sounds of Joyce shouting through her gag and kicking at the wall of the cage as it dropped closer to the flames.

5

THE HIGH PRIEST SHOUTED ORDERS AND THE MEN IN
the skull masks ran toward Noboru's hiding place.
Gabriel gripped his Colt and charged out of the woods.
He was tempted to try to take down some of the men
from behind, even up the sides a bit, but instead he
headed straight for the lever. He had to stop Joyce's
cage from going into the fire before he could deal with
this would-be army of the dead.

As he ran, the cage continued its descent toward
the flames. On either side of the bowed tree trunks,
massive stone counterweights slowly lifted into view,
giant tablets carved with hideous, leering faces.

The high priest turned suddenly—Gabriel figured
the man must have heard his racing footsteps or
spotted him out of the corner of his eye. He frantically
barked out a new order and pointed. Four of the
masked men broke away from the group heading for
Noboru and moved to intercept Gabriel, shouting and

swinging their swords above their heads.

Gabriel pulled the trigger of his Colt on the run, knocking the closest of the charging swordsmen off his feet. He smashed mask-first into the ground.

Shots rang out from Noboru's hiding place as well, as the remaining men reached the edge of the jungle. Two of them fell before the others swarmed into the trees.

Gabriel kept racing for the lever. There were three men still coming at him, and the fastest of them caught up with him when he was two yards short of his goal. The man swung his sword in a wide arc, and Gabriel desperately ducked below it. He swung out with his free hand, burying it deep in the man's belly. But the next swordsman was right behind him, leaping over his fallen comrade's body as the man collapsed.

Gabriel fell back, the descending blade narrowly missing him. He continued retreating as the swordsman aggressively bulled forward. The nearest of the posts planted around the perimeter of the clearing was just steps behind him—he could feel the heat from the flames on his back—and he ducked behind it as the blade swept toward his head again. The sword buried itself deep in the wood of the post. As the swordsman tried to yank his blade free, Gabriel threw himself against the post, striking it as hard as he could with his shoulder. The bowl at the top wobbled, then toppled over, showering the man with burning oil. He screamed as his robe burst into flames. He relinquished his sword and staggered blindly away, leaving a flaming trail behind him.

The last of the four swordsmen immediately took his place. He slashed at Gabriel, who leapt to one side, trying to circle around toward the lever again. He heard the gears turning and the links of chain slowly paying out; he could hear Joyce's muffled screams from within the cage. There was no more time. He swung his Colt up and put a bullet through the forehead of the man's mask, snatched the dead man's sword out of his hand as he fell, and ran all-out for the lever.

As Gabriel neared it, he saw Noboru in the distance, being dragged from his hiding place. The older man was empty-handed; one of the robed men had seized his gun. But Gabriel knew that didn't mean he was unarmed. Demonstrating that he'd kept up his combat training even in retirement, Noboru twisted suddenly out of their grasp and in the same fluid motion pulled the long knife from his ankle sheath. He drove it into one masked man's chest, grabbing the man's sword with his other hand as he drew his own blade out. When another of the men rushed him, Noboru blocked the man's thrust with the sword and slashed across his throat with the knife. A spray of blood stained the man's mask a dark red. Seeing two of their fellows fall in quick succession, the others hesitated, took a step back. Noboru pressed his momentary advantage, letting loose with a martial shout and rushing them with both blades swinging mercilessly.

Gabriel, meanwhile, slid to a stop beside the lever, holstered his Colt, and—with Joyce's cage less than a half dozen feet above the fire and sinking lower—reached out to take hold of the metal pole. But before he could close his fist around it, a sword sliced toward his arm. He jumped back, turning to face the second swordsman, who'd apparently recovered from the punch to the midsection that had taken him down earlier. Gabriel swung his sword around with both hands on the hilt, but his opponent parried and came back with another thrust. Gabriel knocked the blade aside, then stretched out a leg and kicked the lever back into its upright position. Behind him, the chains halted their descent and the massive counterweights shuddered to a stop. Gabriel swung his sword at his adversary's neck, but the man met his blade and, kicking out with one sandal-clad foot, shoved the lever forward again. The gears groaned back into motion and the cage started to lower once more.

They chopped at each other, the clash of metal ringing in Gabriel's ears as he struggled to push the swordsman back. He maneuvered around until the lever was at his back and as his opponent's blade swept through the air beneath his chin, Gabriel fell backwards against the lever, shoving it to the 'off' position. Then he let go of his sword, spun, and grabbed the lever in both hands. He twisted it mightily and yanked it out of its socket. Swinging with all his strength, Gabriel smashed it into the side of the masked swordsman's head, like a home run hitter aiming for the fences. The pole may not have been a regulation Louisville Slugger, but it packed plenty of heat. The man staggered back, back, teetered on the edge of the flaming pit—and was gone, his passage marked only by a momentary rush of flame and ash from below.

Gabriel looked to the side. The wooden cage was no longer overhead—it was right next to him, and Gabriel could look directly through the side of it into Joyce's terrified eyes. She was on her knees, and her forehead was glistening with sweat. For that matter, so was his. Her eyes went wide suddenly as she stared past him. *"Ook ow!"*

Something slammed into him from behind, knocking him to the ground. He rolled onto his back and saw the high priest standing above him, staff in hand, his eyes flashing with rage. He spun the staff so that the bronze blade at its end was pointing at Gabriel's chest. Gabriel rolled, and the blade sank into the ground behind him. He grabbed the sword he'd dropped and scrambled to his feet.

The high priest pulled the blade free and charged him, holding the staff like a bayonet. Gabriel parried with the sword, knocking the staff aside, but the man kept coming, striking at him with the side of the staff and trying to bring the blade around for another thrust. Gabriel knocked it aside each time, stepping backwards to buy some room, until he felt the intense heat of the fire pit at his back. He knew he must be close to the edge—he could feel the heat melting through the heels of his boots.

The high priest thrust his staff at him again, and this time Gabriel swung his sword down from above, driving the bronze blade to the ground. As it jabbed into the dirt, Gabriel lunged forward, grabbed hold of the shaft, and pulled it toward him, wedging one foot against the base to serve as a fulcrum. The high priest made the mistake of clinging to the staff stubbornly— as Gabriel had hoped he would—and went up in the air as Gabriel dragged the staff toward him. By the time the high priest realized he should have let go, it was too late: Gabriel had pivoted, and the man was dangling by his hands above the pit.

"Stop!"

The voice came from twenty yards away, the opposite end of the clearing, and Gabriel looked up to see Noboru with a curved sword at his throat, each of his arms held in the tight grip of one of the skull-face acolytes.

"I'm sorry, Gabriel," he called. "I tried—"

"Silence." The man holding the sword to his throat shouted to Gabriel: "If you let him drop, your friend dies. Both of your friends, and then you." His accent was thick—but Gabriel had no difficulty understanding what he was saying.

What Gabriel was having difficulty doing was keeping the staff from sinking in his arms. The high priest wasn't a small man, and that damn headdress must have weighed fifteen pounds by itself. He tried not to let the strain show in his voice. "And if I don't?" Gabriel called. "If I let him go? Free, I mean. Let him go free, not let him go into the pit."

There was some angry muttering among the robed men, but the one who had spoken silenced them with a gesture. "If you let him go, we let you go."

"You first," Gabriel said. The man didn't lower his sword. "You'd better make up your mind fast. I don't know how much longer he can hold on."

The high priest's hands were clutching and re-clutching the staff sweatily. He cried out in the unrecognizable tongue they'd spoken in earlier and instantly the men released Noboru's arms. The one holding the sword reluctantly lowered his blade.

"Get over here," Gabriel shouted and Noboru darted over, covering the distance between them in seconds. He took hold of the shaft of the spear just above where Gabriel was holding it, and together they dragged it over till the high priest was over solid ground again. He let go and collapsed in a heap. His robes were singed and smoking.

"Now, get out of here," Gabriel shouted, pulling his Colt again. He aimed it at the high priest, who scuttled backwards on his hands and heels. "Go." He trained his sights on one after another of the men till they'd all faded into the darkness of the jungle. The sound of their footsteps receded as they fled.

"I feel terrible," Noboru said, "I should never have let them—"

"Feel terrible later," Gabriel said. "Right now I need you to keep an eye out for them, make sure they don't come back."

He raised one foot carefully and smashed his heel against one of the cage's upright slats—but instead of the wood splintering as he'd hoped, the cage as a whole swung further out over the pit. Inside, Joyce moaned.

"Careful," Noboru said, glancing over. "That chain's going to give."

He was right: as the cage swung, the heavy chain shifted ominously in the narrow track that held it, and one end of the cage dipped precariously toward the flames.

There was no more time. Gabriel holstered his gun and jumped for the nearest link of the chain. It burned his palms as he caught it but he held on and pulled himself up until he was standing on the uneven upper surface of the cage. It was slanting like a barn roof and hot as hell. He could only imagine what it felt like for Joyce inside. Straining to keep his balance, he made his way to the far side—the side the cage's door was on— and lowered himself hand-over-hand till he was level with the padlock. Letting go with one hand, he pulled his Colt and struck the padlock with its butt. The lock didn't budge.

"Come on," he muttered and tried again.

The cage shook and dropped some more. He could feel the fire beneath him. Through the bars, Joyce stared at him. "Oo ih," she said, sounding exasperated. "*Oo* ih!"

What?

Oh. Shoot it.

Gabriel said, "Move back," needlessly—Joyce had already sensibly crawled to the farthest corner she could reach—and took aim. The hasp of the lock flew apart as a bullet plowed through it. He yanked the remnants loose and tossed them aside, then unlatched the door and stuck an arm inside. Joyce tumbled into it and he hoisted her up onto his shoulder. The cage shifted again, dipping lower.

"Gabriel!" Noboru shouted. "The chain!"

Gabriel didn't look to see what the chain was doing. It wouldn't be anything good. Instead, he jumped, pushing off against the cage. They were in midair for a moment, and then there was solid ground beneath them, and they were rolling across it, Joyce beside him.

He looked back and saw the cage swinging wildly toward the trees. Above it, the chains groaned and, as the cage started swinging back, jumped their tracks. The giant wooden box came crashing down, smashing into the edge of the pit. It broke into pieces, the largest of which plunged directly into the fire; but the next largest kept going, spinning through the air toward them, its jagged edges aimed directly at Gabriel's face. He fell forward, taking Joyce to the ground beneath him, and the deadly slab of wood passed overhead, just inches away. It caromed off the trunk of a tree seconds later.

Gabriel looked down at Joyce. She was grimacing through the gag. He tugged the filthy strip of cloth out of her mouth, and she took in a huge breath gratefully.

Gabriel rolled off her, got to his feet and helped her stand with one hand under her arm. Noboru had retrieved his knife and used it now to carefully cut through the ropes at her hands and feet. She rubbed her wrists, grimacing in pain.

"We'd better get out of here," Noboru said. "They could come back at any time."

But Joyce wasn't listening. She turned to Gabriel. "How could you? How could you leave me in that cage and walk away? I could have died!"

"You still might," Gabriel said. "Now get moving."

6

THEY MADE THEIR WAY OUT OF THE JUNGLE WARILY,
but didn't encounter any of the robed men. Gabriel led
the way back into the center of the village and banged
on the door of the guesthouse until a window lit up
on the top floor. Merpati leaned her wizened face out
to see who it was, frowning until she spied Joyce. She
exclaimed then and disappeared back into her room.
There was the muffled sound of footsteps racing down
the stairs, and then the front door burst open.

Merpati rushed out and clamped her skinny arms
around Joyce, whispering nonstop in Bidayuh. There
were tears in her eyes, Gabriel saw. She seemed
reluctant to release her, and even when she did, she
held onto one of Joyce's wrists as she led them inside.
Joyce made a remark to her in the same language and a
smile appeared on Merpati's face. She said something
and tugged Joyce into the kitchen.

"She's going to cook something for us," Joyce

said. She eyed the small pile of vegetables and spices Merpati was assembling on the counter with a look only five days in a cage can inspire. "She says we should clean up first."

Joyce led the way upstairs, followed by Noboru; Gabriel brought up the rear. He saw Noboru wince once as they climbed, when he brushed the banister with his right arm. The sleeve of Noboru's shirt had been sliced open and looking closer Gabriel saw a still-wet streak of blood below.

"You're hurt."

"Not too bad. You should see the other guy."

"I did," Gabriel said. They reached the landing and turned toward Joyce's room. "Did they teach you how to fight like that in Intelligence?"

"Surprised that a man my age can still take care of himself?"

"If you couldn't," Gabriel said, "you'd never have made it to your age."

Joyce opened the door to her room. "Damn it," she said, eyeing the mess.

"Worse than you remembered?" Gabriel said.

Noboru crossed to the bed and sat down to inspect the wound on his arm. "Do you have any bandages?"

Joyce shook her head. She picked up a white tank top from the floor and handed it to him. "Here, use this." Noboru nodded his thanks and tied it around his arm.

"Who were those people in the jungle?" Gabriel asked her.

She squatted in the middle of the room and started pulling up one corner of the carpet. "They're a cult, quite an old one. The Cult of Ulikummis," she explained. "They're mostly Georgian, Russian and

Ukrainian by birth, but they're spread out all over the world. Their presence here is actually a good sign. It means I'm close."

"There's nothing good about those people," Noboru said.

"Ulikummis," Gabriel said. "I've heard that name before."

"One of the gods of the Hittite Empire," Joyce said. "Ulikummis was the enemy of the storm god Teshub."

Joyce folded the rug over, clearing a portion of the wooden floor beneath it. She started digging her fingernails into the floorboards. Noboru shot Gabriel a curious look.

"When the Hittite Empire collapsed in 1160 B.C.," Joyce continued, "most of their people stayed put in what is now Turkey, but some of the religious orders fled north into what became Russia. Over the years, they gave the appearance of assimilating into the local culture, but they kept the old religion alive in secret cults. Most of these cults are gone now—all but one, really. The Cult of Ulikummis was pretty ruthless and basically they slaughtered all the others. Thousands of people were killed, many of them in ritual sacrifices like the one they were planning for me. The only reason I'm still alive is that they were waiting for the full moon before performing the sacrifice."

"Why did they come after you in the first place?" Gabriel said.

Joyce blew a lock of blonde hair out of her eyes. "They thought I had something that properly belongs to them."

"Do you?" Gabriel said.

"If they didn't find it." She located the floorboard she'd been searching for and pried it free. She reached into the hole in the floor. "Ah." Joyce straightened, pulling something wrapped in an oilcloth out of the hole. She stood, put the object down on top of the dresser and gently unwrapped it.

In the folds of the oilcloth was a flat, circular object with intricate designs cut into its golden surface. It wasn't a single solid piece but rather seemed to be made up of several concentric rings set one inside the next, with a protruding bit in the center, like a handle or a knob. The sharp, angular designs along the outer rim were cuneiform symbols, Gabriel realized, and had been cut all the way through, like stencil letters—light shone through them from underneath. The bit in the center was shaped like a starburst, each of its three arms a different length and each tipped with a small jewel. Two of the gemstones were green, one red.

"This," she said, lifting it carefully out of its swaddling, "was known as the Star of Arnuwanda." The gold glittered in the lamplight.

SOA. The acronym in Joyce's journal entry.

"Arnu—?" Noboru said.

"Arnuwanda the Second. He was king of the Hittites around 1320 B.C., and supposedly the last custodian of the Three Eyes of Teshub. Shortly before he died, he had this device constructed to his specifications. Then he had the man who made it for him executed. He didn't trust anyone to know how it worked, for fear that they might use it to find the Three Eyes."

Noboru looked over at Gabriel. "Do you know what she's talking about?"

"Some," Gabriel said. "The Three Eyes of Teshub are these legendary jewels that were supposed to unlock an ancient hidden weapon of the Hittites. But the jewels themselves were also hidden, or lost, or something."

"Cast to the three winds," Joyce said, "by Teshub himself. But the Star is supposed to show their resting place. Teshub spoke to Arnuwanda in a dream and told him how to build it."

"Thoughtful of him," Gabriel said. "Where did you find the thing?"

"Not me. My uncle. He dug it up in Turkey last month. He didn't trust the locals he'd hired, he thought they might try to steal it for the gold, so he shipped it to me for safekeeping."

"And you brought it to Borneo," Gabriel said. "Does he know?"

"Not exactly."

"How not exactly?"

"He thinks I'm still in the States. I asked Michael not to tell him about the grant."

"And Michael agreed?" Gabriel asked.

She shrugged. "I told him I didn't want to worry Uncle Daniel, that he'd be anxious for no reason. Remember, Michael just thought I was going to be studying in a library."

"Yeah," Gabriel said. "You sure fooled everyone."

"Are you going to tell me you've never told a lie when you've been on the trail of something big?" she said. She returned to the oilcloth and pulled out a second item, a folded piece of paper. She kicked aside a pile of clothing to clear a space on the floor, then opened the paper and spread it out. It was a copy of an ancient map of the eastern hemisphere with penciled-in grid lines crisscrossing over the crude drawings of continents and landmasses, dividing the map into little squares. Cuneiform symbols similar to the ones on the Star appeared in various of the squares.

"This is an enlargement of Arnuwanda's map,"

Joyce continued. "The cult has one too. It's easy enough to get, you can copy it out of any book on ancient Anatolian history. Without the Star it's nothing. But *with* the Star... here I'll show you. Hold your flashlight above the Star and shine it down." Gabriel pulled the flashlight from his belt and switched it on. He positioned the beam to shine through the Star so that its shadow fell on the map.

Gabriel smiled. "The symbols."

"Exactly," Joyce said. The beam passed through the cuneiform symbols around the perimeter of the Star and projected them onto the map. "It's Nesili, the language of the ancient Hittites. Now check this out." She gripped the starburst shape at the center of the device and turned it. It clicked along a hidden track and as it did the outer perimeter rotated in the opposite direction. She kept turning it, apparently trying to align the symbols from the Star with those on the map, but the ones on the map were printed in a different order—they didn't match.

"How confident are you," Gabriel said, "that it's the real Star?"

"Oh, it's real," Joyce said. "This is just Arnuwanda being a sneaky bastard." She kept turning the starburst slowly, one click at a time. "Obviously it's a puzzle of some kind, and for the longest time I had no idea what the key could be. But I had a lot of time to think in that cage."

Gabriel kept his eyes on the map, trying to find a pattern to the symbols.

"The legend says that when Teshub scattered the Three Eyes around the world, he gave each for protection to a different one of the three natural elements," Joyce continued. "Earth, water and... well, no one's sure what the third one is. In the earliest translations of the legend, they couldn't decipher the difference between earth and whatever the third element is, so they called it 'loose earth,' but that was just a way of saying 'We don't know what this symbol means.' Unfortunately the original tablet the legend was carved on was destroyed centuries ago, and ever since we've only had those faulty translations to work from."

"You think the three elements are the key to making this thing work?" Gabriel asked.

"I do," Joyce said. She pointed to one of the Nesili symbols. "This is the one that means 'earth'—ordinary earth, like dirt or soil." She turned the starburst until the symbol was directly opposite her on the rim, then held the Star so the projected image lined up perfectly with an identical symbol on the map. The beam from Gabriel's flashlight passed through one of the tiny green jewels and hit the map with a virescent pinpoint.

Right in the center of Borneo.

Joyce said in a hushed voice, "Arnuwanda made several trips to Borneo. I've been convinced for years that one of the Eyes of Teshub had to be here. This just confirms it." She dug through the piles on the floor. While Gabriel held the Star and flashlight steady, she turned up a pencil, a scrap of paper, a protractor and a compass from the pile by the bed. "If I can just figure out these coordinates…" Squatting next to the map, she quickly jotted down notes, muttering to herself and estimating measurements.

A knock at the door made her spring up. She grabbed the map and the Star and rapidly covered them both with the oilcloth. Gabriel approached the door with one hand on the grip of his Colt. He turned the knob and pulled the door open.

Merpati stood in the doorway. She held a tray with a big plate of steaming dumplings on it.

Joyce ran over and took the tray from her. "My god, food." She grabbed a dumpling and jammed it into her mouth. Her eyelids fluttered.

Gabriel nodded his thanks to Merpati and closed the door after she had left. He turned to Joyce, who was shoving another dumpling into her mouth. "I take it the cult didn't bother feeding you."

She shook her head, chewing. "Rainwater and roots," she said around a mouthful. She swallowed and added, "They didn't want me to die before the sacrifice, but they didn't go out of their way to keep me fat and happy either."

Gabriel picked up a dumpling and bit into it. Warm, salty liquid flowed onto his tongue, flavored by the scraps of pork and scallion nestled inside the dough. Noboru came over and helped himself. It had been a while since they eaten, too.

The Star of Arnuwanda lay untouched under the oilcloth until the plate had been emptied. Gabriel wiped his fingers on the sides of his pants and picked it up, turned it this way and that under the light. "It's quite a find," he said, finally. "And your figuring out how to use it—it's impressive, Joyce."

She walked over to him, a slight swagger to her step. "You don't know how I used to dream about hearing those words come out of your mouth. When I was fifteen and sixteen and hearing about the things you were doing. When I was twenty or twenty-five, for that matter. The great Gabriel Hunt, impressed."

"Well, I am. Once we've gotten it and you both home, I'll want your help identifying the three locations—"

"My *help*?" She snatched the Star out of his hands. "At home? What are you talking about?"

"I think it'll be safe for us to sleep here tonight," Gabriel said, "though we should probably sleep in shifts, in case our faceless ghosts make another attempt." He looked over at Noboru, who nodded. "Then tomorrow we'll drive you to the airport, you can take the Foundation's jet back to the States…"

Joyce was shaking her head. "Who the hell do you think you are? You think you can walk in here and take this away from me?"

"We're not taking it away from you, we're sending it back with you—"

"I don't mean the Star, goddamn it! I mean the find!"

"The find nearly got you killed tonight," Gabriel said.

"And? How many times have *you* nearly gotten killed? How would you feel if when it happened some big hero swept in and carried you to 'safety,' i.e. the sidelines, while other people finished what you started?"

"Any time someone wants to save my life," Gabriel said, "that's fine with me."

"Sure," Joyce said. "But you wouldn't fly home afterwards and leave the rest of the expedition to someone else."

No, Gabriel said, to himself. But to her he said, "I promised Michael I'd get you home safely."

"Don't you think I should have a say in this? Jesus. You're worse than they are." She began wrapping the Star up again. "You want to put me in a cage, too. At least the cult respected me enough to try to kill me."

Noboru stepped forward, put one hand on Gabriel's arm and one on Joyce's. "If I may—"

"*What?*" Joyce snapped.

"I think she's right," Noboru said.

"Oh," Joyce said, as Gabriel snapped, *"What?"*

"If this cult operates internationally, she won't necessarily be safer in the U.S. than here. As long as they think she has this thing, they'll keep coming after her. And if we send it back with her, they'll be right. Meanwhile, if that map's correct, what everyone's looking for is somewhere around here. If we're going to have to face them somewhere, better to do it where we can put an end to it."

"Thank you," Joyce said, with a tone of satisfaction. "I knew there was a reason I liked you."

"All that business about liking your job," Gabriel muttered, "and not wanting to make Michael angry...?"

Noboru shrugged. "He won't like it any more if they kill her back in New York."

Gabriel nodded. Noboru was right, of course. And so, for that matter, was Joyce. If someone had ever tried to take something like this out of his hands, he'd never have stood for it. But—

"It'll be dangerous," Gabriel said. "You might get killed. I can't promise I'll be able to keep you alive the next time."

"—and airplanes can crash, and peanuts can give you anaphylactic shock," Joyce said. "Life's a thing of risks. You know that better than anyone."

"You're so right," Gabriel said. "Next time we're facing a dozen men with swords and a bowl of peanuts, you can deal with the swordsmen, I'll handle the peanuts."

They stared at each other in tense, unblinking confrontation till a grin broke out on Joyce's face. "I'm picturing you throwing yourself on a bowl of peanuts," she said, "like a soldier on a grenade."

"Well, we really wouldn't want you to go into anaphylactic shock," Gabriel said.

"I wouldn't," Joyce said. "That was just an example. I'm not allergic to…"

But Gabriel had already turned away. "You want the first shift or the second?" he asked Noboru.

"Either's fine with me," Noboru said. "But first I'd be grateful if someone could tell me just what this ancient treasure is that everyone's getting so excited over."

"You mean the Three Eyes…?" Gabriel said.

"No," Noboru said. "I mean whatever it is that the Three Eyes unlock."

"The Spearhead," Joyce said.

"It's a weapon," Gabriel said.

Joyce shook her head. "It's much more than that. Hold on a sec, I want to show you something." She went over to the corner of the room where they'd piled her books earlier, rummaged through them and pulled one out. She flipped through the pages and said, "When Teshub gave the Spearhead to the Hittites, the first thing they were supposed to have done with it was turn it on their enemies, the Kaska. In 2005, the Kaskan city of Sargonia was excavated in the northern hill country between Hatti and the Black Sea." She handed Gabriel the book, open to a photograph of the excavated village. In it, Gabriel saw a stone structure, its pillars and walls black and cracked, the rest of it in ruins. "That was a temple," Joyce went on. "The stone was charred and baked all the way through by some sort of extreme, concentrated blast of heat. And you see that at the bottom?"

There was a reflective pool surrounding the base of the temple. "What, the water?"

"That's not water," she said. "It's glass."

He looked up from the photograph.

"Whatever destroyed Sargonia was strong enough, hot enough, to turn the sand around the base of that temple into glass."

Gabriel looked at the photograph again, studying the reflective surface. On closer inspection, he saw what might be faint fissures or cracks—something you wouldn't see in water.

"Of course, we don't know what did this," he said. "We don't know that it was the Spearhead."

"Of course," Joyce said. "But we know something did. And how many things in the ancient world could?"

"Lightning?" Noboru said, looking at the photo over Gabriel's shoulder.

"You're on the right track," Joyce said. "A bolt of lightning might fuse the sand in a limited area, right where it struck. But not an area that large. A thousand bolts of lightning, though, directed simultaneously at a single target…"

"The wrath of the storm god," Gabriel said.

"Precisely," Joyce said. "Teshub was a storm god the way Thor or Zeus were storm gods. He wasn't the god of rain or wind or hail, he was the god of thunder and lightning. And what is lightning but raw, unbridled electricity? A sufficiently strong blast… it could do to Sargonia what you saw in the photo. If it had the power of a small nuclear reactor."

Noboru whistled softly. "Sounds like a weapon to me."

"Sure," Joyce said, "if you use it to attack a city. But what if you used it to *power* a city? I think the Spearhead is a source of power—not military power, not necessarily, but electrical power. Some sort of natural generator. And according to the descriptions in Hittite literature, it required no fuel to operate, gave off no byproducts—just pure, clean energy." Her eyes lit up as she spoke about it. "Can you imagine the good that kind of technology could do for the world? Think of it. Cheap, efficient energy. No pollution, no radiation. You could use it to power entire nations. It could power water purification plants, hydrobotanical gardens. It could wipe out the need for oil, coal, gas, nuclear energy." She touched Gabriel's hand. "That's the potential of this discovery. It could change the world."

Gabriel studied her face. She was sincere. All traces of the mischievous child he remembered were gone, but there remained a childlike quality, a belief in the potential for a discovery like this to improve the world rather than destroy it.

He handed the book to Noboru. "It's a weapon," he said.

7

"GET SOME SLEEP," GABRIEL SAID. "I'LL TAKE FIRST watch." They'd moved Joyce into a room whose mattress and window were intact and had dragged another mattress into the hallway outside the door. Noboru was lying on the mattress, his shoes beside him, his knife in its sheath within easy reach. Gabriel sat across the hall with his back to the wall and his Colt in his lap.

"You think they're going to come back tonight?" Noboru said. He fished a small, square pillbox out of his pants pocket, opened it, popped a pill in his mouth and snapped his head back to swallow it. When he saw Gabriel watching him with a raised eyebrow, he said, "To help me sleep," and put the pillbox back in his pocket. He rubbed his chest with a grimace and then lay back on the mattress.

"I don't know," Gabriel said. "But I don't like them knowing where we are."

Gabriel should have been tired, but his nerves were still in tight coils after the fight with the cult. He sat in the dark, facing the door, listening for any sudden noises. Despite the reassurances he had given Joyce, he knew it was a bad idea to stay at the guesthouse tonight. But they didn't have any better alternative. Joyce needed food and rest after her ordeal and Noboru did, too; in any event, it was too late to make the long drive back to Balikpapan safely. But even one night was a risk he would have preferred not to take. The guesthouse was the first place the cult would look for Joyce again, and for the Star of Arnuwanda. So Gabriel waited, and listened. Through a narrow window at the far end of the hall he watched the stars grow brighter, then begin to dim as dawn approached. Even with the sun still hours away, the room grew warmer. He peeled off his shirt and used it to wipe the sweat off his face and chest.

Still nothing. No sign of the cult, just Noboru's gentle snores. Gabriel thought about waking him to let him take second watch, but he decided to let Noboru sleep.

When the stars disappeared from the window altogether and the sky faded from gray to blue, the door to Joyce's room suddenly swung open.

Gabriel grabbed his Colt, leaped to his feet.

Joyce grinned at him from the doorway. Somewhere during the night she'd used the pitcher and basin in the room to wash herself clean of the mud and grime of the jungle and had donned a fresh set of clothes. Gabriel was once again struck by what a beautiful woman she had become. She opened the door wider and leaned against the jamb. Noboru woke and turned to face her, rubbing sleep out of the corners of his eyes.

"Rise and shine," Joyce said. "We've got a big day ahead of us. I spent the past hour narrowing down the coordinates and I think I know where the first Eye should be. It's not far from here, maybe an hour's drive."

Gabriel nodded. "All right. Pack up your things and bring them down to the jeep. We'll meet you there."

"Way ahead of you," Joyce said. She slung a heavy knapsack over one shoulder and stepped out into the hallway. "See you downstairs." She headed for the stairway, then stopped and smirked at him over her shoulder. "Oh, and you might want to put on a shirt. Not that it isn't a pretty sight, but... the sun can be pretty fierce around here. Wouldn't want you to burn."

NOBORU DROVE THE JEEP OUT OF THE VILLAGE AND back onto the same unpaved road they'd taken from Balikpapan yesterday, continuing away from the city toward Central Kalamitan. In the passenger seat, Joyce looked over the notes she'd scribbled in her book. Periodically, she would consult her compass and either nod or give a new direction to Noboru: a bit farther, take the next right. Gabriel sat in the back seat, crammed in beside their suitcases, and wondered what, if anything, they would find. If the map and the Star were authentic, at the very least they could discover a gemstone whose value as an artifact would be enormous. Or maybe, if Joyce was right, they would find the first key to a revolutionary source of energy that could change the world. Either way, his interest was piqued. More than piqued.

The only problem, as he saw it, was Joyce herself. Could he trust her? She'd already lied to her uncle, lied to Michael, and nearly gotten herself killed. She was stubborn and foolhardy, rushing headlong into dangers she didn't understand. True, he'd often been accused of the same thing himself, but he'd demonstrated he could handle it. Joyce, on the other hand…

Maybe he was just being overprotective. But that didn't sit any better with him, because it forced him to think about *why* he was being so protective. Was it because she was Daniel Wingard's niece? Because he'd promised Michael he'd bring her home safely? Or was it something else?

Like the charge he'd felt when she'd looked him up and down in the hallway.

There'd been no shortage of women in Gabriel's life over the years. But there was undeniably something special about this one…

Pull yourself together, he thought. He couldn't let himself become distracted, not with the Cult of Ulikummis still out there. Not only were they still desperate to get their hands on the Star of Arnuwanda, they had also been humiliated in defeat, and that made them doubly dangerous. That the cult hadn't returned to the guesthouse last night meant nothing, except the likelihood that they were regrouping. If he let himself get sidetracked, if he lost focus, they could all wind up hanging over a fire pit.

"Stop here!" Joyce cried suddenly.

Noboru hit the brakes, bringing the jeep to a halt on the side of the road, and cut the engine.

"This is the spot." Joyce hopped out of the jeep and gestured toward the trees. "It should be about five hundred yards in."

Gabriel followed her out, then reached back into the jeep and took a machete from the back seat.

Noboru glanced at the morning sun and loosened his collar. "If it's that far, you'd better start walking. It's only going to get hotter out."

"You're not coming?" Gabriel said.

"Someone's got to stay with the jeep and keep an eye out for trouble." He patted the glove compartment. "If I see anyone coming, especially anyone wearing a skull mask, I'll send up a flare. You should be able to see it through the trees."

Gabriel led the way into the forest. The vegetation seemed more tightly packed here. He made judicious use of the machete, cutting away vines and branches to clear a trail. Behind him, Joyce kept an eye on her notebook and compass, shouting directions at him as if he were a shady New York City cab driver looking to jack up the fare.

"No, wait, to the left," she said. "We're getting all turned around."

"You just said right."

"Yeah, left. See if you can get those vines out of the way so we can keep going."

He sighed and started chopping again. "This better be one hell of a gemstone," he muttered.

The jungle in daytime was just as active as night, only with different kinds of wildlife. Instead of the buzzing of nocturnal insects, the air was filled with the sound of fluttering wings and screeching birdcalls. Proboscis monkeys and long-tailed macaques jumped from branch to branch in the canopy above, barely visible blurs of white, gray and tan hair. The terrain was hillier here too, slowing their progress and forcing them to exert more energy in the rising heat.

Gabriel glanced back. Joyce was breathing hard and fanning herself with her notebook. Her face and neck were glistening. His own body was already soaked in sweat, and the intense humidity didn't seem like it was going to let up anytime soon.

"Do you want to rest?" he asked.

Joyce shook her head, catching her breath. "No, I'm fine. We should keep going." She undid the top few buttons of her thin cotton blouse. Gabriel quickly turned away to chop at the vines again.

Stay focused.

"It shouldn't be much farther now," she said. "Maybe another fifty yards."

Gabriel hacked some more branches out of their way. "Any idea what we should be looking for? Did the Hittites say how the Eyes were hidden?"

"The legends say this Eye was 'buried in the earth's embrace, where only the dead shall see its beauty.' Scholars think this means the gemstone is hidden in a cemetery." Gabriel remembered Noboru's comment on their way out from the airport, that Joyce had been asking about a cemetery in the jungle. He also remembered Noboru saying there wasn't any in Borneo. But Borneo was a big place, most of it covered with jungle. With the right map…

They came out of the densely packed trees into a small clearing, roughly forty yards across. On the far side, the ground rose up in a steep slope before the thick foliage resumed. Gabriel sheathed the machete in his belt. Joyce pushed her sunglasses up to the top of her head.

"This isn't right," she said, her eyes darting over the layer of twigs and leaves covering the grass. She checked the compass against her notes. "This is the spot. The first Eye of Teshub is supposed to be here."

"Well, it doesn't *look* like a cemetery," Gabriel said.

She shook the compass, as if that would somehow change its reading. She flipped through the pages of her notebook. "It should be here."

"First lesson of field work," Gabriel said. "Don't rely on maps to stay accurate for more than, oh, a thousand years." He squatted, scanning the clearing. "Even assuming you read the Star right, any number of things could have changed."

"For instance, a cemetery could get buried, right?" Joyce said. "We're probably standing right on top of it."

Gabriel shook his head and ran a hand through the grass. "Maybe," he said, "but didn't Hittite death rituals mostly involve cremation? As I recall, only high priests and kings were preserved and buried—and they got huge stone tombs built for them. If something that size had ever been here, there would still be some sign of it. But there's nothing." He stood.

"No." Joyce shook her head. "It's here, I know it is. It has to be."

Gabriel walked over to her. "Look, I know you were excited about your first find, but—"

Joyce grabbed the handle of the machete and pulled it out of his belt so fast he didn't have time to stop her. She started marching toward the slope at the far end of the clearing. "I'm going to keep looking," she called back to him. "Come or don't come, it's up to you."

He sprinted up behind her. "Joyce… don't let yourself be blinded by what you *want* to find. For every legend that points to something real, there are dozens that are just stories. You have to prepare yourself for the fact that sometimes what you're looking for just isn't there. Believe me, it's happened to me plenty of times."

She ignored him and continued storming up the slope. Nearly at the top she lost her footing amid the twigs and roots littering the hillside. She slipped suddenly, cried out, and slid back down toward the clearing.

"Joyce!" Gabriel ran to her. She had tumbled to the

base of the hill. When he got to her, her cheek was smeared with dirt, but thankfully she looked okay otherwise. He held his hands out. She glared at him, then cursed under her breath, took his hands and let him help her back to her feet.

"I'm *fine*," she snapped, yanking her hands away. She bent to pick up the machete she'd dropped. Then she froze and stared at the grass on the side of the hill. "Gabriel," she whispered. "Come here. Look at this."

He bent down next to her. "What is it?"

"There," she said. She pointed at a patch of grass that had been torn up by her fall. She'd struck a stone with the machete, dislodging it, and where it had been there was now a narrow hole. The sun reflected off of something inside the depression. She pushed the tip of the machete into the hole. It hit something flat, smooth and hard. Gabriel recognized the sound it made right away: the *tink* of metal on metal.

"Something's buried under there," Gabriel said.

"The first Eye was given to the earth," Joyce murmured.

They looked at each other, then back at the hill. Joyce started scraping the dirt away with the edge of the machete while Gabriel dug with his fingers, pulling out divots of soil and tossing them over his shoulder. It was slow work, but after twenty minutes they'd cleared away enough earth to reveal a stretch of dark metal with a long seam in it. A few minutes later, they uncovered the rusty bulk of a hinge.

"It's a door," Gabriel said. "There must be a whole structure under here."

They attacked the hill again, digging faster now in their excitement. Joyce plunged and scraped with the machete like a coal miner working a pickaxe, and

Gabriel dug until his fingers cramped. Another half hour passed without his even noticing it, and though his back and shoulders ached and he was tired and drenched in sweat, thoughts of what lay beyond the mysterious metal door kept him going. Joyce didn't waver either, didn't even take a break. Finally, they'd cleared away a rough rectangle of earth, exposing the metal door that lay beneath. The seam around it was caked with dirt, as were the ornate carvings that decorated the door. There was no knob or handle visible, but there was a lock.

Gabriel knelt to inspect it. He picked the dirt away and saw that the keyway was shaped almost like an upward-pointing arrow, with not one but three slots. Above the lock was a rough etching of a skull with a diamond between its eye sockets. Gabriel recognized it right away. The muscles in his back tightened.

It was the same design that had been on the Death's Head Key.

Vincenzo de Montoya had found the key somewhere in Asia—but no one knew exactly where. Even de Montoya's own journals were vague on the specifics. Now Gabriel had the answer: Borneo. De Montoya had taken the key with him upon leaving the island and died in the Amazon with it still on a strap around his neck. Five hundred years later, Gabriel had found it, only to lose it again almost immediately.

No, scratch that. He hadn't *lost* it. It had been taken from him at gunpoint. Stolen by someone who claimed to know what the key unlocked.

"Gabriel Hunt, I presume?" a reedy voice called from behind them.

Gabriel whirled around. A man stood at the treeline where Gabriel and Joyce had entered the clearing. He was not tall, maybe five-foot-five, and dressed in khaki shorts and a beige short-sleeved shirt. A Tilley hat the same color as his shirt rested atop his head, throwing a band of shade across his eyes. He looked to be in his late fifties or early sixties. Behind him stood four men in jungle camouflage, their guns drawn.

"And this must be the enchanting Joyce Wingard," the man continued. He tipped his hat. "Allow me to introduce myself. My name is Edgar Grissom, and I owe you my thanks. You have saved me a great deal of time and effort."

Gabriel scanned the treetops. Why hadn't Noboru sent off a flare to warn them?

The answer came a moment later when Noboru came into view, his hands behind his back.

Then Gabriel saw the man behind Noboru. A blond man wearing a thick cargo vest and pressing a Desert Eagle .44 Magnum against Noboru's neck. The sunlight glinted off a ring on the man's hand. A horned stag's head.

"Ah, there you are," Grissom said. "Mr. Hunt, I believe you've already met my son Julian."

8

JULIAN SHOVED NOBORU FORWARD, SENDING HIM stumbling toward Gabriel and Joyce. Gabriel reached out and caught him before he could fall.

"They came up behind me," Noboru began.

"It's all right," Gabriel said. He glanced at Grissom's men. With so many guns drawn and pointed their way, there was no chance of running. Certainly Noboru couldn't, not with his arms tied behind his back.

Gabriel watched Julian walk over to his father. At six feet, he towered over the elder Grissom.

"It was in one of the suitcases," Julian said. He reached inside his cargo vest and pulled out the Star.

Grissom snatched it out of his son's hand and held it up so that it gleamed in the sunlight. "The Star of Arnuwanda," he murmured. "Oh, you have saved me a great deal of time and effort indeed."

"How did you find us?" Joyce demanded.

Grissom handed the Star back to Julian. "It wasn't

difficult. We knew where you were staying, but you'd already left the guesthouse by the time we got there. The old woman there was distinctly unhelpful, but in spite of that we were able to follow your trail here."

Joyce blanched. "Merpati…"

"Was that her name?" Edgar Grissom said. "Remarkable woman, really. Took three bullets before she finally stopped swinging that damned shovel."

Joyce took a step toward Grissom, but suddenly five guns were aimed at her. Gabriel stuck out his arm to block her, shaking his head. Joyce clenched her jaw and stepped back.

Grissom walked toward them, flanked by his men. "Tie them up," he ordered.

The four gunmen came forward, surrounding them. One reached into Gabriel's holster and pulled out his Colt, while the others yanked his and Joyce's arms behind their backs and knotted lengths of rope around their wrists.

Julian and his father inspected the door excavated from the hillside. Grissom ran a hand over the metal. "Iron," he said. "The Hittite Empire was always ahead of its time. They were working with iron as early as the fourteenth century B.C., almost two hundred years before the rest of the ancient world." He turned to Joyce. "But that wasn't all that set them apart, eh, Ms. Wingard? There is also the little matter of the Spearhead. The power of the storm, harnessed and ready to be wielded like a broom to sweep their enemies from the face of the earth."

"So that's what you're after," Joyce said. "Destruction."

"A weapon so powerful no army can stand against it?" Grissom replied. "Oh yes, Ms. Wingard, I want that very, very much. Julian, the key."

Julian reached into his collar and lifted the Death's Head Key, still on its leather strap, from around his neck. He passed it to Grissom, who bent forward to inspect the lock in the door. He blew at it, picked out the dirt that clogged it and lined up the three blades of the Death's Head Key with the lock's triple keyway. Before he could slide it in, the key jumped out of his hand and sank by itself into the lock. Grissom looked at Julian. "Magnetized?" He gripped the key's skull-shaped bow and struggled to turn it in the ancient lock, his face turning red with effort. As he completed a single rotation, a loud click echoed from the door, and it began to scrape open on its hinges, swinging toward Grissom. He stepped back to give it room. Dirt rained from the seams between the door and its frame. The old, rusty hinges groaned, squeaked and cracked under the pressure of being pushed open again by some ancient mechanism after thousands of years.

"The first Eye of Teshub," Grissom said. "Thrown with its brothers into the wind by the storm god himself, separated from the others and given to the earth. Isn't that how the legend goes, Ms. Wingard?"

Joyce glared at him.

"Bring them forward," Grissom ordered his men. "They should see this. After all, it was their hard work that led us to this glorious moment."

The gunmen shoved Gabriel, Joyce and Noboru up to the doorway. Julian caught Gabriel by the shoulder as he passed. "Nice scar," he said, nodding toward the mark of stitches on Gabriel's cheek. Gabriel let it pass.

From inside the doorway, dusty, stale air swirled out of the darkness. Grissom coughed, pulled a handkerchief from his pocket and covered his nose and mouth with it. He gestured impatiently at Julian, who handed him a flashlight. Grissom switched it on as the opening door finally ground to a halt. He pointed the beam into the darkness, illuminating the cobwebs that hung in the corners of the doorway. Beyond was only empty space, until Grissom lowered the beam and revealed a flight of stone steps leading down. He folded the handkerchief back into his pocket and walked toward the doorway.

One of Grissom's men pushed Gabriel again, the gun pressed to his spine. He stepped into the darkness, watching Grissom's flashlight beam bob down the steps ahead of him. Gabriel carefully descended the stairs. The air inside the crypt was stifling and oppressive. The stone steps were covered in loose dirt and grit, making it tricky to find his footing. Cobwebs hung everywhere, tickling his face and sticking to his hair. Behind him, he heard Joyce stumble and one of the gunmen bark angrily at her to keep moving.

At the bottom of the steps was a long corridor. Grissom had stopped in the middle and was shining his flashlight along the walls. Six alcoves had been carved into the walls, and inside each was a skeleton, the bones brown with rot and age. Their jaws hung open—the ones that still had their jaws attached—and their bodies were twisted into frightful positions, their hands curled into claws. Hittite warriors, Gabriel guessed from the rusted, crumbling armor hanging off the bones. They'd been buried alive with the Eye to stand as eternal guardians, most likely dying from asphyxiation long before starvation set in. While the door wasn't a perfect airtight seal, the fact that these millennia-old skeletons weren't piles of dust was evidence enough of how little air had gotten inside once it was closed.

A cemetery in the jungle, Gabriel thought. Joyce had been on the right track. Only the cemetery in question was two stories underground.

The corridor ended in a large archway that was draped with a gossamer film of long-abandoned webs. Beyond, Gabriel could just make out a shimmering green light playing along the stone wall of the next chamber. Grissom led the way with Julian at his side, tearing the webs open as if he were parting curtains. The gunman behind Gabriel prodded him to follow. He glanced back at Joyce and Noboru to make sure they were all right. Noboru looked stoic, unwilling to show their captors any emotion: no fear, no anger. Joyce, however, did look angry. Furious. Gabriel knew what she was feeling. This was supposed to be her find, her moment of triumph. She'd worked hard for it, put her life on the line for it, only to see it snatched away by a couple of thugs with guns. Gabriel glared at the back of Julian's head. Oh yes, he knew exactly what she was feeling.

As they filed into the chamber beyond the arch, Gabriel took in their surroundings. To one side of the chamber was a stone pedestal that looked like a natural formation, a stalagmite with its sides and top smoothed flat by ancient tools. On top of the pedestal was a stone carving of a hand, rising up on a thick wrist. Nestled in the grip of its fingers was an enormous, octagonal emerald. The jewel was flat and wide like a saucer, with a circumference roughly the size of a softball. Where everything around it was corroded, rotted or covered in dust, the emerald looked as clean and polished as the day it had been cut. It seemed to be lit from within by a natural iridescence, sending green light gleaming against the walls and illuminating the paintings there. Gabriel recognized the faded art as scenes from the myths of Teshub: the storm god riding a chariot pulled by two bulls, wrestling the sea serpent Hedammu, slaying the dragon Illuyanka, battling the stone god Ulikummis, sitting on a throne beside the sun goddess Arinna and their son Sarruma. And one final image: Teshub hurling what appeared to be three separate thunderbolts away from a horde of angry-looking men in traditional Hittite armor. The scattering of the Three Eyes.

A low hum reached his ears. He glanced around the chamber, trying to find the source, until he realized it was coming from the emerald itself.

Grissom stepped up to the pedestal. His whole body seemed to tremble in anticipation. His flashlight beam struck the wall behind the pedestal and revealed large cuneiform symbols etched across the stone. It was the same alphabet as on the Star and the map.

Grissom swept his beam slowly across the symbols. "'The fire at world's end,'" he translated. "The end of the world! An apocalyptic prophecy. How perfect."

"Light," Joyce said.

Grissom turned to her. "What?"

"It's doesn't say the *fire* at world's end, it says the *light* at world's end," Joyce replied. "The Nesili cuneiforms for light and fire are close, but they're not the same. It's an easy mistake to make, for an amateur."

Grissom frowned. "If you're expecting to get a rise out of me, Ms. Wingard, you're sorely mistaken." He turned back to the gemstone. They barely heard him mutter, "My son, on the other hand..."

Julian whirled around and punched Joyce in the stomach so quickly Gabriel didn't even see it coming. Joyce doubled over, coughing and trying to catch her breath.

"Leave her alone!" Gabriel shouted. He struggled

against his bonds, but the barrel of the gun behind him dug deeper into his back, a reminder to behave himself.

"What kind of a coward do you have to be," Noboru said, "to hit a defenseless woman?"

Julian stepped up to Noboru and pulled back his fist, the time the one with the silver stag's head ring. Without even turning around to see what his son was doing, Grissom said, "That's enough, Julian." Glowering at Noboru, the blond man lowered his hand and returned to his father's side.

The gunman behind Joyce pulled on the ropes around her wrists, yanking her upright. She coughed again, her face red with exertion, tears squeezing from the corners of her eyes.

"Are you all right?" Gabriel asked.

She nodded and spat on the ground. "He just caught me off guard." She shouted at Julian, "Next time try that when my hands aren't tied!"

"Hold your tongue, Ms. Wingard, or I will remove it," Grissom said. He reached for the gemstone. As his hands moved closer to it, the humming seemed to grow higher in pitch. "An energy field," he marveled. "Given off by the stone itself. There can be no doubt it's just as the legend describes. Not only a key to Teshub's weapon, but a kind of battery that powers it." He lifted the emerald out of the stone hand's grasp and laughed with excitement. "I can feel it. Like the pulse of the storm god himself!"

Julian pulled a black velvet sack out of a pocket in his vest. Grissom deposited the emerald into it. Julian pulled the strings around the sack's mouth tight and returned it to his pocket.

A strange grinding sound came from the pedestal. The fingers of the stone hand suddenly bent inward on hidden hinges, forming a fist around the space where the emerald had been. Above, the ceiling rumbled and started to pull back from where it met the wall. Thick brown clods of dirt rained down over the pedestal. The ceiling continued to slide away on ancient tracks, dumping more dirt into the chamber. Gears within the walls groaned, and a thick stone slab started slowly descending in front of the archway, gradually sealing off the way they'd come in.

Grissom, Julian and the four gunmen all made a dash for the archway. Gabriel glanced around quickly, desperate to find another way out of the chamber. But there was no other exit, only the arch, and that was rapidly vanishing behind the descending slab. The dirt, meanwhile, was already up to his shins, with more raining down as the ceiling continued to withdraw.

Joyce and Noboru hurried toward the archway, their steps uneven. Joyce stumbled and dropped to one knee. Gabriel came up behind her and tried to help her to her feet again. It wasn't easy with his hands tied behind him. He nudged his shoulder under her arm, and she leaned back against him, levering herself upright. The level of dirt was rising higher, with some piles already at waist height. More rained down continuously, making it harder to move. By the time they reached the archway, only a narrow opening remained between the growing pile of dirt on the floor and the slab of stone dropping from above.

Joyce plunged through, tumbling forward headfirst, her feet kicking as she fell forward. Then Noboru slid through, his back scraping the underside of the stone slab. Gabriel struggled forward. He threw himself at the shrinking hole, ducking under the slab and eeling out into the corridor on his belly. A moment later, the bottom of the slab hit the top of the dirt mound below it, closing off the chamber.

Pushing himself back onto his feet, he could hear the dirt, tons of it, pouring against the other side of the stone slab. If they'd been trapped inside, they would shortly have joined the six Hittites in being buried alive. But not for long.

Grissom and his men were standing around them in a half-circle, their guns drawn.

"Well," Grissom said, brushing dirt from his legs. "That's one down, two to go."

Gabriel shook the dirt from his hair. "What are you going to do with us?"

"Never fear. I have uses for you and your friends yet, Mr. Hunt," Grissom replied. He started back along the corridor toward the steps to the surface.

As they were marched along behind Grissom, Gabriel tried to loosen the knot around his wrists, but the ropes wouldn't budge.

When they emerged into the sunlight, Grissom kept walking toward the forest. Julian stayed behind, hovering by the door of the crypt. Gabriel kept his eyes on him even as the gunman behind him shoved him forward, watching intently as Julian pulled the Death's Head Key out of the lock of the still-open iron door and hung it around his neck again.

By this point, Grissom had reached the treeline. He turned to face them. "We're done here," he called to Julian. "Destroy the crypt."

"What?" Gabriel said. He turned around to see one of Grissom's men passing Julian a bundle of dynamite.

"You can't!" Joyce cried. "Do you have any idea how old that crypt is? Who knows what else can be learned from it?"

Grissom shrugged. "Undoubtedly. But I don't want anyone to know where we've been, or what we have found. I'm afraid certain sacrifices must be made." He turned his back on them and kept walking into the trees.

Gabriel watched as Julian flicked a lighter under the long fuse attached to the dynamite. Julian threw the lit bundle into the open door and began tearing across the clearing toward the spot where his father had vanished. "Move!" the gunman behind Gabriel shouted. "Now!"

They had just reached the edge of the clearing when a loud explosion rocked the trees. Birds screamed and flew out of the canopy, soaring away from the cloud of dark smoke that billowed into the sky.

FROM HIS VANTAGE POINT AMID THE TREES ON THE opposite side, Vassily Platonov saw the blond man toss the dynamite into the doorway, then watched him and the others run off, the armed men and their three bound captives. The blond man was not one of those who had deprived Ulikummis of his sacrifice the night before, but it hardly mattered. In following the interlopers who had dared come to their sacred ground and free the American girl, Vassily now saw there were even more trespassers to be dealt with. The ground shook suddenly with an enormous subterranean explosion. Black smoke erupted from the doorway as the structure collapsed, taking half the hillside with it.

In the jungle beyond, Vassily's followers slipped silently to the ground from their places in the trees, like ghosts emerging from the darkness. Vassily gestured at them with his staff, and they lowered the skull masks over their faces.

The interlopers had destroyed a holy site, surely a tomb of their ancestors. Just as surely, they had found and taken the gemstone that he as the high priest of Ulikummis had vowed to find himself. The time for merely watching and following was over. He would make them pay for the affronts they had committed. Then he would locate the second and third Eyes of Teshub, secure the Spearhead, and use it to wipe the followers of all false gods from the face of the earth.

Vassily motioned to his followers, and together they disappeared into the jungle.

9

A HEAVY, WARM RAIN HAD BEGUN TO FALL IN SHEETS by the time Grissom's men marched Gabriel and the others out of the jungle and onto the road. Noboru's jeep stood wet and muddy where they'd left it. Parked right beside it was Grissom's much larger one, military-style with three rows of seats. Gabriel, Joyce and Noboru were shoved into Grissom's jeep, Gabriel and Joyce in the middle, and Noboru in the back with two of Grissom's men. Grissom took the wheel, and Julian sat in the passenger seat. The other two men got into Noboru's jeep.

The engines roared to life and the jeeps pulled out. The bumpy, unpaved road jostled Gabriel and Joyce into each other. The ropes around his wrists bit into his skin. The rain soaked through his clothes.

Joyce shook a wet strand of hair out of her face and shouted over the downpour, "Where are you taking us?"

Grissom smiled at her in the rearview mirror.

"Patience, Ms. Wingard. You'll find out soon enough."

Julian glanced into the rearview too. Gabriel stared at him in the reflection, not breaking eye contact. Julian's gaze returned to the road, then flitted back to the mirror a moment later. Gabriel didn't blink. Memories of Julian pistol-whipping him back at the Discoverers League and stealing the Death's Head Key replayed in his head and it must have shown in his eyes, since Julian looked away quickly.

Joyce leaned against him, her sopping wet hair falling in thick ropes across her face. "I'm sorry you got involved in all this," she said.

"Funny," he replied. "That's usually my line."

She leaned closer until a wet strand of hair touched his cheek, and lowered her voice to a whisper. "If we get out of this—"

"We will," he said. "I just need to think."

"If we get out of this," she continued, her voice insistent, "we can't let Grissom keep the Star. We can't let him find the other two Eyes. Whatever it is they activate, whatever the Spearhead turns out to be... it would definitely be a weapon in his hands."

Gabriel thought of Sargonia, a city of ash and cinders and glass after the Spearhead had been turned on it.

Joyce went on, "If it comes down to it, if you have to choose between the Star or me..."

"It won't come to that," he said.

"Promise me if you have to make a choice you'll take the Star and run. Leave me behind if you have to, just keep it out of his hands."

"It won't come to that," Gabriel repeated.

"Goddamn it, promise me."

"Joyce—"

She stared at him, her mouth a tight line. Rainwater dripped from her nose and chin.

"Okay," Gabriel said. "I promise."

"Because it's only fair you know what I'll do if I'm faced with the same decision," she said. Her expression didn't change. He had to admit, she was tougher than he'd given her credit for. Looking in her ice-blue eyes, he had no doubt she'd leave him behind if it meant getting the Star away from Grissom.

The jeeps turned off the road and barreled along a narrow stretch of dirt that cut through the foliage. Eventually the leaves and branches around them thinned and parted, revealing a campsite filled with wide canvas tents. More jeeps were parked around the camp, and men dressed in jungle camo busily passed in and out of the tents. Gabriel counted at least a dozen of them, with god knows how many more out of sight. Who knew how long Grissom had been on the trail of the Spearhead, but he'd amassed a small army along the way.

The jeep stopped suddenly, and Gabriel lurched forward, banging his chest against the front seat. Grissom killed the engine and jumped out of the jeep. His men dragged Gabriel, Joyce and Noboru out of the vehicle and marched them into the nearest tent. Three chairs had been set up in the center and a folding table stood to one side, a small, rectangular wooden box atop it. They were forced to sit and the ropes around their wrists were replaced with new bindings that secured their arms to the chair backs. Gabriel was seated in the middle chair, with Joyce on his left and Noboru on his right.

The tent flap opened, and Grissom entered. Rainwater dripped off the wide brim of his hat. He had a white towel draped over his shoulder. He nodded to his men. They exited the tent, except for one who stayed inside by the flap, one hand on the butt of his holstered gun.

"Well," Grissom said, "I must say, this is better than I could have hoped for." He took off his hat and shook the water from it onto the ground. He pulled the towel off his shoulder and dried his face and hair.

"Why are we here?" Gabriel demanded. "You've already got the Star of Arnuwanda."

"Indeed I do, but what I don't have, Mr. Hunt, is an *understanding* of it. Not yet. We have a copy of Arnuwanda's map, but without knowing how to use the Star to read it, it's merely a curious historical document. Yet in your hands the map and the Star together somehow led you to the crypt in the jungle. What I want to know is how." He placed the hat back on his head.

Gabriel glared at him and kept his mouth shut. Grissom looked at Joyce and then Noboru. After a moment, he nodded solemnly. "You're reluctant to tell me. That's understandable. I haven't been the most pleasant host." He folded the towel carefully, and put it down on the table beside the wooden box. He opened the box, pulled out a long object wrapped in a thick purple cloth and began to unwrap it. "But let me assure you, I can be even *less* pleasant."

Grissom lifted a dagger out of the cloth. He held it up so that the light from the generator-fed lamp in the corner glinted off the edges of the long, sharp blade. The handle was made of ivory, a curling dragon carved along the hilt from the pommel to the crossguard. "Thousands of years ago, the Chinese of the Shang and Zhou dynasties sacrificed young men and women to the gods of their rivers. They did this to prevent flooding, and to ensure the supply of fish continued for another year. A government minister named Ximen Bao put an end to the practice a few centuries later, but not before that famous Chinese ingenuity took hold. They liked to put their sacrifices in the rivers bleeding copiously, you see, and they needed a device to speed the process of preparing them." He touched a hidden button in the dragon's eye, and two additional blades sprang out of the handle alongside the first. He crossed to Gabriel's chair. "Of course, this isn't an original. They only had bronze to work with back then. But I do so like the design, don't you? It's far more of a precision instrument than it appears."

He touched the tips of the blades to Gabriel's face. Gabriel fought the urge to flinch as they neared his eye. The sharp metal slid along his skin, finally stopping when Grissom reached the stitches on his cheek. "I see my son was quite vehement in retrieving the Death's Head Key from you, Mr. Hunt. He's a good boy, but he doesn't always know when to stop. Doesn't know how much is too much. Perhaps he gets that from me." Grissom flicked his wrist suddenly, and the tip of the central blade cut through a stitch. Gabriel clenched his jaw as a drop of blood rolled down his cheek. "We can both be quite persistent. Neither of us lets people stand in the way of our goals. Like father, like son. It's best when things match, don't you think? The important things, anyway." He moved the knife to Gabriel's other cheek and flicked it again, opening a second wound to mirror the first. "Tell me how the Star is used."

Gabriel didn't answer. Blood trickled down both cheeks. He grit his teeth against the pain radiating from the incisions.

For a moment the tent was silent except for the

drumming of the rain on the canvas roof. Then Grissom said, "Very well." He grabbed Gabriel's collar in his fist and tore his shirt down the front. "I don't know how well you know knives, Mr. Hunt, but I had this one made from the best high-carbon steel there is. It never dulls, no matter how much flesh it slices." His hand shot forward suddenly, and the tips of all three blades stopped less than an inch from Gabriel's chest. "Or so I'm told. Shall we put it to the test?"

With another flick of his wrist, Grissom slashed a new wound into Gabriel's skin. Blood welled up in the three parallel cuts the dagger left in his chest, then spilled out, painting three red lines down to his ribs. Behind his back, Gabriel's hands clenched into fists. The ropes chewed into his wrists.

"I see you're a stubborn man," Grissom went on. "I understand this. I am one myself. When I want something, I'll do whatever it takes to make it mine. I've never cared for the word no. I care even less for those who say it to me." He swung his arm in a quick arc, drawing three more lines of blood across Gabriel's chest, like a claw mark. Gabriel gritted his teeth and shut his eyes against the sharp pain until it dulled. When he opened his eyes again, Grissom smiled. "Still with us, Mr. Hunt? Good. I'd be sorely disappointed if you didn't make it past the opening act."

Grissom coughed suddenly, his whole body shaking with the effort. Another cough followed, and another, wracking his frame so strongly he doubled over. He pulled the handkerchief from his pocket and coughed into it. A few seconds later, the coughing fit stopped and Grissom put the handkerchief back in his pocket. Gabriel caught a flash of red in its folds. Blood?

"Perhaps you don't know what it's like to be weak,

Mr. Hunt. To be a ticking clock, counting down to your own death as your body eats itself alive. To have nothing to look forward to but a few remaining years of misery, immobility and pain. To have more than enough money for anything you want, and yet still not enough to extend your life. Time is a thief, Mr. Hunt. It steals everything from you, little by little. I watched Julian's mother waste away on her deathbed. I saw the pity in everyone's eyes, heard it in the pitch of their voices. I won't allow that to happen to me. Pity is what you get when people don't fear you. Other people's pity only makes you weaker. But fear..." He swung the dagger once more, slicing three fresh cuts across Gabriel's chest. Gabriel grunted in pain from between his clenched teeth. "Fear makes you much, much stronger. Now, tell me how to use the Star."

Streams of sweat rolled off Gabriel's forehead. Each new cut felt like a fire burning just under his skin. But as long as he could keep Grissom talking, keep the madman thinking he was the one with the answers and not Joyce, he would take it for as long as he had to. There was no other choice.

Grissom slashed his abdomen. This time Gabriel cried out. Judging from the smile on the old man's face, it seemed to make Grissom happy.

"Can you imagine," Grissom continued, "how intrigued I was when I heard the legend of the Spearhead? What I could do with such a thing. The fire at world's end. Why should it just be *my* end that approaches? Why not the whole world's, just like the legend says, only with my hand setting the blaze? When my wife died, the world didn't care. It carried on as if nothing had happened. The next morning was like all the ones before it: birds sang, breezes blew, politicians lied, all of it. There will be no ordinary next morning when I die, Mr. Hunt. For me, the world will sit up and take notice. There will be no forgetting the name Edgar Grissom."

"You're…" Gabriel began, and then shook his head. The words were so inadequate. But he said them anyway. "You're crazy."

Grissom smiled. "And now we finally hear from Gabriel Hunt! Has your tongue been loosened at last? Tell me what I need to know and the pain stops."

Gabriel looked away. The patter of the rain on the canvas roof slowed to a stop, amplifying the silence that filled the tent.

"A pity," Grissom said. "I was hoping you'd be more cooperative." He looked down at the three blood-tipped blades of his dagger. "You see, until I have what I want, I need you alive. Your friends, however, are of no such importance to me." Grissom turned to Joyce. She kept her head down, her eyes to the ground. "There's something wonderful about women, don't you think?" He reached out with the knife until the blades' tips just brushed the skin of her clavicle. "The way the fear stays in their eyes even after they die."

He moved the dagger to the base of her neck, then up to her throat. Joyce tilted her head away from the sharp blades and glared up at Grissom, her lips pulled back from her teeth.

"Tell me how to use the Star, Mr. Hunt," Grissom insisted, "or I will open her lovely neck."

Gabriel sat silently, his skin singing with pain, blood rolling down his ribs and abdomen. Beside him, Noboru tugged against the ropes that bound him to his chair. Gabriel met Joyce's eyes, and she shot him a look of steely resolve that erased any doubt whether she meant what she'd said. She was willing to die to keep the Spearhead out of Grissom's hands.

But what if the legend was wrong? They'd found one gemstone, but what if there weren't any others? Or what if the Spearhead didn't exist anymore, or if it never had? He couldn't let her die for something no one even knew for sure was real. He met her eyes again, then looked over at Grissom, and saw an equal determination in each pair of eyes. Rock, meet hard place. Gabriel struggled against his bindings, trying to slip a hand free, but the knot was too tight.

Grissom frowned. "I'm disappointed in you, Mr. Hunt. You've backed me into a corner. I dislike hurting women, but I'm afraid I have no choice now. When you look back at this moment in the future—should I allow you a future—I want you to remember whose fault this really was." He grabbed Joyce's hair in one hand and pulled her head back. She gritted her teeth and clamped her eyes shut. Grissom swung the dagger back, preparing to slash it across her throat.

"It's a code!" Noboru shouted suddenly. "It's a code."

Grissom stayed his hand. Joyce opened her eyes. Gabriel turned to Noboru and saw the pained, desperate look on the older man's face.

"Of course it's a code," Grissom said. "But how does it *work*? What is the *key*?"

"The elements," Noboru said. "Earth, water. The symbols for the elements."

"Don't!" Joyce yelled at him.

Grissom let go of her hair and walked over to stand in front of Noboru. "The elements, you say. You mean the three elements from the Teshub legend, of course."

"Noboru," Joyce pleaded.

He looked at her and shook his head. "I couldn't let him do it."

"Go on," Grissom said, raising his voice impatiently.

"The first gemstone, the one you have… it's the one for earth," Noboru said. "The second is water."

"Noboru, don't," Joyce warned again.

Grissom shot a silencing a glance her way.

"Yes, but the third one, that's the mystery," Grissom said. "Any fool with half a brain knows the original translation is wrong. 'Loose soil' makes no sense. But you've figured out what it means, haven't you? Tell me."

Noboru swallowed hard and looked away from Grissom's eyes. "No. We haven't. None of us has."

Grissom grabbed a fistful of Noboru's hair and held the three-bladed dagger to his throat. "I don't have time for games. What is the third element?"

"We don't know," Noboru insisted. "I swear."

"You're trying my patience," Grissom hissed. "Hunt, speak to me or he dies." He pulled back the dagger, ready to strike.

"Sorry, Joyce," Gabriel said. "You are I are one thing, but Noboru didn't make you any promises. I'll tell you what you want to know, Grissom. Just let them—"

A shout of alarm came from outside the tent. The report of a gunshot rang out. Grissom straightened, letting go of Noboru's hair. Another shot exploded, followed by more shouting, a confused clamor, the sound of boots running through mud. Grissom touched the eye of the dragon on the dagger's hilt again and the two outer blades slid back into the handle. He tossed the dagger back in the wooden box. "Watch them," he barked at the guard stationed at the tent flap. Then he exited.

"How could you?" Joyce said. "Both of you! If he

finds the other gemstones and activates the Spearhead, he'll use it to slaughter thousands—maybe millions."

"I'm sorry," Noboru said. "But I couldn't let him kill you."

More angry shouts erupted outside, more gunfire, and another sound, like the twanging of a guitar string.

"What the hell is going on out there?" Joyce asked.

Gabriel shook his head. "Your guess is as good as mine."

The guard stiffened suddenly and a strange gurgling came from his throat. He fell backwards, clutching at his neck. The shaft of an arrow protruded from his Adam's apple.

The dying man's fingers grabbed at the tent flap, pulling the canvas to one side.

Just long enough for Gabriel to see someone run past holding a wooden longbow, a quiver of arrows strapped to the back of his white robe.

A skull mask covered his face.

10

THE CULT, HERE? NOW? GABRIEL HAD NEVER THOUGHT he'd be grateful to see them. But it was only a temporary reprieve. Both groups wanted them dead and whichever came out on top would see to it that they wound up that way.

"This can't end well," Gabriel said. "We have to get out of here."

Noboru pulled hard against the ropes tying him to his chair, to no avail. "Any suggestions?"

Gabriel eyed the table with the box on it. "One. But it depends on my getting over there." He began rocking back and forth in his chair, tipping it farther and farther until it finally fell forward. He shifted as he fell so that he landed on his side. The jolt of the impact made the fresh cuts on his torso flare with pain again.

He wriggled on the ground, making slow progress toward the table, dragging the chair with him. The strain it put on his shoulders made it feel like they would snap out of their sockets at any moment. He backed up against the table and knocked the chair into it as hard as he could. The wooden box on top shifted but didn't fall. He hit the table again, gritting his teeth against the pain. The box jolted, crept closer to the edge. Looking up, he saw that it was within centimeters. He struck the table one more time. The box jumped, teetered on the edge. *Come on, damn it…* It teetered on the table's edge, then fell. He swung his head to the side and it smashed beside him, kicking off splinters. One nicked his ear as it shot past. Grissom's ivory-handled dagger spilled out on the floor and rolled a yard or so. He rotated till it was in reach of one of his feet, then kicked it toward Noboru. The other man caught it between his boots.

More shouting came from outside the tent. Gabriel could hear people running past, the crack of gunfire and the *shuk* of arrows landing in the mud. They had to hurry. All it would take was one cult member to stumble upon them, or one of Grissom's men to catch them in the middle of an escape attempt, and they might as well have spent the time digging their own graves.

"Turn it around," he told Noboru. "The other way. Upright." With the sides of his boot soles, Noboru turned the knife till it was pointing straight up. He steadied the pommel against the ground. Gabriel squirmed painfully back to him, angling himself so his back was to the blade. "Just hold it steady," he said. "Despite the position we find ourselves in, I don't really want to slit my wrists." He started working the rope holding his arms together against the blade. The angle was difficult, and it hurt like hell to raise and lower his arms, but after half a minute he could feel the tension in the rope weakening.

"Go faster," Joyce called. "You've got to go faster."

Gabriel grimaced. It felt like his arms were about to break. He thrust the ropes against the blade savagely—again—once more—and suddenly his hands were free. He threw the rope off to either side and scrambled to his feet. He grabbed the knife and pressed the hidden button. The extra blades snapped into view. He used their razor edges to make short work of the ropes holding Noboru and Joyce to their chairs.

"We've got to get the Star back," she said, rubbing circulation back into her wrists.

"The only problem," Gabriel said, "is that there's a battlefield between us and wherever Grissom's got it. Assuming he's not lying face down in the mud." *We should be so lucky.* Gabriel crossed to the tent flap, stepping over the dead guard, and pulled it back an inch to peer out. It was chaos outside, with Grissom's men running back and forth, shouting and firing their weapons. Everywhere, the feathered ends of arrows stuck up out of the ground like tire spikes. One of Grissom's men ran past, pistol in hand, shooting at a target Gabriel couldn't see, and then an arrow hit him in the back. The man fell forward, his body skidding to a halt in the mud. The arrow had come from the direction of the jungle. Aside from the one cult member he'd seen running past the tent, it looked like the others were hanging back and trying to pick off Grissom's men from the trees. There was no sign of Grissom himself, or of Julian.

"I can't see much from here," he said. "We have to move, find a better vantage point. Someplace a little safer, too."

Gabriel handed Grissom's dagger to Noboru. "Here, take this."

Noboru weighed it in his hand and nodded. "What about you?"

"I'll find something." Gabriel looked outside again. The chaos hadn't abated. He saw a jeep full of Grissom's men barreling toward them.

"When I say run, run," Gabriel said. Joyce and Noboru nodded. He waited until the jeep was just before the tent, the gunmen in back firing into the trees, and then shouted, "Run!"

He threw open the tent flap and sprinted out into the open, using the passing jeep for cover. Joyce followed right behind him, then Noboru. Gabriel kept running, head down, pumping his legs as hard as he could to carry him toward a tent directly across the open center of the camp. Arrows hissed through the air toward them, one going by directly over his head and three more embedding themselves in the ground near his feet.

When he reached the other tent, he ducked around the corner. Joyce and Noboru dove for cover behind him, breathing hard.

"Where to now?" Joyce asked.

Gabriel peeked out. He had a better view of the scene from here. Dead bodies littered the ground, mostly Grissom's men but also a few members of the Cult of Ulikummis, their white robes stained with mud and gore. Grissom's remaining soldiers were running for the jeeps, squeezing off shots into the forest as they went. Arrows continued to fly from the trees, though not as many as before. Gabriel couldn't make out the cultists' positions in the trees. For men whose choice of camouflage was more suited to the Arctic, they did a hell of a job of blending in.

The jeeps pulled out and roared toward the treeline,

the men standing in back exchanging their pistols for shotguns. He didn't see Grissom or Julian in any of them. Had they already evacuated the camp?

No, Gabriel thought. Grissom wouldn't. He was too stubborn and arrogant to alter his plans just because he suddenly found himself under siege. He'd still be in the camp somewhere, letting his henchmen fight for him while he…

While he *what*?

The Star. Grissom had gotten a portion of what he needed from Noboru and would be trying to use the Star and the map even now, in the middle of a pitched battle, to get as much information as possible before moving on. Gabriel looked around. At the far end of the camp, he spotted a tent with two gunmen posted outside. Everyone in Grissom's army was fighting the cultists except those two. They were protecting something. Or someone.

"There," he said, pointing.

"How will we get past the guards?" Joyce asked.

"I don't know," Gabriel said. "We'll think of something." He led them behind the row of tents, hoping the jungle beside them wasn't filled with cultists waiting to unleash their arrows. He kept his head down and hurried, counting on the continuing gunfire to cloak the sound of their running footsteps. He stopped one tent short of their destination, motioned to the others to stay low, then peeked around the corner.

The guards. How to get past—

At that instant, an arrow flew out of the jungle and landed squarely in the chest of the guard on the left. He crumpled to the ground. The other guard turned and started shooting into the trees.

"Now," Gabriel said.

While the guard's back was turned, they ran toward the tent. Halfway there, he glanced back and spotted an arrow cutting through the air in a perfect arc right toward Joyce. He spun and tackled her around the knees, pulling her down into the mud. The arrow whizzed through the air where she'd been.

Unfortunately, their motion caught the surviving guard's attention. His mouth fell open in surprise and he swung his pistol toward them. Noboru, still running, hurled the dagger. It spun end over end, its triple blade glinting in the sun before sinking with a meaty *thock* into the guard's chest. The guard dropped his gun, tilted his head down to look at the ivory handle sticking out of his chest, and dropped to his knees. He tipped forward, landing in the dirt.

Gabriel helped Joyce stand up. Her hand felt small in his and he could feel it trembling. Together they ran toward the tent, staying low. He didn't let go of her hand till they'd made it to the tent's entrance. He was acutely aware of her gaze on him, those piercing blue eyes staring out at him from her mud-caked face.

"You saved my life back there," she said. "Again."

He bent to pick up one of guards' guns. Next to him, Noboru pulled the dagger out of the guard's chest and wiped the blood on the corpse's shirt. "Easy," Gabriel whispered. "Not a peanut in sight."

Gabriel put a finger to his lips, then slid the muzzle of the guard's pistol through the tent flap and nudged it aside an inch.

Inside, a half dozen chairs and a pair of folding tables had been pushed to the side. Grissom stood in the empty center of the tent, looking down at something on the floor. It had to be the map. When

Grissom shifted position, Gabriel saw he was holding the Star of Arnuwanda over the map with one hand and shining a flashlight through it with the other. So he'd figured out that much. Gabriel moved slightly for a better view of the tent's interior. He saw Julian standing with his back to them. The grip of his Magnum was visible at the waistband of his pants. He had his hands up at chest height and it looked like he was writing something down. Coordinates of the second Eye? Just how far had they gotten?

There was no time to waste. Gabriel stepped through the flap and had his arm around Julian's neck before he could turn around. The pen and paper he'd been holding fell to the floor. Gabriel pulled Julian's Magnum from his belt, dropped it and kicked it behind him so it slid under the tables. "Remember when I said you better hope I never see you again?" he whispered in Julian's ear. "I wasn't kidding." He dug the barrel of the guard's gun into Julian's ribs. Julian's eyes widened.

Grissom spun around, dropping the flashlight but keeping a tight grip on the Star. His eyes darted toward a table by the wall, where their confiscated weapons lay: the two Colts, Noboru's knife, even the flare gun from the jeep. Grissom made a break for the weapons, but Noboru, darting in, managed to get between him and the table. He raised the dagger. Grissom turned to run the other way and found Joyce blocking his path. She lifted the second guard's gun.

Joyce held out her other hand palm up. "The Star," she said.

Grissom looked over at Julian gasping for breath in Gabriel's chokehold, then at Noboru, who had snatched up one of the Colt revolvers from the table and was pointing it at him. He swallowed hard and held out the Star. "This isn't over," he said.

Joyce reached out to take the Star. Grissom started coughing so hard he doubled over, his hands on his knees. As Joyce bent to pull the Star out of his hand, Grissom swung it at her. The heavy metal disk connected with her stomach, and she went down, the gun skittering out of her grasp. But she managed to hold onto the Star. For an instant, Grissom looked like he was going to try to get it back from her, but she rolled over, clutching it to her chest and cradling it beneath her. Noboru drew back the safety on his Colt and advanced on him. Grissom settled for snatching up the pistol at his feet and, shooting it blindly in Noboru's direction, bolted through the tent flap. Ducking, Noboru fired off two shots that punched holes in the canvas but it was too late—Grissom was gone.

Joyce stood again, brushing dirt off the artifact in her hands. "It's all right. Let him go. The Star's the only thing that matters."

"Not exactly," Gabriel said. "Getting out of here alive matters, too." Julian was still struggling in Gabriel's chokehold. "Looks like your father left you all alone," Gabriel said into Julian's ear. "What do you suppose we should do with you? What you would do to us if our positions were reversed?"

Julian squirmed against his arm, but the hold was too tight. Gabriel started to squeeze, cutting off his air supply, and Julian clawed at him. Then Julian snapped his elbow back into Gabriel's gut. Normally it would have been the sort of blow he could take easily—but the cuts on his abdomen turned it into a symphony of pain. Gabriel doubled over. But he held on tight, clamping down on Julian's throat. The younger man struggled wildly, but Gabriel didn't give an inch. After a minute, the struggles slowed and finally stopped.

"Is he…?" Joyce said.

"Not to say I'm not tempted, but no," Gabriel said. "Just unconscious." He lowered Julian to the ground and tore the unconscious man's collar open. He pulled the Death's Head Key from around his neck. He hung it around his own. Then he took his Colt .45 and holster from the table and buckled it on while Noboru did the same with his knife and ankle sheath. Noboru also stuffed the flare gun into his belt. While they were doing this, Joyce was rifling through everything else on the tables, overturning boxes, opening document folders, and throwing them to the ground in frustration.

"What is it?" Noboru asked.

She bent over Julian's unconscious body and patted the pockets of his cargo vest, then his pants.

"The Jewel," she said. "The Eye. It's gone."

"Grissom must have it on him," Gabriel said. He looked outside. The battle was still raging, but there was no sign of Grissom. "We can't go after him now. We need to get out of here."

They exited the tent cautiously, headed toward Noboru's jeep. Gabriel stayed low, his revolver in his fist, Noboru by his side, Joyce directly behind him. They reached the jeep without incident. Just as Noboru jumped into the driver's seat, though, a muffled scream from behind Gabriel made him turn.

Another jeep had rolled up out of nowhere; there were three men inside. One of the three was leaning out and had snatched Joyce off her feet with an arm around her waist and the other clamped over her mouth. She was lifted, struggling and screaming, into the vehicle.

"Joyce!" Gabriel shouted. She still had the Star in her hands, and she tried to throw it to him, but the man holding her grabbed it out of her hand. The driver stomped on the gas then and the jeep rocketed forward, vanishing into the distance even as Gabriel fruitlessly chased after it on foot. Borneo covered two hundred eighty-eight thousand square miles, with plenty of places to hide a struggling captive—or to bury one. If they didn't catch the other jeep quickly, they would lose the Star *and* Joyce for good.

11

GABRIEL WHIRLED AROUND AND SAW NOBORU, TEN
yards back, starting the jeep's engine. Noboru pulled
out, spun the jeep to face him and sped toward him.
Arrows zipped over the jeep, banged off the hood.
Gabriel ran toward it as it approached. He grabbed the
side of the jeep as it skidded to a halt, pulled himself
up onto the side bar and jumped over the door into the
passenger seat.

Behind him and off to one side, a white-robed man
emerged from the jungle and ran toward them, a long,
curved sword swinging overhead in both hands. The
mud didn't seem to be slowing him down at all.

Noboru cranked the gearshift and stepped on the
gas. "Hold on to something!" he shouted. Gabriel
dropped back into his seat as the jeep picked up speed.
The man darted into their path, running toward them
as they accelerated. At the instant they ought to have
hit him, he leapt lightly onto their front bumper, then

from there onto the jeep's hood, swinging the sword at Noboru's head. Gabriel pulled the trigger on his Colt. The man flew backwards from the impact. He landed in the mud several feet away and didn't get up again.

Noboru spun the wheel, turning them back toward the path that led to the main road. Gunfire crackled around them as they sped past a last cluster of Grissom's men shooting at the cultists in the trees. "What are they doing here?"

"They must have followed us," Gabriel said. "But they can't just be after us for taking Joyce away from them. It's got to be the Star they want. Everybody's after that damn thing."

Noboru raced along the jungle path, leaving the camp behind, and turned onto the main road. It ran for at least a mile straight ahead, and in the distance they saw the other jeep barreling along it in the direction of Balikpapan. Noboru increased his speed, the two of them bouncing and jostling in their seats as the jeep raced over the unpaved road.

"Get right up next to them," Gabriel shouted over the engine's roar as they closed on the other jeep. He aimed his Colt again, then thought better of it. He didn't want to risk hitting the driver. If they went off the road, Joyce could be killed in the crash.

Noboru narrowed the gap between the two vehicles, the jeep shuddering under the strain like it was about to fall apart.

As they drew closer, Gabriel saw Joyce and one of Grissom's men, a big man with a close-cropped beard, struggling in the back. The man was trying to get the Star away from her, but she was clinging to it, spitting curses and kicking at him. The man swung at her with his free hand, clocking her in the side of the head and she cried out, but didn't lose her grip on the Star.

Noboru pulled up beside the other jeep, matching its speed. Gabriel stood, the wind whipping his hair. He balanced himself against the roll bar and kept an eye on the space between the vehicles, knowing a single misstep would send him hurtling to the road below.

The bearded man punched Joyce again. This time she fell onto the back seat, finally releasing her grip on the Star; this sent the man reeling back too.

"Joyce!" Gabriel shouted. Her head popped up over the side of the jeep. He held out his arms. "Jump!"

"Not without the Star," she shouted back.

The man in the passenger seat, a short, evil-looking fellow with a long scar down his cheek, reached for her, but she knocked his hands aside.

"You have to jump," Gabriel shouted. Then, to Noboru, "Get us closer!"

Noboru brought them as close as he could without contacting the other car's chassis. The other driver glared at him and stepped on the accelerator. Noboru fell behind for a moment, then pulled up alongside again. Joyce stood in the back of the jeep, staring with a look of terror at the road ripping by between them. Behind her, the bearded man got back on his feet, holding the Star. Tucking it under one arm, he reached for her with the other.

"Now," Gabriel yelled.

Glancing back—could she really leave the Star in their hands?—Joyce took a deep breath, put one foot on the back seat and launched herself into the air. Noboru cursed, trying to keep the vehicle steady. Joyce cried out as she hurtled toward them and slammed into Gabriel, nearly knocking him over. With one arm around the roll bar for support, he wrapped the other around her to hold her steady. She breathed hard in his ear.

"The Star," she said. "We can't leave it with them."

"We won't," Gabriel said. He let go of her. She dropped into the seatwell. In the other jeep, Grissom's men were shouting at each other. Their vehicle turned suddenly, moving farther away, toward the edge of the road. The man in the front passenger seat leveled a handgun at them and fired. Bullets punched craters in the door and ricocheted off the roll bar inches from Gabriel's head.

"Stay on them!" he shouted to Noboru.

They swung closer again, and when the two jeeps were side by side once more Gabriel jumped across the divide. He landed on top of the bearded man in back, tackling him to the floor. The Star dropped from the man's hand and rolled under the driver's seat. Gabriel and the bearded man stood up at the same time, the bumps in the road as they raced along it threatening to knock them off their feet again.

The other man punched first, but Gabriel caught his fist in his hand and brought his knee up into the man's gut. He doubled over, and Gabriel haymakered him on the back of the neck, driving him to the floor. The scar-faced man in the passenger seat stood up and climbed over his seat into the back of the jeep, brandishing his gun. Gabriel backhanded it out of his grip before he could fire. It clattered to the floor, landing between the front seats. The man punched Gabriel, stunning him for a moment and sending him reeling back. The scarred man swung at him again, but Gabriel jerked his head back, the man's fist just missing his jaw. Gabriel's own fist connected, though, knocking his opponent backwards. He collided with the driver's back and the jeep swerved dangerously.

The bearded man rose from the floor. He'd retrieved the Star from under the driver's seat.

Gabriel elbowed him in the face and grabbed the Star out of his hands.

Looking over, he saw that Noboru had kept pace, their jeep jouncing alongside the one he was in. Joyce had her hands cupped around her mouth and was shouting something at him, but he couldn't make it out.

Gabriel stepped up on the side of the jeep and was about to jump back when the bearded man grabbed him from behind, his thick arm snaking around Gabriel's neck. Now he knew what it had felt like for Julian: his windpipe was compressing, the oxygen flow to his brain cutting off. The man reached forward to snatch the Star back. Gabriel couldn't let that happen.

He threw the Star. Tossed it flat and spinning like a metal frisbee and watched it sail toward Noboru's jeep. Joyce stretched for it, snagging it out of the air.

Gabriel elbowed the bearded man in the ribs and felt the hold around his throat slacken. He spun and punched the man in the jaw, knocking him back.

The scarred man rose from the passenger seat, meanwhile, climbed over the driver's back, and leaped across to Noboru's jeep, landing right next to Joyce. He grabbed her neck in one calloused hand and tried to seize the Star with the other. Noboru swerved the vehicle from side to side, trying to knock the intruder off balance, but the man kept his footing.

Her face turning red, Joyce hurled the Star just as Gabriel had. It flew back across the divide and into Gabriel's hands.

"What are you doing?" Gabriel shouted, just before the bearded man threw a punch at him again. Jamming the Star under his arm, Gabriel sidestepped the punch and drove his fist into the man's nose. He felt bone and cartilage snap and the bearded man fell back, blood spilling down his face.

In Noboru's jeep, the scarred man let go of Joyce's neck and turned to jump back across. Joyce grabbed at him, snagging a fistful of his uniform shirt and tugging fiercely. The man went off balance for a second and she tried to push him out of the jeep, but he regained his footing and stepped up onto the back seat.

He jumped across—and at the same moment exactly, Gabriel leapt back the other way. They passed each other in the air, so close that Gabriel could read the anger in the man's face as he realized his mistake. Gabriel landed in Noboru's jeep, grabbing the roll bar with one hand and holding onto the Star with the other.

The scarred man landed in the other jeep and whirled around. His face a mask of fury, the man reached down between the front seats and came back up with his gun.

Joyce ducked to the floor and Gabriel dropped into the passenger seat. Noboru spun the steering wheel, trying to put distance between them. A spray of bullets pounded the metal chassis of the jeep. Gabriel put the Star down and pulled his revolver. He fired off two shots, but they both went wide, missing their targets. He pulled the trigger again, but the Colt only clicked emptily.

The driver of the other jeep shouted, "He's done! Finish him!" The scarred man lined up another shot.

Reaching behind him, Gabriel pulled the flare gun out of Noboru's belt, swung it around in the direction of the other jeep, and pulled the trigger.

The scarred man ducked but Gabriel hadn't been aiming at him. The sparking red magnesium projectile flew directly at the driver, slamming into his shirt. The man panicked as his clothing erupted in flames. He let go of the steering wheel and slapped at the burning flare. The jeep careened away, skidded off the road and slammed into a tree with an enormous impact. Seconds later, the site of the crash exploded into flame.

Noboru kept his foot on the gas. Gabriel turned around and watched the smoking wreckage disappear into the distance.

He handed the Star to Joyce in the back seat. "I believe this is yours."

She took it from him and inspected it for damage. "I thought it was gone for sure."

Gabriel leaned back in his seat, letting the wind cool the sweat off his body. "It nearly was. You nearly were, too."

She gave him a look he found it hard to interpret. There was gratitude in it, but also indignation, as though she half resented him for saving her life.

Ahead of them, the skyline of Balikpapan rose up at the horizon.

12

AS THEY DROVE INTO BALIKPAPAN, THE CITY FOLDED ITS
arms around them in the form of skyscrapers and high-
rise hotels, office towers and apartment buildings.
Covered in bruises and blood, their clothes torn and
filthy, their jeep battered and pocked with bullet holes,
they attracted more than a few glances every time
they stopped at a red light. Gabriel didn't much care.
He was glad to have a moment to breathe, away at last
from both Grissom and the Cult of Ulikummis.

Neon advertisements on the sides of the buildings
threw bright colors across the windshield and onto
Noboru's face as he grimaced and took one hand off
the steering wheel to rub his chest.

"Are you okay?" Gabriel asked.

"It's nothing, I'm fine," Noboru said. "Just thinking
about what my wife's going to say when she sees our jeep."

"I'm sure she'll just be happy you're alive," Joyce
said.

"You haven't met Michiko. She'll kill me herself."

Noboru drove through the city center and over the hills until they reached the shore, where Balikpapan's rampant, glossy urban expansion slowed and signs of its centuries-long history as a fishing village returned. The houses were smaller, more modest, and along the harbor dozens of fishermen were gathered, standing by their poles and chatting while they waited for something to tug at their lines. Noboru turned onto a lane that rose up the gentle slope of a hill lined with houses painted bright shades of red, yellow and green, their walls fashioned of thick cement to withstand the gale-force winds of storm season. He pulled the jeep over in front of a pale blue house with a white roof and killed the engine.

"Home," he said, his voice unsteady.

They climbed out of the jeep, and Noboru fished his keys from his pocket. He tried to fit the key into the lock in the front door, but his hand was shaking and the blade kept sliding against the lock plate, missing the keyway.

"Is something wrong?" Gabriel asked.

"Michiko—" Noboru said, and his face twisted in pain. The door suddenly opened from the inside, and Noboru collapsed into the arms of a Japanese woman about his age. She cried out as she caught him, and glanced with confusion at Gabriel and Joyce. Gabriel rushed forward to help her carry Noboru into the house. They brought him through a polished wooden moon gate standing at the entrance to the living room and laid him gently on the couch.

The woman dabbed Noboru's forehead with a tissue. "Who are you?" she asked Gabriel in Japanese.

"Your husband works with my brother," he replied in the same language. "I'm Gabriel Hunt, this is Joyce

Wingard. He was helping us."

Michiko looked down at her husband resting on the couch, his face coated with a sheen of sweat. He was breathing shallowly. "It's his heart. I told him this would happen."

"Will he be all right?" Joyce asked.

Michiko pointed to a doorway off the living room. "Bring me a glass of water from the kitchen," she said, in English. "And a wet towel." Joyce hurried off. Michiko knelt beside the couch. She reached into Noboru's pocket and pulled out the small pillbox Gabriel had seen before. She opened it and took out two pills, small white tablets that Gabriel suddenly realized weren't sleep aids but nitroglycerine pills. "His heart is poor," Michiko said. "He had a heart attack when he was only forty-nine. It's why he had to retire early."

Gabriel frowned. "He didn't tell me."

"Why would he? He likes his job."

Joyce rushed back into the room with a glass of water and a wet cloth and put them down on the table. Michiko gently opened Noboru's mouth and slipped the pills onto his tongue. She tipped the water glass against his lips and made him swallow. "After we left Japan, I begged him to take it easy, just enjoy his retirement, not work for your Foundation. His heart can't take the exertion. And it's not as though we need the money—I make plenty, enough for both of us. But he insisted. He said if he didn't do anything he'd feel like he was already dead."

"Should we bring him to the hospital?" Joyce asked.

Michiko shook her head. "It wasn't a heart attack, only an arrhythmia. The pills are enough. He'll be fine, we just have to give it some time."

"Are you sure?" Gabriel asked.

"Of course," Michiko said, dabbing Noboru's forehead with the wet cloth. "I'm a doctor."

IT DIDN'T TAKE LONG FOR NOBORU TO COME AROUND, but when Gabriel asked if he was feeling better, he was too embarrassed to talk about it. Michiko cleaned Noboru's wounds while he lay on the couch, re-bandaging the slash on his arm and dabbing ointment on the bruises and cuts on his face. By the time she was finished, he had slipped back into a deep sleep, untroubled even by the snores Gabriel remembered from their night in the hallway of Merpati's house.

Michiko tended to Joyce's bruises next, while Joyce sat in a chair and chewed her thumbnail anxiously. Something was going on behind her eyes, but Gabriel still couldn't quite figure it out. When Michiko finished, Joyce asked if she could use her phone. Michiko sent her back to the kitchen, where a cordless unit was sitting on the counter. Then she turned to Gabriel. "You're next."

"You don't have to worry about me," Gabriel said. "I'm fine."

Michiko gave him a stare that said she was not in a mood to argue. "You look like you got it the worst of everyone. Sit." Gabriel sighed and sat in the chair. She examined the cuts on his face, chest and abdomen, and shook her head. "My god, what did they do to you?" Gabriel winced as she dabbed alcohol on the wounds to sterilize them. Michiko nodded. "Someone cuts you to ribbons, but it's the alcohol that hurts. I'll never, ever understand men. At least you're lucky: the cuts aren't deep. You won't need more stitches."

"The man who did it was going for pain, not lasting damage," Gabriel said.

As she cleaned his wounds, he turned to watch Joyce in the kitchen. She was leaning against the refrigerator with her back to them. She spoke into the phone so quietly he couldn't hear what she was saying.

"I don't know what I would do without her," Noboru said. Gabriel turned to the couch and saw Noboru's eyes were open again. "Michiko, I mean." His voice was weak and raspy, but he looked less pale than he had before, less clammy. He seemed to be regaining a bit of his strength.

Michiko glared at her husband. "I don't know what I'd do without you either, you stupid old man. You're not a boy anymore. You have a daughter, you have a family. I can't have you running around, fighting, not when your heart keeps warning you not to. One of these days it'll be a heart attack again, and then what? It's bad enough you still smoke when you think I'm not looking." She shook her head. "You have to think about your health—and if that's not a good enough reason, think about me. In the morning, I want you to call Michael Hunt and tell him you're resigning. I don't want you doing any more work for the Hunt Foundation unless it's stuffing envelopes."

Noboru laced his fingers behind his head. "I'll think about it."

Annoyed, Michiko turned back to Gabriel and jabbed the alcohol-soaked cotton ball against one of his cuts so hard that he winced again. "He'll *think* about it, he says." She practically punched him with the bandage she applied over the cut. "This is all your fault. You and your brother. Don't you care what happens to other people?"

"Stop it," Noboru said. "If it weren't for Gabriel, I wouldn't be here right now."

"If it weren't for Gabriel, you wouldn't have been in danger in the first place." She glared at Gabriel and he looked away. He couldn't say she was wrong.

She picked up a double handful of used cotton balls and leftover bits of gauze, got up and carried it into the kitchen to throw away.

Noboru groaned and rubbed his chest as he watched her go. "Michiko has saved my life more times and in more ways than I can count. She's a good woman. The best. You need to find a woman like that, Gabriel. Someone who'll take care of you. Or have you found one already?"

Gabriel shook his head. "I'm not the type to..." He trailed off, unsure how to finish that sentence. He wasn't the type to what? Let someone take care of him? Stick around long enough to find out? Both were true, he supposed. He'd lost more than a few good women over the years, women he'd cared about and cared for, who claimed they couldn't compete with whatever it was that kept pulling him back to the forests and jungles, mountains and deserts half a world away. On top of that was an uneasy feeling that came over him whenever he got too close to someone, a fear that she'd be in danger because of him—or, maybe worse, that he'd be forced to give up being in danger for her. The way Michiko wanted Noboru to give it up.

"That's too bad," Noboru said. "You've saved so many people, Gabriel. When will you let someone save you?"

GABRIEL LEANED ON THE WOODEN BANISTER THAT ran around the deck behind Noboru's house, sipping warm tea out a ceramic cup. A small back yard sloped gently downward away from the house until the lawn ended and the land dropped off in a steep incline. Beyond it he could see the waters of the Makassar Strait glistening in the twilight, and the lights of the oil refineries on the far shore twinkling like stars.

He took the Death's Head Key from around his neck and looked at it. When Edgar Grissom surprised them in the jungle, he'd already known about it—he'd recognized Gabriel and known that Julian had taken the key from him. That was understandable. Gabriel was a public figure; a lot of people knew what he looked like from his appearances on television and the articles written about him. And of course Julian would have told his father what had happened at the Discoverers League. But—Grissom had recognized Joyce, too. And that was troubling. Why would Grissom know the name of a random graduate student on a research trip to Borneo?

That wasn't the end of what was nagging at Gabriel. There was also the matter of how Julian had known Gabriel had come back from the Amazon with the Death's Head Key, and where to find him. There was only one possible answer. Grissom was being fed information. Someone must have told him about Gabriel finding the Death's Head Key, someone must have told him that Joyce was in possession of the Star of Arnuwanda.

Someone had sold them out. The only question was who.

"You've got that look on your face again," Noboru said. He was stretched out on a lounge chair by the sliding glass door of the house, a cup of tea resting on the small table by his hand. "That 'something's not right' look."

"You've known me for how long? A few days?"

"I've seen it plenty. I'm guessing you wear it a lot."

Gabriel smiled. "It's nothing." He didn't want to worry Noboru.

Noboru raised a doubtful eyebrow and sipped his tea.

Gabriel looked through the glass door as Joyce finally came out of the kitchen. She'd been on the phone for nearly an hour. Michiko, sitting at a small breakfast table reading hospital reports, pointed toward the tea kettle on the range and Joyce poured herself a cup. Gabriel watched her walk toward them, holding the cup between her palms, blowing on the tea and taking a tentative sip. The bruise around her eye had grown darker, but Michiko's treatment had kept it from swelling too badly. Joyce slid the door open, stepped out onto the deck and slid it closed again behind her.

She joined Gabriel by the banister and put her cup down next to his.

"Who were you talking to?" he asked.

She stared out at the water. The sky grew darker, the first stars appearing in the sky. "That was Uncle Daniel. He's still working at the dig site in Turkey and wants me to come there. I think it's a good idea. I can't stay in Borneo—it's too dangerous now. And besides, we don't know how much Grissom was able to work out before we got the Star back. For all we know, he's already on his way to finding the second gemstone. I can't let that happen."

"You want to go after Grissom again?" Gabriel said. "You barely survived this time. And he'll be ready for you next time."

She shook her head. "I know I can't take him on.

No, my plan is to get to the second gemstone before he does. Uncle Daniel can help with that. He's got the resources and expertise. If anyone can help me find it, it's him. He found the Star itself, after all."

Gabriel reached for his tea and took a sip, taking the time to think. Daniel Wingard was certainly an accomplished archaeologist; he knew what he was doing when it came to locating lost artifacts. But Daniel Wingard didn't know his way around a gun and wouldn't stand a chance if he were facing one. He could probably help her beat Grissom to the second Eye of Teshub, and if this were a simple case of professional rivalry among colleagues, that would be enough. But Edgar Grissom wasn't just another academic looking to notch up a publication for his CV. He had an army at his command and no compunction about leaving a trail of corpses in his wake. Even if they succeeded in finding the other gemstones before Grissom did, there wasn't a chance in hell Joyce and Daniel would come back alive.

He tossed back the rest of his tea and put the cup back on the railing. "I can't let you do this. Grissom is too dangerous."

Her eyes narrowed. "You can't *let* me? Didn't we have this conversation already?"

"Let me clarify," he said. "I can't let you do this alone. I'm coming with you."

She looked surprised. She started to say something, but Gabriel cut her off.

"You're right," he said. "Grissom can't be allowed to find the other gemstones. If it exists, he can't be allowed to get his hands on the Spearhead. It would be catastrophic, Sargonia all over again, only on a global scale. And, no disrespect to your uncle, but Daniel's not prepared to face a man like Grissom."

She studied his face for a moment. "You're willing to put yourself back in Grissom's crosshairs just for me?"

"And for your uncle," he said. "And the rest of the human race."

"And," she said. "And." She rose up on her toes took his face gently between her hands and kissed him. Her lips felt tender against his.

"Joyce," he said, "you don't have to—"

"Oh, I didn't do it for you," she said, her voice all innocence. "I did it for humanity."

She picked up her tea and walked over to Noboru.

"I can't go with you," he told her. He smiled sadly. "I wish I could, but…" He touched his chest. "Tomomi is coming back from Singapore to check up on me. I haven't seen her in so long. But you'll be in good hands with Gabriel. The best."

"Thank you, Noboru," Joyce said. She bent down and hugged him. "For everything."

"Any time," he said. "Just give me a chance to recover from *this* time first."

She turned to Gabriel. "Uncle Daniel said he's gotten us tickets for an early flight to Antalya tomorrow morning. They'll be waiting for us at the airport. Get some sleep—I'll knock at six." She slid open the glass door and stepped inside.

After she'd slid it closed again, Noboru looked at him curiously.

"What?" Gabriel asked.

"Is there something you want to tell me about you two?"

He shook his head. "There's nothing to tell. She's an old friend of the family, that's all."

"Really." Noboru raised his eyebrows and took a

sip of tea. "I guess she must feel she can count on her old friends."

"What do you mean?"

"Didn't you hear what she said? Her uncle told her he was buying two tickets. She knew from the start you would go with her."

Gabriel turned to the glass door, but Joyce was already walking with Michiko down the hallway toward the guest room.

13

ANTALYA WAS NESTLED AT THE INLAND TIP OF A LARGE
bay along Turkey's Mediterranean coast. From the
air, it looked like any other resort town. Gabriel saw
enormous luxury hotels sprawled along the coast,
each surrounded by swimming pools, golf courses and
beaches. A few miles to the northwest was the country's
more desolate mountain region, where archeological
digs had been taking place non-stop for nearly a
century. Just a few years ago, he remembered, a new
site of ancient Hittite temples had been unearthed in
the western city of Burdur, and the remarkably intact
foundations of a Roman village had been dug up outside
Ankara. It was no surprise, then, that Daniel Wingard
had been drawn to Turkey. How could any archeologist
resist the seemingly limitless treasures still waiting to
be unearthed? And he'd been right to come, given what
he'd wound up finding, even if he hadn't had a clue at
the time what the consequences would be. The entrance

of Edgar Grissom and the Cult of Ulikummis into their lives could be traced back to the moment Daniel Wingard pulled the Star of Arnuwanda out of the dirt.

On the ground, Antalya was a good deal less generic than it had seemed from above. The Mediterranean had a flavor all its own. The smell of the sea, the ancient sunbaked features of the people, the sounds of the Turkish sea birds calling to one another as they circled over the water. It was as warm as Borneo had been but noticeably less humid, the breeze off the sea like a cool fan on the back of Gabriel's neck.

They deplaned and took a taxi to the Peninsula Hotel, in the city's center. Thirty floors of concrete and glass that covered most of a block, flanked by smaller buildings on either side. Balconies dotted the building's façade. Thick cement ledges, each carved with traditional Turkish designs, wrapped around the hotel in bands between the floors. It was the city's highest-end luxury hotel and as Gabriel and Joyce walked into the vast air-conditioned lobby, Gabriel carrying his beat-up suitcase, Joyce with her rucksack hanging from one shoulder, the guests sitting on the couches and at the bar by the piano turned to watch them, murmuring among themselves.

At the front desk, the concierge, a young man in a gray blazer, looked up from what he was doing and blanched. "Are you all right?" he asked in Turkish. "Do you and your wife require assistance?"

"We're fine," Gabriel replied in the same tongue. He could see their reflection in the mirrored wall behind the desk. Their faces were covered in bruises and cuts, and there was still a dark raccoon circle around one of Joyce's eyes. "Just visited some rough spots before coming here."

The concierge looked like he wanted to ask more but he was too well trained. As long as they paid their bill, guests were free to do what they liked, even if it left bruises. "You're certain you don't need anything?"

"One thing," Gabriel said. "We need Daniel Wingard's room number."

The concierge flipped through a box of index cards, found one marked "Wingard," and read through the notes penciled on it. "You are checking in to stay with Professor Wingard? Mister, uh, Hunt, is it?"

"Yes," Gabriel said. "He's expecting us."

The concierge told them to go to the penthouse, room 3002, and pointed to the elevators. He offered to have their bags taken up by the bell captain, but Joyce snatched her arm away when he tried to take hers off her shoulder. She wasn't letting anyone near it. Not while the Star of Arnuwanda was nestled inside, wrapped in one of her old t-shirts. They crossed to the elevator bank, hit the call button beside the silver-plated doors, and as they waited Gabriel watched all the reflected faces in the doors watching them. Were they just curious bystanders? Joyce had said the Cult of Ulikummis had members all over the world. It would make sense that they'd at least be in Turkey, the ancestral home of the Hittite Empire. Any of the men staring at them from the lobby might have his own skull mask hidden away in his attaché case or tucked in a drawer back home.

The elevator doors slid open and they stepped inside. They rode to the penthouse floor in silence, soft jazz playing through the speakers in the ceiling. When the elevator pinged and the doors started to open, Joyce said, "I'm glad you came, Gabriel." She walked out of the elevator before he could answer.

He followed her into a long hallway with plush carpeting and creamy silk wallpaper. He watched Joyce walk ahead of him and thought about how she'd slept through most of the flight from Borneo, turning in her sleep at one point so that her head fell against his shoulder. She'd looked calm, peaceful for the first time since he'd pulled her out of that cage in the jungle.

She'd looked beautiful.

Cool it, he thought, carrying his suitcase down the hallway. *You knew her when she was seven, for God's sake.*

But she's not seven anymore, another part of his mind pointed out.

They found room 3002 around the corner from the elevators. When Joyce knocked on the door, it swung open and Daniel Wingard rushed out, crushing Joyce in a bear hug.

"Thank god you're all right," he said. He looked her over, frowning over her bruises and black eye. "Oh, my dear girl, what did they do to you?"

"I'm fine," Joyce said. "Really, I'm okay."

"And Gabriel! Thank you for finding her, thank you!" He pumped Gabriel's hand like he expected to draw water. "My god, look at you. I haven't seen you since the memorial service. That's what, eight years now?"

"Nine," Gabriel said. "It's good to see you, professor." Daniel Wingard looked exactly as Gabriel remembered him, if a little grayer on top and a little more wrinkled around the eyes and mouth. He was a full head shorter than Gabriel, with round features and the belly of a man who enjoyed hotel buffets.

"Only my students call me professor," he said, waving a dismissing hand. "It's Daniel, my boy. Ambrose and Cordelia were among my dearest friends—I won't stand on ceremony with their son. Now, come in, come in." He held the door open for them.

Directly inside was the suite's living room, an enormous chamber with arched doorways leading off on either side to bedroom and bathroom, study and kitchenette. Daniel had them to put their bags in the study, and when they returned to the living room he held out two glasses of scotch for them.

"Tell me everything, my dear," Daniel said. "From the beginning, don't leave anything out."

While Joyce brought him up to speed, Gabriel sipped his scotch—it tasted smooth, smoky and expensive—and walked restlessly around the room. Hadn't they gone over this on the phone already? If not, what had made that call last an hour? He didn't begrudge Daniel the information, of course, but every minute they delayed setting off to find the second Eye gave Grissom that much more of a head start.

He walked over to a set of three metal cylinders standing against the living room wall beside a long wooden table. Each cylinder stood about three feet tall and bore a sticker in German that warned the contents were under pressure.

"Oh, be careful," Daniel said, rushing over. "You shouldn't touch those. They're acetylene gas for the dig site. They only just arrived today, I haven't had a chance to bring them over yet."

"You had them delivered to your hotel room?" Gabriel asked.

Daniel nodded. "We've had a lot of items go missing from the site. It seems we have a thief on our hands, probably one of the local kids we hired. They can make a lot of money selling tools and instruments on the black market. They could get a lot for acetylene. Better to keep it here until it's needed. Out of harm's way." He turned back to Joyce. "Same reason I sent the Star to you. Speaking of which, I am dying to see what you worked out, the way it operates with the map—will you show me?"

Joyce fetched her bag from the study, took out the Star and unfolded the map. "Grissom has the first of the Eyes—but you'll help us find the second, won't you?"

"Absolutely, my dear." He shook his head disbelievingly. "To think that the Three Eyes of Teshub, the Spearhead, might all be *real*. How could I possibly say no to that?"

Joyce set the map on the floor. "We'll need a light," she said. Gabriel fished a flashlight out of his suitcase while Daniel went around the room drawing the curtains in front of all the windows and the glass doors to the terrace.

As Daniel pulled this last curtain shut, Gabriel thought he saw something, a movement glimpsed out of the corner of one eye. He looked over more closely. A man's silhouette crouched outside—

"Get down!" he shouted, and Joyce and Daniel dropped to the floor. Gabriel ran for the curtain and threw it open. Beyond, the terrace was empty. He blinked in surprise.

Joyce came up behind him. "What is it?"

"I thought I saw someone," he said. He unlocked the door, slid it open and stepped out onto the terrace, a rectangle of tiled cement enclosed by a waist-high brick wall. A table stood at the far end, its umbrella folded, flanked by two matching lounge chairs. There was no one in sight. With all the carvings providing handholds and footholds, the wall of the hotel would be easy enough to scale; and the neighboring terraces were close enough to jump to, or from. Someone *could* have been there. He scanned the row of terraces stretching to either side, then leaned over the edge of the terrace and looked down. No one. He turned to look up at the roof of the hotel, just above their room. There was no sign of movement.

Maybe it was just his nerves. He'd felt on edge in the lobby too.

Daniel poked his head out. "What was it?"

Gabriel walked back inside. "Don't know. Maybe I'm jumping at shadows."

Daniel slid the door closed and locked it again. "I'm not surprised, after what you've been through."

Daniel may not have been surprised, but Gabriel was. He could have sworn he'd seen a shape moving out there. He glanced at the terrace one more time. There was nothing but sunlight and the cityscape beyond.

"Can we... get back to the...?" Daniel waved an arm at the map on the floor.

Joyce held the Star in position over the map and Gabriel switched on the flashlight. He angled the beam so the light passed directly through the artifact. Joyce rotated the inner ring till the projected cuneiforms began to line up.

"All right, I see it," Daniel said. "That's the one you found in Borneo, the one marked with the symbol for earth."

"Right," Joyce said. "Now let's see the second." She turned the central starburst further until the Nesili symbol for "water" was opposite her. She moved the Star until the symbol's silhouette lined up perfectly with its twin below. The beam from Gabriel's flashlight passed through the tiny green jewel at the end of the starburst's shortest arm, sending a pinpoint of emerald light down to strike right in the open Mediterranean Sea.

"Mm," Daniel said. He got down on his hands and knees next to the map and peered at the penciled-in grid. "The question is, what's there? An island, perhaps?" He rose to his feet. "Wait here, I'm going to get my atlas." He hurried off into the bedroom and returned a moment later with a big hardcover volume in his hands. "Here we go." He sat next to the map again and flipped through the pages of the atlas until he found one showing a detailed view of the relevant portion of the Mediterranean. He pulled a small stub of a pencil from one of his pockets, licked its tip and made a mark on the page. "It appears to be about thirty-three degrees longitude," he looked at the map again, then back at the atlas, "twenty-seven degrees latitude." He made another mark and put the pencil down, frowning in confusion. "But there's…" He looked at the atlas again. "There's nothing there, just open sea all the way from Rhodes to Egypt."

"There's plenty there," Gabriel said and he switched off the light. He fixed both of the Wingards, father and daughter, with a concerned stare. "Remember, the first element was earth, and the crypt was underground. What we're looking for isn't *on* the water. It's under it."

14

THE CAVE SMELLED OF SPICE AND SMOKE. DEEP IN meditation, Vassily Platonov knelt before the altar, a low, flat boulder surrounded by candles whose flames illuminated the cave with a flickering glow. Incense smoldered from inside a stone brazier next to the boulder. With his headdress on the ground by his knees, he bowed his bald head in reverence. No statue of Ulikummis graced the altar. Such images were forbidden—theirs was a god of darkness and secrecy, his face so terrible it was said no mortal, not even his most devoted follower, could look upon it. Instead, resting at the center of the altar on a small woven blanket was a human skull that had recently been flensed of its skin.

In a low singsong Vassily chanted verses from memory, the ones he had been taught as a child and the ones he had only been permitted to learn upon turning twenty-one. He had recited them morning and night for decades now, and the words blended together as he sang them rapidly, his tongue flicking against his palate. With both hands he made the signs of Ulikummis and traced them along his chest. The time was coming near: World's End, as the prophecies described it. When it came, the ancient stories would be played out again Just as Ulikummis had been born to defeat Teshub, Vassily had been born to become Ulikummis' renewed vessel on earth, a shell for their god to inhabit when he once again descended to their plane to plunge the world into darkness and despair.

A rustle of movement drew Vassily from his thoughts as someone entered the cave behind him. "High Priest," a voice said in Russian.

Vassily got up from where he knelt, placing the headdress back on his head. One of the younger brethren stood in the doorway, dressed in his street clothes instead of the ritual robe and skull mask. The young man was breathing hard and rubbing his hands anxiously on the thighs of his jeans. It was clear he had run to the cave with important news, but as with so many the younger brethren, he had to be taught proper respect first.

"In the presence of our god's altar, Arkady," Vassily said, "you will address me in the sacred tongue, not the corrupt language of our adopted land. Is that clear?"

Arkady's face flushed with embarrassment. "Yes, High Priest," he answered in Nesili.

"Deliver your news," Vassily said.

"We have confirmation our enemies have left Borneo," Arkady said. "Our brother in the…" He paused, struggling to find words that didn't exist in the ancient language. Vassily nodded, allowing him to substitute Russian words for them. "…in the *airport* reports both the man and the woman were on a flight to Turkey this morning."

"And the Star of Arnuwanda is with them?"

"Yes. Our brother caught it on the…" He struggled for the words again. Vassily was losing patience with this young one, as he often did with so many of them. The younger generation seemed less interested in serving Ulikummis than in the mere fellow-feeling of being a member of the group—that and indulging in the occasional violence their god demanded. Vassily wearily signaled permission with a wave of his hand, allowing Arkady to use Russian words again. "Our brother caught sight of the Star in the *baggage X-ray,* but without privacy he could take no action at the time. The flight landed in Antalya this afternoon. The man and woman were spotted checking into a hotel."

Vassily nodded. "Have our brothers in Turkey keep eyes on them at all times. I must be informed of their every move."

"Yes, High Priest." Arkady bowed stiffly. "Shall I gather the brethren and tell them to ready themselves for travel?"

"Not yet. Have the thieves followed for now, but take no action against them until my order." Vassily picked his staff up from the ground. "What news of the others we fought? The army of outsiders?"

"They are gone," Arkady replied. "They left us no trail to follow."

Bad luck, Vassily thought. The first Eye was in their possession and would have to be retrieved. But the Star of Arnuwanda was the priority. It had to be captured at all costs. Only the Star could lead them to Teshub's Spearhead.

Vassily returned to the altar, knelt before it. How

foolish the old storm god had been, hiding such immense power from men in the name of mercy. Mercy was a word without meaning to Ulikummis, as the world would soon find out.

THE BOAT WAS NAMED THE *ASHINA TUWU* AND belonged to one of Daniel Wingard's colleagues, an engineering professor at Akdeniz University who had made a bundle from an invention of his, something involving lasers. He reluctantly agreed to lend the boat to them. A Hatteras 77 Convertible, the *Ashina Tuwu* was more yacht than fishing boat, with black-tinted windows lining the flybridge, two luxury cabins below deck, and a streamlined white fiberglass hull that sliced effortlessly through the water as Gabriel steered it out of its mooring at the Setur Antalya Marina and into the open Mediterranean Sea. Traveling at a speed of 33 knots, it wouldn't take them long to reach the coordinates they'd calculated from the map.

Daniel joined Gabriel on the flybridge, taking one of the riding seats beside the helm chair. Four state-of-the-art displays were embedded in the forward console just past the steering station: compass, speedometer, sonar, and a touch-screen where the ship's computerized system monitored everything from engine diagnostics to fuel transfer and tank levels. Gabriel would have preferred a more old-fashioned bridge, with fewer controls—fewer things to go wrong—but you made do with what you had.

"Where's Joyce?" Daniel asked over the low hum of the engine.

"Below deck," Gabriel replied, his eyes scanning the horizon. "She's checking on the dive equipment."

Daniel nodded. "I don't know what I would have done if you hadn't found her, Gabriel," he said. "She came very close to dying, didn't she?"

"Yes. We both did."

"This isn't what I wanted for her," Daniel said. "This life. Don't get me wrong, I was happy when she showed an interest in archeology and anthropology. In fact, I took quite a bit of pride in it, knowing I'd had a hand in it. Her favorite uncle." He smiled weakly. "When she was younger, she would spend more time with me than with her parents. I would tell her stories about all the amazing things I found whenever I went on digs. You should have seen the way her eyes lit up, hearing about it. I knew even then that she had the bug. I hoped she might find a good university to teach at, do some traveling, work a dig site or two during her off time. The usual routine. But that's not how it turned out."

"What happened?" Gabriel said.

"You did," Daniel said. Gabriel didn't say anything, just continued steering. "I remember the day she brought me a copy of *National Geographic* and asked me if the man on the cover was the same boy she'd met all those years ago at my house in Maryland. I told her yes, it was. You remember that article?"

How could he forget? He'd only been on the cover the one time, shortly after his discovery of the tomb of the Mugalik Emperor. He hadn't meant for it to become public, at least not as quickly and as widely as it had. But there'd been a spy in his crew, not in an enemy's pay but in CNN's, and his face had been all over the world the next day.

"After that," Daniel said, "she never stopped following your career. All your adventures in the papers and magazines. That TV special on the Discovery Channel a few years back." That *unauthorized* TV special, Gabriel thought. "She became obsessed with you, Gabriel. She headed off to follow in your footsteps, and she almost died because of it."

Gabriel didn't know what to say. He'd never set out to be anyone's role model, least of all Joyce Wingard's. But that didn't absolve him of responsibility if that's what had happened. He remembered her comment to him back in Merpati's place: "You don't know how I used to dream about hearing those words come out of your mouth... The great Gabriel Hunt, impressed."

And he remembered the touch of her lips.

"I'm not blaming you," Daniel went on. "She's an adult now. She makes her own decisions. But I thought it was important for you to know. And if you were to talk to her, I think she'd listen."

Gabriel shifted uncomfortably. "What do you mean?"

"You might be able to talk her out of this life, Gabriel. When this is all over, convince her she'd be better off with a university job where the only attacks she'll ever have to fend off will be to her funding, or her tenure application. Where she'll be safe. She's like a daughter to me, Gabriel. I couldn't stand it if something happened to her."

"I doubt she'd listen to me," he said. "I don't think she's one for taking advice from anyone."

"I'd appreciate it if you'd try," Daniel said.

GABRIEL STOOD ON THE WOODEN PLANKS OF THE AFT deck, leaning against the steel railing with the sun beating down on his shoulders. In the distance, the

Turkish skyline retreated toward the horizon until it was little more than a dark band at the far end of a field of rippling turquoise. The waters were calm. The nearest boat, a massive cruise ship anchored some miles away, looked like a bathtub toy. He felt the engine cut out before he heard it, the vibrations below his feet slowing to a stop. He'd left Daniel to steer and keep an eye on the coordinates; the man wasn't a seasoned sailor, but he knew more about all the machinery in the pilot house than Gabriel did.

As the *Ashina Tuwu* bobbed gently in the waves of its own wake, Daniel emerged from the flybridge and climbed down the steps to the deck. "This is the spot," he announced.

"You're sure?" Gabriel asked.

"Have you seen the computers up there? This boat could find Amelia Earhart if you plugged in enough numbers."

Gabriel nodded and turned back to the water. According to Arnuwanda's ancient map, the second of the Three Eyes of Teshub waited somewhere below the undulating blue waves. He only hoped Grissom hadn't beaten them to it.

Below the flybridge, the door to the cabin opened. Joyce stepped down the shallow steps to the deck, her hair tied back in a tight ponytail. She'd changed into a black bikini while she'd been below, and the sunlight glistened off her bronzed skin. She held an oxygen tank in each hand and planted them before Gabriel on the deck.

"I take it we're here?" she asked.

"The exact coordinates," Daniel said. "Assuming the map was correct to begin with and nothing has changed in the centuries since it was drawn, the Eye should be right below us." He ducked into the cabin and came back a moment later with the rest of the equipment.

Gabriel and Joyce put on their scuba masks, fins and gloves. They hooked dive lights and small knives to their weight belts. Gabriel unzipped the nylon backpack he'd brought with him, pulled out the Death's Head Key and hung it around his neck in case they needed it to deal with whatever was waiting for them down there. As he zipped the backpack again, the Star of Arnuwanda caught the sunlight, glittering at him from inside. Joyce had insisted on bringing it with them when they left the hotel. After all they'd been through, she didn't wanted to let it out of her sight. Gabriel felt the same way about his Colt, which rested at the bottom of the backpack. Old habits died hard.

Daniel checked the tanks and regulators to make sure they were working properly, then brought them over to where Gabriel and Joyce sat at the edge of the deck. There was no railing behind them, only a short drop to the water below.

"There are deep trenches in the sea floor all along this part of the Mediterranean," Daniel said. "If the structure housing the second Eye hasn't been found in all this time, it's a safe bet it's at the bottom of one of them. I don't know how deep you'll have to go, but if the pressure gets too much for you, if you get light-headed or sick, come back to the boat right away. Please—" He caught Joyce's eye. "Don't put yourself in any more danger than necessary. Worse comes to worst, we can always come back tomorrow and try again."

"We won't get a second chance," Joyce said. She slipped her arms through the straps of an oxygen tank and straightened it on her back. "If we don't get the Eye, Grissom will. Tomorrow's not an option."

Gabriel strapped on his tank too. "Keep the boat here," he told Daniel. "And turn on the dive lights on the bottom so we can find you again."

"Already done," Daniel said. He turned to Joyce as she fitted the regulator into her mouth. "Be careful," he said. Joyce gave him the thumbs-up, then tipped backward into the water with a loud splash.

Daniel shook his head. "You see what I'm dealing with? She's completely reckless."

"I'll try to bring her back in one piece," Gabriel said.

"Yes," Daniel said, "do that, please."

Gabriel slipped the regulator into his mouth. He took a couple of breaths to test the action, then dropped backward off the deck and followed Joyce into the sun-warmed water. Though the salinity levels were low in this part of the Mediterranean, his scars stung as the water washed over them. A moment later the stinging subsided, or at least he got used to it, and he kicked his way deeper. Above him, bright red lights ran along the bottom of the ship's hull, a beacon to guide them back. He spotted Joyce ahead of him, her body tipped downward, coursing lower into the depths where the shimmering columns of sunlight that broke through the surface grew diffuse. He hurried to follow her, angling his body and kicking his fins. The Death's Head Key swung on the strap around his neck and floated behind him as he swam. Roughly four hundred feet below, he could make out swaying masses of seaweed at the bottom, and a dark, jagged crack cutting across the sand and stone of the sea floor. A trench.

Schools of fish darted around him as he descended, gray bullet tuna and long, thin silver garpikes parting to either side in undulating sheets. Joyce was still ahead of him, kicking her fins hard, not waiting for him to catch up, not even looking back to see if he was still there. At that moment, it was hard to imagine her giving a damn about anything he or anyone else had to say about her career choices.

He had to admit, there was a dichotomy to her he found intriguing. Sometimes she was funny, tender, even affectionate, and other times she was stubborn, single-minded, even hostile. It was almost as if she became a different person when they were in the field, like she was trying to compete with him, desperate to prove her mettle. It fascinated and frustrated him at the same time. He didn't want to see her risk her neck again and again taking foolish risks, but it was when she was like this, barreling full steam ahead into the unknown, that he felt more drawn to her than ever. It was foolish, he knew. And a little uncomfortable—his family and hers had been so close she felt almost like a relative. Yet the more he was around her, the more he realized there was something about her he couldn't shake. And didn't want to.

Joyce continued toward the trench in the sea floor, her slender form gliding gracefully through the water. Gabriel followed, closing the distance between them. The water grew colder the farther they got from the surface and the reach of the sun. Ahead, Joyce passed into the shadows of the trench, disappearing from view. A moment later, her dive light went on, a bright shaft that cut through the darkness and illuminated her body in silhouette. Gabriel approached the mouth of the trench, pulling his own dive light from his weight belt and switching it on. A fat spotted eel dove into the sand to hide as he passed, descending into the trench, the darkness and cold closing in around him.

In the glare of his dive light, he saw rugged stone walls on either side. Tufts of marine plant life grew out of the cracks and swayed in the gentle current. The deeper he swam, the more the pressure built, making the bruises and wounds on his torso and face throb dully.

He caught up to Joyce as she passed a rounded outcropping in the trench wall. She glanced at him, her eyes hidden in the shadows of her swim mask, then shone her light deeper into the trench. The beam pierced the darkness for a hundred feet, then faded without touching anything. There was no telling how far they were from the floor, only that at this height the trench seemed bottomless.

The Death's Head Key floated up in front of his mask. He reached up to push it out of the way, but before he could touch it the key jolted suddenly to the side. He pulled it down, but the key yanked up to the side again, too insistent for it to be due solely to the current. It felt like it was pulling against the strap of its own accord. He signaled to Joyce to follow him, then swam in the direction the key was pointing. It remained floating in front of him as he swam, which wasn't right—his momentum should have caused the key to trail behind him.

He remembered the key leaping out of Grissom's hand into the lock of the crypt in Borneo. Grissom had muttered a word Gabriel almost hadn't caught.

Magnetized.

The key angled up suddenly as he neared the trench wall, pulling at the strap with such force that Gabriel thought the leather might break. He shone his light up and saw he was directly beneath the large outcropping, the rock's surface slick with sea moss and thick weeds. Joyce swam up beside him, adding her light to his in illuminating the enormous stone above. The key kept tugging forward.

He swam closer, Joyce right beside him. The Death's Head Key rose over his head, almost pulling the strap from around his neck before he could grab it. It was aiming itself directly at the outcropping. Gabriel released the key. It sped a few inches through the water and attached itself to the bed of moss.

Grissom had been right. Somehow the key was magnetized, responding to something in the outcropping.

He started pulling at the weeds around the key, tearing them off the surface of the rock. Joyce dug at the moss as well, scraping handfuls away. Together they cleared a wide swath, enough to see that the surface underneath was made of metal. As they pulled away more vegetation, it revealed itself to be a large, square hatch, decorated under a thick patina of rust with the same sorts of ornate designs as the door in Borneo. As before, there was no knob or handle, only a lock featuring the same peculiar triple-slotted keyway and the same etching above it of a skull with a diamond shape between its eyes.

Gabriel retrieved the Death's Head Key from where it was stuck, quivering, in the moss and angled its three blades toward the keyway. The key leapt from his fingers to sink into the lock. Joyce looked at him in amazement. He tried to turn the key, but the pins and tumblers inside the lock hadn't moved in thousands of years, and the water had all but rusted them in place. He kept forcing it, and just when he thought either the key or his arm would snap in half, he felt something give inside the lock. Using both hands, he managed to turn the key, first just forty-five degrees, then the rest of the way around. He felt a powerful vibration inside the door, then a heavy *clonk,* as of a bolt sliding aside.

Taking hold of the key, he planted both flippered feet against the rock and pulled as hard as he could. Joyce slid her knife into the edge between the hatch and the surrounding rock, to try to help wedge it open. It felt like he was trying to pull the entire outcropping out of the trench wall with his bare hands. The hatch refused to budge. He wondered if it even would be possible to open it after all this time. Then he felt something give. The hatch popped open a crack and slowly swung wide. Behind it, Gabriel saw nothing but pitch black, a tunnel into the rock. He pulled the key from the lock, struggling against the magnetic force that tried to keep it in place, and hung it around his neck again. He shone his dive light into the opening.

Something moved in the distance, heading toward the hatch.

Joyce shone her light in as well, then recoiled and screamed into her regulator, sending a rush of bubbles over her head.

Long, white arms reached suddenly toward them, followed by the leering face of a skull.

15

GABRIEL SWAM ASIDE TO LET THE SKELETON DRIFT
harmlessly past. It bumped against the trench wall and
its bones broke apart, tumbling away loosely with the
current. He turned his light on Joyce. She put a hand
out and pushed the light away. In the brief glimpse
he'd gotten of her face, she'd looked embarrassed.

It was nothing to be embarrassed about. Most
people would scream if they saw a skeleton apparently
swimming toward them, even if they hadn't just spent
five days imprisoned by men wearing skull masks.
But here again Joyce seemed to need to prove she was
every bit the hardened veteran he was. He just hoped
this tendency on her part wouldn't lead to her doing
something that would be worse than embarrassing—
possibly even fatal.

In any event, he wasn't going to give her the
chance to do so here. Gabriel swam into the tunnel
first, the beam from his dive light leading the way.

Joyce followed, shining her light along the walls. The entire stone outcropping was hollow, angling slightly upward from the hatch and extending some thirty feet into the trench wall. Rough alcoves had been carved into the walls on either side, just as there had been in the crypt in Borneo. Inside all but one alcove was a skeleton, wrists and ankles manacled to the stone. In the empty alcove, broken manacles hung where they'd once held the skeleton that had floated away. All traces of skin and clothing on the skeletons were long gone, and the Hittite armor they had worn when buried had corroded to shapeless patches covering their ribcages and in a few cases the tops of their skulls.

Gabriel's heart beat faster at the sight of a familiar shimmering green light playing along the walls at the far end of the chamber. As he swam closer, he saw a pedestal on the floor, and atop it a huge emerald, the same shape and size as the one in Borneo, clutched in a similar stone hand. Like its twin, this jewel glowed from within, painting the walls around it with flickering green rays that illuminated a row of carved cuneiform symbols. Gabriel recognized them as the same Nesili words they'd seen in Borneo.

The light at world's end.

The stone fingers looked like they had a firm grip on the gemstone; at minimum they had prevented it from floating away all this time. Remembering what had happened in Borneo, Gabriel examined the walls and ceiling for any sign of booby traps before touching the stone hand. Nothing.

He signaled to Joyce to keep an eye out, then pulled the knife from his belt. He placed one palm over the emerald to brace it and felt a strange vibration travel up his arm. What Grissom had felt, presumably; the power of the storm god, he'd called it.

Gabriel slid the blade of his knife between the emerald and the stone thumb. The hand in Borneo had had hidden hinges in the knuckles. If he could bend the thumb away, he might be able to pry the gemstone free. He pushed with the knife, trying to lift the thumb. It didn't budge. He pushed harder. It was difficult to gain leverage while floating, but finally the thumb started to give. He slid the knife deeper between the emerald and the thumb and pushed again, but instead of bending on its hinge, the thumb broke off entirely. The oblong bit of stone spun away from the pedestal and sank slowly to the floor.

He put the knife away in its sheath and grasped the emerald carefully with both hands. With the thumb gone, he was able to shift the gemstone easily within the confines of the other fingers. He maneuvered it toward the space where the thumb had been and with a little finessing and a lot of yanking, he managed to pull it free.

Joyce swam over to him, her eyes flashing with excitement. She gave him a thumbs-up.

Movement at the corner of his eye brought Gabriel's attention back to the pedestal. The stone fingers began to bend inward on their hinges to form a thumbless fist. Just like in Borneo, before they'd almost gotten buried alive in the chamber. He pointed in the direction of the hatch and started swimming, gripping the emerald tightly and kicking his legs as fast as he could. He glanced back to make sure Joyce was still behind him. Past her, at the far end of the underwater crypt, a panel in the ceiling was sliding open (damn it, he hadn't seen a seam!), and a large, jagged stone fell through, moving at a tremendous pace as though hurled by some sort of spring mechanism. It smashed the pedestal beneath it and careened off the floor. Because the chamber was angled downward toward the hatch, the stone caromed toward them. It banged off the walls, smashing off shards of stone that spun through the water like shrapnel. Behind it, another stone, even larger than the first, shot out of the hole and barreled toward them in the first one's wake. Then a third. Gabriel twisted back around and kicked as fast as he could toward the hatch.

The water slowed the speed of the oncoming boulders, but not enough. He'd seen the damage they were capable of doing. If one of them hit him or Joyce, they'd be pulped.

As they swam desperately along the channel, he felt Joyce beside him, tugging at his arm. He looked where she was pointing—at the alcoves with the skeletons inside. She swam toward one of the alcoves and started wedging herself inside.

Not a crazy idea on the face of it—hide in an alcove, let the stones pass—but in fact it would be suicide, for reasons he had neither the time nor the ability, underwater, to explain. Instead, he yanked Joyce out of the alcove she'd swum halfway into and shoved her furiously toward the hatch. She plunged through, disappearing outside. He gave one last glance over his shoulder and saw the first boulder bearing down on him. Gabriel launched himself through the hatch.

He made it through a fraction of a second before the boulder slammed against the hatch from inside, blocking the opening. The second boulder hit the first from behind a second later, then the third, and with each impact the metal frame of the hatch warped and bulged under the weight, forming a tight seal. If they hadn't made it out—if they'd tried to duck into the alcoves instead of fleeing—there was no way they would have gotten out now.

Joyce stared at him through her mask, the look on her face once again tinged with embarrassment. Gabriel pointed toward the surface and started swimming up. *Let her feel embarrassed all she wants. I promised her uncle I'd keep her alive.*

A few minutes later he spied the bright beacon lights along the bottom of the *Ashina Tuwu* and headed for them. Joyce followed close behind. When they broke the surface, Gabriel saw Daniel rushing down the steps from the flybridge toward them. They pulled themselves up the ladder on the side of the ship, Gabriel clutching the emerald in one arm. He took the regulator out of his mouth and slipped out of the air tank's straps, putting it down on the deck next to Joyce's.

Daniel handed them each a towel and said breathlessly, "Dear god, is that it?"

Gabriel held up the emerald. "Right where Arnuwanda said it would be."

"My God," Daniel said, "it's huge. It would be worth a fortune to any jeweler, never mind the historical value."

"Right, never mind that," Joyce said. She flipped her ponytail to her shoulder and squeezed the water out of it. "That's only the reason dozens of people are trying to kill us right now."

"Oh, I know, I know," Daniel said, still staring at the gemstone. He reached for it tentatively. "May I?" Gabriel handed it to him. "Oh, my word. Is it… vibrating?" He put his ear to it. "And humming? It's incredible! I can feel something, like an electrical charge." He shook his head in wonder. "Fantastic."

Daniel handed the gemstone back to Gabriel. "I'll turn the ship around. We should be back in time for dinner. I know a place on the Atatürk Caddesi. A bit pricy, but this calls for a celebration." He climbed the steps to the flybridge again and disappeared behind the tinted windows.

Gabriel stood by the railing, letting the sunlight play off the facets of the emerald in his hand. They'd beaten Grissom to the second Eye of Teshub. That was good, but it didn't mean they were out of danger yet. Grissom still had the first gemstone, and quite possibly had a better idea of where the final one was hidden than they did. Of course, even if Grissom found the third Eye before they did, the Spearhead was presumably useless, inert, without all three to activate it. But that only put their lives in further danger. It meant Grissom would come looking for the missing piece, and he wouldn't stop until he had it.

Briefly Gabriel thought about whether they could use Grissom's determination to their advantage somehow—maybe they could stay put in Turkey and let him come to them. But no, it was too dangerous. Grissom had too many men under his command, too many resources. Besides, Joyce would never go for it. Watching her walk toward him across the deck, tying a towel around her hips like a skirt, Gabriel knew exactly what she was going to say. He could have written the script for her.

"The third gemstone is still out there somewhere," she said. "We have to find it before Grissom does. It's the only way to keep him from getting his hands on the Spearhead."

"You still don't have any idea what that third element from the legend is?"

She shook her head. The light from the emerald reflected in her eyes as she stared at it. She lifted it out of his hands and cradled it between her palms. "Whoa! You guys weren't kidding about the vibrations. How is it possible? It's just an emerald, isn't it?"

He cupped his hands around hers, feeling the gemstone's muffled vibrations through her flesh. "I met a medicine woman in Paraguay once, one of the last of her tribe, who claimed to be able to use crystals to heal the sick. Her line was that all crystals are in a constant state of vibration, which gives them special conductive properties. She said it was what made it possible for her to heal her patients."

"Did it work?"

Gabriel shrugged. "I don't know if it was the crystals or not, but a lot of sick people got well in her care. Maybe it was purely psychological. Maybe there was more to it."

"But you couldn't actually feel the vibrations in her crystals, could you?"

Gabriel shook his head.

"So this is different."

"That's putting it mildly," Gabriel said.

"It's like these gemstones are so charged up that they can barely contain the energy inside them. But what kind of energy is it? Where did it come from?"

"Don't you remember the legend?" Gabriel said. "It came from Teshub."

She laughed sarcastically, but only for a moment. He wasn't laughing, and with the giant emerald thrumming powerfully in their hands, no explanation felt like it was worth dismissing.

They stood for a moment in silence.

"So... Gabriel," she said, looking up at him. "Are

we up to four now, or have I lost count?"

"Four what?"

"Four times you've saved my life."

"Someone's got to," Gabriel said. "You keep risking it." He smiled. "And what would the world do without Joyce Wingard to keep things interesting?"

A questioning look came into her eyes, for once an unguarded one, and she tilted her head back. There was no embarrassment in her expression now, nor any hostility. Her lips were slightly parted, and it was clear what she was waiting for. He bent his head forward and kissed her, felt her lips soft against his, her tongue slipping gently between them, her eyes sliding shut. She released the gemstone with one hand and moved it up to behind his head, her fingers curling in his wet hair. Her grip tightened and she pressed her lips harder against his—and then she broke away suddenly. She turned her face aside.

"I should…" she said. Her breathing was unsteady. "I'm going to get changed."

"Sure," Gabriel said, though sure was the last thing he felt. "That's a good idea."

He took the emerald back from her and watched her walk to the door.

"I'm sorry," he called to her. "I shouldn't have…"

She glanced back at him over her shoulder. "What in the world are you talking about, Hunt? Of course you should have." A half-smile played about her face, then she disappeared below deck.

He shook his head. *What have you gotten yourself into now?*

He opened the backpack and placed the gemstone and the Death's Head Key inside. He looked up at the tinted rear windows of the flybridge. The ship had turned around, heading back for Antalya, and with the sun now on the other side of the bridge he could make out Daniel's silhouette through the dark glass. He thought he saw Daniel move something small away from his ear—a cell phone?—and slip it into his pants pocket.

16

IF DANIEL HAD SEEN THEIR KISS ON THE BOAT, HE didn't mention it. In fact, Daniel didn't talk much at all on their trip back from the marina to the hotel. It seemed unlike him, especially after he'd been so excited when they'd brought the Eye up. Gabriel, back in his street clothes, adjusted the heavy backpack on his shoulders as they rode the elevator to the penthouse and tried to guess what was going through the older man's head. Daniel stood at the front of the elevator car, shifting his weight anxiously from one foot to the other. Something was definitely up; he'd have to ask Daniel about it when they were next alone.

Which they weren't right now. Standing in the back of the elevator beside Gabriel, Joyce surreptitiously wrapped her fingers around his. He glanced at her, but she didn't meet his eye, keeping her gaze forward and her face expressionless, entirely professional. The elevator pinged and the doors opened, and she quickly pulled her hand back.

Daniel led the way to his room, pulling the keycard from his pocket. He slid it into the lock mechanism on the door, waited for the little light beside the slot to turn green, and then pushed the door open. As they walked through, Gabriel saw Daniel raise his hands over his head. His heart sank even before he saw Edgar Grissom sitting on a chair in the living room, one leg casually crossed over the other. It wasn't until the door slammed behind him that he noticed the other men standing in key positions around the room. Three stood near Grissom, another by the side table along the wall, and a fifth was behind them, covering the door. All five had guns drawn and pointed at them.

"Frisk them," Grissom said. The man behind them left his post at the door and patted Gabriel down. Not finding anything, he moved on to Joyce.

"No weapons," the man said.

Grissom beckoned. "The backpack." Gabriel shrugged out of it and the man who'd frisked him carried it over. Grissom unzipped it, looked inside, and chuckled. "Excellent. The Star, the Death's Head Key, the second gemstone, even your gun. I couldn't have gotten a better gift if it were Christmas." He lifted the emerald out of the backpack and regarded it in the light. "Once again I ought to thank you. You have done all the heavy lifting for me, Mr. Hunt. Killing you seems like such a waste. I really ought to hire you instead." Grissom replaced the emerald in the backpack and zipped it closed. He smiled at Daniel. His hands, no longer raised, hung feebly at his sides. "Professor Wingard can tell you that I am a fair man to work with."

Joyce's face clouded over with anger. "You... helped them?"

Gabriel suspected his own face was displaying a similar combination of disbelief and disappointment. How could Daniel have sold them out? Not just Gabriel, the son of two of his oldest and closest friends, but Joyce, his own niece, whom he'd spoken so sincerely of wanting to protect. Or maybe he thought this was a good way to protect her? Get the Eyes and the Star out of her hands once and for all, never mind whose he was putting them in?

Daniel looked on the verge of tears. "I'm so sorry, my dear. You must believe me when I say that. Mr. Grissom contacted me a week ago, told me you'd been kidnapped in Borneo. He said he would bring you back safely if I helped him with his search for the gemstones."

"And you believed him?" Joyce demanded.

"Why shouldn't he?" Grissom said. "I'm a man of my word. But imagine my surprise when I discovered that the famous Gabriel Hunt had beaten me to it. Of course, even before I contacted your uncle, I already knew you were in possession of the Star of Arnuwanda, Miss Wingard. It's amazing what spreading a little cash around can accomplish with the locals here in Turkey."

Gabriel glanced at the three metal cylinders standing by the side table and remembered Daniel mentioning how the expensive acetylene gas was safer in his room than at the dig site because the place was full of thieves. Well, one of those thieves had signed their death warrants with a phone call to Grissom, and for what? A few extra coins?

Daniel turned to Gabriel, tears streaming down his cheeks. "I didn't know you would get involved, Gabriel. I thought they would just take the key from you in New York and that would be the end of it."

Gabriel's eyes narrowed. "What?"

Grissom laughed. "You mean you haven't figured it out yet? How we knew you had the Death's Head Key?"

Daniel hung his head and wiped at his eyes with the heel of his hand.

"Tell me," Gabriel said. Grissom started to speak, but Gabriel cut him off. "Not you. You," he said to Daniel. "You tell me."

Daniel took a deep breath. "You know I still talk with your brother from time to time, right? The last time, Michael mentioned that you'd gone to the Amazon to find the key. When Mr. Grissom mentioned he was looking for it, too, I thought…" He shook his head and looked at Joyce. "I'm no fool. I knew the kind of man I was dealing with. But I thought if I got him the key, it would ensure your safety. Please, Joyce, I'm so sorry. I only did it for you."

She turned away from him.

"Please—"

Grissom smiled. "Don't beg, professor. It's not seemly for a man of your experience. She is a petulant child and doesn't appreciate what you've done for her."

"Speaking of petulant children," Gabriel said, "where's your son? I'd have expected to see him here, carrying your bags."

"Julian will be joining us momentarily, Mr. Hunt. I know how much he's looking forward to seeing you again after your last encounter."

The door behind Gabriel opened.

"Ah, speak of the devil," Grissom said.

"The stairwells are manned, and the security cameras on this floor will be down for half an hour," Julian reported. "Any longer than that and hotel security will get suspicious. We're going to want to be long gone by then."

"Well done," Grissom said. He nodded toward Gabriel. "Our friend here was just asking about you."

Julian came around. He had a gun in his hand and Gabriel saw that his throat still bore the angry red marks of the chokehold that had rendered him unconscious.

Gabriel smiled. "Nice scar."

Julian turned the gun toward Gabriel's face.

"Not yet, Julian," Grissom said. "You'll have your chance soon enough, my boy. But Mr. Hunt and I have some unfinished business of our own." From his jacket pocket he pulled the ivory-handled dagger. He pressed the eye of the dragon carved along the handle and the two additional blades sprang out to flank the central one. Grissom rose from the chair, leaving the backpack on the cushion behind him.

"Step aside, Julian," Grissom said.

Julian obediently stepped to one side—but in doing so, he came within Gabriel's reach. Gabriel swept one hand up, grabbing Julian's gun arm and yanking it so the weapon pointed toward the side table. The gunman standing there ducked aside, but he wasn't the target. Gabriel squeezed Julian's fingers against the trigger.

One of the acetylene cylinders exploded in a violent eruption of fire and thick black smoke. Everyone hit the floor except the gunman who'd been nearest to the table; a large piece of the canister's outer shell sliced crosswise through his torso and pinned him to the wall. His clothing erupted into flames.

A shrill alarm sounded from the smoke detector on the ceiling. The sprinkler system turned on, drenching the room in a cold rain. Gabriel wrestled the gun out of Julian's hands, sprang to his feet and broke for the chair across the room, where Grissom had left the backpack.

Undeterred by the sprinklers, the fire climbed up the wall, devouring the wallpaper and charring the wooden frame of the mirror above the side table. Thick black smoke filled the room. Gabriel felt lightheaded, and realized the acetylene gas was mixing with the smoke. Through the haze, he saw Grissom kneeling and coughing violently into a handkerchief, the dagger on the floor by his knees.

Shapes moved in the thick smoke as Grissom's men got back to their feet. Gunshots sounded. Gabriel heard a bullet zip past his head and smash a ceramic lamp by the couch. Another smashed the mirror into shards of glass. With Grissom's men unable to see, they were shooting in all directions. He heard voices shouting but none of them sounded like Joyce's. He'd lost track of her—but he didn't dare call her name, not while the gunmen were looking for any indication of a direction to fire in.

He snatched the backpack off the chair and, hearing footsteps behind him, spun around. A man rushed toward him through the smoke, gun in hand. Gabriel swung the backpack, hitting the gunman in the head and knocking him to the floor. The man rolled away and came back up with his weapon blazing. Bullets tore through the air beside Gabriel, so close he could feel their heat on his skin. Gabriel lifted Julian's gun, aimed into the center of the dark mass in the smoke and fired. The man fell and didn't get back up.

Sopping wet from the sprinklers, eyes burning, throat raw, he slung the backpack over one shoulder and dropped to a crouch. A breeze from a shattered window swept through the thick smoke, clearing it a little, and he was suddenly able to make out two figures grappling on the other side of the room. One was tall and thick, the other shorter and with a ponytail flapping at the back of her head. Joyce! He saw her elbow her opponent in the side of the head. When he fell forward, she brought her knee up into his face. He hit the floor hard and stayed there. As Joyce turned, another man came up behind her, snatching her off her feet.

Gabriel sprang toward them, but something grabbed him from behind. Hands wrapped around his throat and he heard Julian's voice hissing in his ear. Gabriel tried to swing his gun around, but Julian batted it away. The gun slipped from Gabriel's fingers and flew across the floor. Then Julian's hands tightened around his throat again.

A massive explosion rocked the room. The other two cylinders, Gabriel thought—the heat of the fire must have set them off. The blast knocked Julian off his feet and Gabriel was able to pull himself free from the other man's grip as they fell. Flames leapt across the wall and licked at the ceiling. More smoke poured into the room. He heard Grissom coughing again somewhere off to his side. Gabriel rolled away from Julian. His hand touched something hard. He grabbed it—Grissom's triple-bladed dagger.

Gabriel stood, the smoke stinging his eyes. The gas in the air made him dizzy. He stumbled forward, hitting the sliding glass door that led out to the terrace. Closed. Gabriel reached for the handle to open it when he saw Julian lurching out of the smoke toward him, his hands extended before him. He'd found another gun somewhere and had it pointed at Gabriel's face. Gabriel ducked, stepped toward him, and drove the dagger in his fist upwards. He felt it sink into Julian's gut. Julian collapsed on top of him, the gun falling from his hands. His face was just inches away and Gabriel saw the fury drain from his expression. In its place, shock. Fear. Pain. His mouth opened, and he drooped forward. Gabriel let Julian's body slide to the floor.

Another figure came running toward him through the smoke. Gabriel groped along the floor for the gun Julian had dropped until he saw Joyce break through the wall of black haze.

"We have to get out of here," Gabriel said as she reached him. A bullet whizzed past them, cracking the glass of the terrace door.

"Where's Daniel?" Joyce asked.

"I don't know," Gabriel said, "but I think he's shown he can take care of himself."

"Daniel!" she yelled.

"After what he did?" Gabriel said. "You still—"

"*Daniel!*"

A short figure rose up slowly from the floor nearby and Gabriel realized Daniel Wingard had been cowering behind the couch.

"Joyce," Daniel said, coughing, "thank god you're all right."

Gabriel shouted in Joyce's ear, "Give me one good reason we shouldn't leave him here with his friends."

"I can't do that," Joyce replied. "I can't just leave him. Whatever he's done."

"Then he's your responsibility, not mine." Without waiting for an answer, he plowed through the smoke toward the door of the suite. Flames roared along the wall near the door, bathing them in heat. Gabriel put one arm up, covering his nose and mouth. He touched the doorknob. The metal was hot from the flames, but not too hot to touch. He turned it and pulled the door open. Smoke billowed out over his head as he thrust his head into the penthouse hallway, gulping air. The fire alarm was sounding even louder out here, wave after wave of shrill electronic pulses. Gabriel looked left and right, trying to spot the fire stairs. The prospect of climbing down thirty floors didn't thrill him, but it was better than staying here.

He spotted the stairwell door at the far end of the hall. As he set one foot out of Grissom's suite in that direction, though, the door burst open—and men began pouring out, running toward him with guns drawn.

17

GABRIEL SLAMMED THE DOOR SHUT AND QUICKLY fastened the deadbolt lock. It wouldn't hold them out for long, but hopefully long enough to find another way out of here. He led them back across the burning, smoke-filled hotel room toward the terrace. Behind them, fists pounded on the door, barely audible above the blasting alarm. Gabriel slid the glass door open and shepherded Joyce and Daniel onto the terrace.

Joyce looked around. "Now what?"

Gabriel walked to the edge, skirting the table and chairs, and looked down. A crowd had gathered on the street below, pointing up at the smoke billowing out of their room. From where he stood, a column of terraces extended thirty stories down. As he'd noted earlier, it would be possible to climb from one to the next—for him, at least; maybe even for Joyce—but getting back inside the hotel would be a challenge. There was no guarantee anyone would let them into their room, and the glass of the terrace door had barely spiderwebbed even from multiple gunshot strikes—it wouldn't break easily, not with just a couple of light lounge chairs to swing at it. And if they couldn't get in, they would be sitting ducks, easy pickings for any of Grissom's men who followed them down.

But up—up was another matter.

He dragged one of the chairs away from the table and placed it against the side of the building. He could hear Grissom's men pounding and kicking the door. He had to hurry. Any moment they would switch to using their weapons to blast the lock open.

Even standing on the chair, the roof was too high for him to reach. However, there was a thick cement ledge, maybe ten inches high, running along the wall just below the roof. He reached for it, his fingers brushing the Turkish designs carved into the cement. The banging on the door stopped. He could picture them aiming their guns at the lock. He stepped up onto the back of the chair, got a firm hold on the ledge and pulled himself up. From there he hoisted himself onto the gravel and tarpaper surface of the roof. He bent down to help Joyce up, then left her to help Daniel while he took off the backpack, unzipped it, and pulled out his Colt. He put the backpack back on his shoulders as the sound of gunshots and splintering wood came from under them.

Daniel threw one fat, stubby leg onto the roof and hauled himself up, then lay on his back, huffing the fresh air and trying to catch his breath. Below, Gabriel heard the terrace door sliding open. Glancing over the roof's edge, Gabriel saw Grissom's men burst onto the balcony. Two of them raised guns his way.

"Move!" Gabriel shouted, ducking back from the

edge as gunfire sped his way. Joyce helped Daniel to his feet, and the three of them ran across the roof, the gravel crunching under their heels. The hotel covered the better part of a city block and in the light of the setting sun, the roof seemed to extend forever. Halfway across, he ducked around a metal shed to find the roof access doorway, but it was locked from the inside. He rattled the knob once and kept moving. Behind them, Grissom's men were still climbing up from the terrace below. Ahead, an obstacle course of turbine roof ventilators stretched for yards like a sea of low, gray onion domes. He started weaving around them as bullets began flying their way. Fortunately, climbing up to the roof had slowed Grissom's men, so there was room enough between them to make aiming hard. But the sprint had taken its toll: Daniel was already out of breath and lagging behind, and Joyce was hanging back to help him. "Come on," Gabriel said. "They'll catch up if—"

The roof access door slammed open. Half a dozen men ran out onto the roof in pursuit. Gunshots cracked. Bullets ricocheted off the ventilators, dug into the gravel at their feet. Gabriel stopped, raising his Colt, but he couldn't get a clear shot with Joyce and Daniel in the way. He let them rush by, then fired. One of the gunmen spun and fell. The others kept coming, filling the air with bullets. Gabriel ran, keeping his head down. A bullet ricocheted off a ventilator by his feet.

The field of ventilators ended and, a moment later, he saw the edge of the roof approaching. Joyce reached it first, skidding to a halt. She looked down, turned back to Gabriel.

Gabriel stopped at the edge, his heart pounding. He looked over and saw the white cement roof of the apartment building that abutted the hotel. The drop looked to be about fifteen feet. He could hear the shouts of the gunmen drawing closer. Their only chance was to keep moving.

"You're going to have to hang down and drop. I'll hold them off as long as I can. Go!" Joyce climbed over the edge, holding onto the concrete rim with a white-knuckled grip. Out of the corner of his eye, Gabriel saw Daniel doing the same. Gabriel covered them, picking his shots carefully. He only had so many bullets, so he had to make each shot count. "Are you down?" he shouted. Joyce's voice came from a distance: "Yes."

Gabriel swung around and without pausing to look, jumped off the roof. He braced himself for a hard landing and rolled as his feet his the surface below. The impact was jarring and one of his palms got badly scraped, but he lurched back to his feet and kept running, sprinting after Joyce and Daniel. They were climbing over a low brick wall separating this building from the next. Behind him, Grissom's men reached the edge of the hotel's roof and opened fire. Bullets chipped the cement all around him. He kept sprinting, pausing only once to toss a gunshot back their way.

"Gabriel!" It was Joyce shouting to him from the next building over. She had reached the roof access shed for this building and had her hand on the knob. "This one's unlocked!"

He raced toward her as she pulled the door open. She stepped back with a startled expression on her face. An instant later, two burly men barreled out of the shed carrying axes in their hands.

Gabriel lowered his gun and hid it behind his back as they turned to face him.

"Miss," one of the men said, "we'll need you to stay back. You, too, sir."

More men were emerging from the shed. They all wore the heavy rubberized uniform of the Turkish municipal fire brigade. One pointed in the direction of the Peninsula and they all began heading that way.

"Please make your way down to the ground floor, sir," one of them said to Gabriel as he passed. "The fire is spreading. It isn't safe for you up here."

"No, it's not," Gabriel said. "Though I have to say, I feel a lot safer now that you're here." He glanced back. Grissom's men had faded—they were nowhere to be seen.

18

THE CARGO VAN RATTLED DOWN A DARK TURKISH side street, carrying Edgar Grissom away from the Peninsula Hotel. He sat on the bare, corrugated metal floor in back while two of his men occupied the front seats. He coughed what he hoped was the last of the smoke out of his lungs and into his handkerchief. Any irritant only worsened his condition further. Back in the hotel room, he'd been immobilized for minutes, unable to do anything but cough and try to suck air into his lungs, air that wasn't there. He'd been lucky that in the confusion he'd been able to drag himself to the door and out into the hallway. Another minute in that smoke…

Grissom looked at the specks of blood in his handkerchief, then folded it, stuffed it in his pocket, and finally allowed himself to look at the horror laid out across the van's floor before him. Julian's body still reeked of smoke. Portions of his clothing were charred. Ash dusted his pallid skin.

His dead skin.

The ivory handle of the dagger still protruded from just below Julian's solar plexus. Grissom's own weapon, modeled to his exact specifications after an ancient Chinese sacrificial dagger. They'd killed their own children, sacrificed them to the river gods, with daggers just like this one.

Julian.

He'd lost his wife to a disease that had cruelly taken her away from him little by little. And now he'd lost his son, his only child, the last of his family.

Lost him to Gabriel Hunt.

What Grissom felt wasn't sadness. There was no mourning or regret. There was only a vast, cold emptiness inside him, surrounding a bright coal of burning heat. This was the vengeance he was preparing for Gabriel Hunt. He would nurse it, stoke it, keep the embers burning until the proper moment came—and then it would erupt into a proper conflagration. Erupt and sweep Hunt from the face of the earth.

The man in the passenger seat turned around. Grissom recognized his face: Wellington, an American mercenary he'd hired back in Southeast Asia. Wellington said something, indicating the walkie-talkie in his hand, but Grissom wasn't listening. He was watching his son's head roll limply on his neck with every turn the van took.

"Forgive me," Grissom whispered to the corpse. "Forgive me." He pulled the dagger from Julian's torso, the three blades sliding out smeared with blood. The weapon that had taken his son's life would take Hunt's. He would make certain of that.

"Sir?" Wellington said.

Grissom stroked his son's blond hair. "There," he

murmured. "That's better, isn't it?"

"Sir," Wellington repeated, louder.

Grissom looked up, his hand tightening around the dagger. "What?"

Wellington indicated the walkie-talkie again. "The strike team's reporting they've lost the targets."

Grissom stood, hunched over beneath the van's low ceiling, and strode to the front. "What?"

"They lost them on the rooftops, sir."

Grissom's lips pulled back from his teeth. He lashed out with the dagger, slitting Wellington's throat with one fluid motion. Blood streaked across half the windshield. The man in the driver's seat flinched but kept his eyes on the road. He didn't dare say anything.

Grissom snatched the walkie-talkie out of the dead man's hand. "Find them!" he roared into it. "Kill the others, but bring me Gabriel Hunt *alive*!"

GABRIEL REACHED THE BOTTOM OF THE STAIRWELL and stepped out onto the sidewalk. Sirens shrieked from the other side of the block, where dark smoke roiled into the sky from the fire. Flames now consumed the upper portions of two buildings and it looked like a third might go at any moment.

Joyce emerged from the stairwell next to him. Daniel came last. He was out of breath, limping from the drop to the roof, and his face was red and sweaty from exertion. The three of them hurried down the street, trying to stay out of the light from the streetlamps.

"What do you think, how long till they come after us again?" Joyce asked.

"Not long," he said. "Grissom won't give up." Not with his son dead, Gabriel said to himself. "We have to get away from here. As far away as possible, as quickly as possible."

Joyce put her arm around Daniel's shoulders, helping him limp along the sidewalk. "We won't get far like this," she said. "His leg is getting worse."

"I'm sorry," Daniel said, sweat glistening on his forehead, grimacing with every step. "I'm slowing you down. You should just leave me and go."

"That's right, we should," Gabriel said. "But your niece inexplicably still wants to help you, so we won't."

"I really am sorry, Gabriel—"

"Save it," Gabriel said. "We can talk about what you did later. If there is a later."

If they wanted to get away fast, they needed transportation. Cars were parked along the curb, but with the crowd around them and firemen and policemen in the street, breaking into one here would be too risky. Gabriel led them away from the hotel and onto a side street. There were no people here, the spectacle of the fire having drawn them all away. But there were cars, and one of them—a black, two-door sports car parked by the mouth of an alley—didn't have an alarm light glowing on the dashboard. Perfect. Looking up the street to make sure no one was watching, he smashed the driver's side window with the butt of his Colt.

He opened the door and tossed the backpack onto the rear seat. After brushing the shattered glass off the driver's seat, he got in and ducked under the dashboard. He had the wires exposed a moment later, and the engine purring a few seconds after that. Joyce got into the back seat and let Daniel take the front, his injured leg requiring the extra space. Gabriel backed the car out of its parking spot and took off down the street.

He kept to side streets, passing dark apartment buildings and garages until they finally found their way onto the open road that led up into the hills. The apartment buildings turned into low one- and two-story houses, and eventually the houses thinned away until there was nothing but dark forest on either side. The head-lights picked up signs marking the distance to Burdur and Isparta in kilometers.

"Where are we heading?" Joyce asked.

"Not sure yet," Gabriel said. "I need to think."

"My students!" Daniel exclaimed suddenly. "They'll hear about the fire. Some of them know I was staying there. I have to let them know I'm all right." He fished his cell phone out of his pocket and opened it, the blue key lights illuminating the interior of the car.

Gabriel snatched the phone from Daniel's hand and tossed it out the broken window. "You're not calling anyone."

"Gabriel!" Joyce exclaimed from the back seat.

Ignoring her, he turned to Daniel. "You don't go anywhere near a phone, a computer, a pair of tom-toms, anything. If I even see you with a tin can and a piece of string in your hand, I'll shoot you. Do you understand me?"

Daniel nodded, staring out the windshield.

"Gabriel," Joyce said, "that was our only phone."

"We're better off without it," Gabriel said. "Grissom knows Daniel's number. He could have used the phone to trace our location."

"All right, so we have no phone," Joyce said. "We have a stolen car, a gun with how many bullets left? Two? Three? And three exhausted people, one of whom can barely walk—and no, we're not leaving him behind. So: what's your plan?"

"We need a place to regroup. Rest a little, tape up that leg—" Gabriel nodded toward Daniel "—and figure out where the third Eye is hidden. No way am I letting Grissom get to it first."

"You know any place around here where we could do all that?"

"One," Gabriel said. "But if she turns us away, I don't know what we're going to do."

"She?"

"A woman I used to know in Anamur."

Joyce was silent for a bit. Then she said, "You used to know her… how?"

"Do you really want me to answer that?"

"No," Joyce said. "I guess I don't."

"Let's just hope she'll let bygones be bygones."

"That doesn't sound good," Joyce said. "How exactly did things end between you two?"

"Could've gone better," Gabriel said. "The last time I saw her, she came at me with a meat cleaver."

HE FOLLOWED THE SIGNS FOR ANAMUR, STICKING TO side streets, the darker and emptier the better. The detours made the trip longer than if he'd taken the highway, but he figured it was better not to risk being out in the open.

He didn't know if Veda Sarafian still lived in her house by the sea, or how she'd feel about seeing him again after so many years, but he couldn't think of anyone else he could call on—not in this part of Turkey, anyway. He drove all night, watching the stars fade and the sky gradually grow lighter. Joyce fell asleep in the back, her head tilted against the window, her hair hiding her face. In the passenger seat, Daniel's head was turned away. Gabriel couldn't tell if he was asleep or just unwilling to face him.

By the time the sun started to peek over the horizon, he had turned onto the winding coastal road that led to Veda's house. The ground dropped off steeply to his right, and past the safety railing there he saw the dawn's light glittering across the Mediterranean. In the distance he could make out the northern, Turkish half of Cyprus and, past it, a hazy sliver of Syria on the horizon.

He turned onto a narrow gravel drive, and there it was, the house, just as he remembered it. A low, two-story wooden home with dark shingles and white painted frames around the curtained windows.

"We're here," he said, setting the handbrake as the car slid to a stop. Joyce stirred in the back, and Daniel stretched, rubbing his neck. They exited the car and walked up the small flight of steps to the door. Gabriel could hear the gentle slosh of the surf from the other side of the house, where Veda had—or at least used to have—a low wooden dock that bobbed on the waves. He knocked.

A few moments later it opened, and a tall, slender woman with olive skin and deep brown eyes appeared. She didn't look a day older than when he'd seen her last, or an iota less enraged. She brushed her black hair out of her eyes and regarded him with a look that could have ignited a fire in a rainstorm. *"Gabriel Hunt?"* She spoke with a smooth British accent, but that didn't mask the emotion behind the words. "What the hell are *you* doing here?"

He raised both hands, palms out, placating. "I wouldn't have come if it weren't important, Veda. I need your help."

"You need *what*?"

"A place to stay for a couple of hours," Gabriel said. "A phone we can use. Some water. That's all. I promise, it won't happen again, but I do need your help now."

One of her hands curled into a fist against the door. "And we both know what your promises are worth."

"You know that's not fair," Gabriel said. "I thought you were dead, Veda. I saw the plane blow up—"

"Oh, and remind me, which ancient culture's mourning rituals involve sleeping with the deceased's sister?"

Joyce and Daniel both looked at him. Joyce especially.

"And who are you, sweetheart?" Veda said, turning to Joyce. "His latest?" She looked Joyce up and down, like she was measuring her for a coffin. "Well, Gabriel, I guess you are maturing. At least this one's not eighteen. Are you, honey?"

"Excuse me," Joyce said, her eyes sparking every bit as much as Veda's. "We just barely escaped being shot at and blown up and chased off a hotel roof, we climbed down thirty stories and stole a car, and all this is after we very nearly got buried alive *twice—and* I spent five days hanging in a goddamn cage—and we're asking you for what, a lousy glass of water and a place to sit down? Lady, maybe he did screw your sister, but right this moment I honestly don't give a damn!"

"Well, now," Veda said. "Little spitfire, aren't you? I'd watch out for this one, Gabriel. She might actually use the cleaver when the time comes."

"The time won't come," Gabriel said. "I'm sorry it ever did with you. Honestly, Veda, I never meant to hurt you."

Veda blew a raspberry. "No, you just meant to deflower my sister. You know the worst part? She still talks about you. Says she never had another man who could measure up to you."

Daniel and Joyce looked at him again. Especially Joyce.

"Do you think, maybe," Gabriel said, in a small voice, "we could have this conversation inside? And maybe also in private? No reason Joyce and Daniel need to hear this. They're tired—"

"I'm not too tired," Joyce said. "And I'm finding this fascinating."

"Well, take notes, love, because with this one you can't be too careful."

"Veda," Gabriel said, "you've got the wrong impression, we're not involved—"

"Shush, you," Veda said, and turned back to Joyce. "What's your name, sweetheart?" Joyce told her. "And that's your father?"

"My uncle," Joyce said.

"Your uncle. I'm sure you have a good reason for carting him around while people shoot at you. Why don't you come to the kitchen with me and tell me all about it…"

Veda took Joyce by the elbow and led her off, leaving the front door open. It was as much of an invitation as he was going to get, Gabriel thought. And maybe more than he deserved.

"You really slept with her sister?" Daniel whispered as they stepped inside.

"Daniel," Gabriel said, "I'd think twice before lecturing anyone else on the subject of betrayal."

* * *

SITTING ON THE COUCH, JOYCE HELD THE STAR OF Arnuwanda and read off the Nesili symbols along the outer rim: *spire, cattle, tilled field, ash, offering, manure, dune, killing, dread, tar pit,* and on and on, dozens of them, like some sort of glossary of the Hittite world. Daniel, sitting beside her and holding a bag of ice on his swollen knee, periodically corrected her translations.

Veda came into the living room. "So that's the Star you were telling me about?"

"The Star of Arnuwanda, that's right," Joyce said. "It'll tell us where the third Eye of Teshub is hidden— but only if we can figure out what the third element is."

"You mean element like hydrogen and helium and uranium?"

"More like earth, air, fire, and water," Daniel said. "This was a very long time ago. And the Hittites made it even simpler: they divided their world into just three fundamental substances, earth, water, and something else, but no one knows what that third one actually was."

"Why not?"

"Because the only tablet on which it was carved that survived the destruction of their civilization was lost nearly a hundred years ago and all we've got are translations that aren't very clear. We don't know which symbol the translator had in mind when he wrote about the third element. 'Loose soil'—there are any number of symbols that could correspond to, especially when some symbols have multiple meanings. *Tilled field,* for instance, also meant 'fertile land'—and fertile soil might be described as 'loose.' Or *manure,* as in 'night soil.' Even *cattle,* which is sometimes translated as 'breakers of the soil.' "

"Or *ash,*" Veda said.

"I suppose," Daniel said, thinking it over. "Ash is certainly loose, and that would at least push in the direction of 'fire,' which would be in keeping with the Greek model…"

"Well, there's the map," Daniel said. "It only covers the eastern hemisphere, so obviously that means all three gemstones were somewhere on these four continents: Europe, Asia, Africa, Australia."

"It could be underwater, like the last one," Gabriel pointed out. "The map also includes the Pacific, the Indian Ocean, the Arabian Sea, the South China Sea…"

"No," Daniel said, shaking his head. "Only one of the elements was water. The other two were definitely solids. Earth and…" He trailed off.

"That's the question," Joyce said. "Earth, water and what?"

"Maybe we're approaching this from the wrong angle," Gabriel said. "Rather than focusing on what the element is, maybe we should be thinking about what we know about the Eyes and how the Hittites hid them."

"What do you mean?" Daniel said.

"I don't know yet," Gabriel said. "But we've seen two of the three hiding places—maybe there's something there that will help us find the third."

Daniel shifted on the couch, adjusting the bag of ice. "All right, let's think it through. What have you seen in the crypts other than the jewels themselves?"

Joyce chewed her lip, thinking back to the underwater crypt in the Mediterranean and the one in Borneo. "They both had corpses stationed as guardians, men in armor who had been buried alive."

"That's generally what you find with the Hittites," Daniel said. "Other cultures, too, for that matter—the Chinese at the Great Wall, even the British used to entomb workers in the foundation when they put up a bridge."

"You're kidding," Veda said.

"No, no, it's quite true," Daniel said. "You know that verse of the song 'London Bridge is Falling Down' that goes 'Set a man to watch all night, watch all night, watch all night'? That's a reference to burying a man in the bridge foundation, as a sort of guardian."

"Learn something new every day," Veda said.

"Come on, what else do we know?" Gabriel said.

Joyce's eyes slid shut. "There were altars in both, with the jewels held in carved stone hands. The hands had hinged fingers that bent inward when the jewels were removed. In each case there was a panel overhead, a trap, that was released when the fingers moved. There was the light from the jewels, flickering on the walls…"

She opened her eyes. "The inscription," she said.

Daniel looked at her. "What inscription?"

"There were the same words written on the wall," Joyce said. "'The light at world's end.'"

Gabriel said, "Or possibly 'The fire at world's end.' Your standard apocalyptic stuff—'the end of the world is coming,' 'the end is near,' that sort of thing."

Daniel pulled at his lower lip in concentration. "But Hittite mythology never had an apocalypse story like Ragnarok or Armageddon. They had no concept of the end of the world."

"Hang on," Veda said, "did it say 'the end of the world' or 'world's end'?"

"Why?" Joyce said. "Does it make a difference?"

"Look, I'm no archaeologist," Veda said, "I'm just a linguist—but speaking as a linguist I'd say yes, word order does matter." She folded her arms over her chest.

"If you say 'the end of the world,' you're generally referring to a time—the 'end of days' if you're an evangelical Christian, Ragnarok for the Norse, and so forth. But 'world's end' sounds more like a *place* to me— you know, the edge of the earth, the place past which you cannot venture, 'here there be monsters,' all that."

Daniel snapped his fingers. "Of course! The Bushmen!"

"In Africa?" Gabriel said. It was a culture he didn't know a great deal about.

"Yes," Daniel said. "It's got to be. The Bushmen— or the *San*, as they're properly known—have lived in Africa for some twenty thousand years, since before the Ice Age, in fact. But in part due to the Ice Age, the San never left their territory to explore or become an empire the way so many other ancient cultures did. They stayed in one place and didn't have any contact with other societies for thousands of years. Throughout that time, they believed there was nothing else out there, that they were alone in the world." He tapped a finger on the landmass of Africa on the map. "There was a remote area at the edge of the Kalahari Desert, in what's now Botswana, where the ancient San wouldn't go. They believed it was the boundary of all existence, occupied by spirits and demons. They called it… well, in their language you might translate it as 'world's end.' "

Gabriel shook his head. It was all so obvious. These things always were, once you figured them out. "Here, let me have the Star."

"But we still don't know what the element is," Joyce said.

"Yes, we do," Gabriel said, taking the ancient device from her and switching on his flashlight. Daniel limped over to the wall to draw the curtains. "The Kalahari Desert. It's not loose soil. It's *sand.*"

Gabriel turned the starburst at the center of the Star to the symbol for *dune* and, holding the flashlight above it, positioned the Star so the projected symbol lined up with its counterpart on the map below. The light shone through the small red jewel this time, casting a thin, scarlet beam of light.

It struck southern Africa, exactly where Daniel had been pointing.

"World's End," he said.

19

EDGAR GRISSOM PULLED THE TRUCK TO A STOP BY the side of the road. They were in the hills outside Antalya, nothing but trees and a narrow band of asphalt extending into the distance. In the passenger seat, DeVoe, his electronics expert, held a small satellite-linked tracking device, the flashing light on the screen accompanied by a loud beeping that had grown faster and more insistent in the past few minutes. Grissom killed the engine and stepped out onto the road. The back door opened and three men climbed out, their handguns drawn. DeVoe came up beside Grissom, studying the device in his hand. His wide, angular face was pockmarked with acne scars. A black eyepatch covered his right eye.

"You're sure they're here?" Grissom asked.

"This way," DeVoe said, pointing toward the forest beside the road.

Grissom let him lead the way. Just a few feet into

the woods, the device's beeping grew so rapid that it turned into a single high-pitched electronic trill. His men lifted their guns in preparation, but there was no one there. Just trees, shrubs and dirt.

"Sir," DeVoe said. He pointed at the ground.

Lying on a bed of dead leaves was Daniel Wingard's cell phone. Grissom stooped and picked it up. Its screen was cracked and the phone's casing was scraped and dirty. He hurled the phone against a tree, where it smashed into bits of metal and plastic. The beeping from the tracking device stopped abruptly.

Grissom whirled on DeVoe like a snarling animal. "Find them. Do you understand me? I don't care how you do it, I don't care who you have to pay off or kill, but you are going to find them. I want to see the passenger manifests of every plane, train, bus and boat out of Turkey! If they're riding goddamn donkeys across the border, I want to know about it!" He jabbed a finger into DeVoe's chest. "You do that for me, DeVoe, or I'll have your other eye. Do we understand each other?"

DeVoe's reply was quiet, but immediate. "Yes, sir." Grissom stormed back to the van.

Gabriel Hunt would not escape again. He wouldn't allow it.

JOYCE SAT IN THE LIVING ROOM ONLY HALF WATCHING CNN on Veda's television. Daniel had been the one to turn it on, eager for some news of the outside world, but he'd had fallen asleep on the couch shortly after.

Gabriel came in, Veda's cordless phone in his hand. He replaced it in its cradle by the couch. "Michael's gotten us passage on a ship to Madagascar leaving tomorrow," he said quietly. "From there it's a short flight to Botswana."

"Why not just fly directly?" Joyce asked.

"Lower profile this way," he said. "Slightly, anyway. He was able to book it under his name rather than ours." He looked over at Daniel, who was stirring in his sleep.

"Don't look at him like that," Joyce said. "You know he was just trying to protect me."

"I do know that," Gabriel said. "I believe it. But it was a terrible decision. He nearly got you killed. And me."

"And himself," Joyce said. "I think he's learned his lesson."

"Maybe."

"I wish you'd give him another chance."

"We'll see," Gabriel said.

VASSILY PLATONOV STOOD IN ARKADY'S APARTMENT in Samarinda, on the eastern coast of Borneo. It felt strange to be wearing street clothes—dirty, heretical—but in order to get to Arkady's apartment he'd had to blend in as best he could, and wearing his ceremonial tunic and headdress would have been a poor way to do that.

The meeting had to be here because this was where Arkady's computer was, and Arkady had insisted that using the computer was the only way to track the movements of their prey. Vassily was skeptical, but he allowed himself to be persuaded. This was the modern world, and one had to accommodate oneself to its devices. For now. Until Ulikummis returned and melted every computer and every cellular telephone and every other modern instrument into so much slag.

But for now, the computer.

He watched Arkady press tiny buttons on the device.

"Look at this, High Priest." He pointed at a line of characters on the device's screen. *HUNT, MICHAEL* it said. *3 BERTHS, AFRICAN PRINCESS, SAILING 10AM.*

"This Michael Hunt," Vassily said, "he is the American?"

"No, High Priest," Arkady said. "Our man at the airport says the American's name is Gabriel Hunt. This Michael Hunt is his brother."

"And you think if we seize his brother...?"

"No, High Priest. I believe he has had his brother make arrangements for him to travel, along with the woman and another—presumably the Japanese who killed Dmitri and Nikolas. He is trying to hide his movements, but he cannot hide from us."

"From the wrath of Ulikummis, you mean," Vassily said.

"Yes, of course, High Priest."

"And this ship they will be on, it goes from where to where?"

"From Turkey to Madagascar, High Priest."

"Madagascar," Vassily said. "We do not have any brethren there."

"No, High Priest," Arkady replied. "But we do have brothers throughout Africa we can mobilize."

"Contact them. Tell them we are coming."

"Yes, High Priest," Arkady said.

THE SETTING SUN SHED A RIPPLING ORANGE BAND OF light across the waters of the Mediterranean. Gabriel sat alone on the dock behind Veda's house, letting the waves gently rock him while he dangled his bare feet in the warm water. Years had passed since he'd last sat in that spot. In the distance, past the sailboats and trawlers that dotted the sea, he could make out the blocky, turreted Fortress of Mamure winding along the shoreline. It was an impressive structure, considering its construction had been started by the Romans in the third century and finished some eight hundred years later by Seljuk Sultan Alaeddin Keykubat I. In the catacombs beneath the fortress, he and Veda had found secret storerooms filled with treasures hoarded by the Sultan, including a set of ornate chess pieces, one side made of solid gold, the other of platinum. A Japanese billionaire who called himself Hachiman had sent a hired team of former yakuza to steal it all, and they'd very nearly succeeded. But Hachiman was now serving a life sentence in a prison in Osaka, and the Sultan's treasure had been divided among several Turkish museums and universities. A happy ending. He wished there were more of them in the world. Something told him things wouldn't end quite so neatly this time. Hachiman seemed like a model of sanity and pacifism compared to Edgar Grissom.

He heard the back door of Veda's house open and close, but didn't turn from the view until Joyce sat down next to him. She kicked off her shoes and let her feet touch the water beside his.

"Are you sure you want to come? You know you don't have to, right?"

"I don't think Veda would let me stay here," Gabriel said.

"You know what I mean. You could fly home from Madagascar. You've done everything Michael asked you to. You don't have to keep helping me."

"And who would watch your back in the desert—Daniel? Even if he deserves the second chance you're so keen on giving him, he can't protect you the way…"

Joyce smiled. "The way you can?"

"The way you need," Gabriel said.

She watched the sunset with him for a while. "Can I ask you something?"

"Sure."

"All this treasure hunting you do, all this exploring… it's like you can't sit still, you're never happy where you are. It's like you're always looking for something, but you never find it."

"And your question is…?"

"What are you really looking for, Gabriel?"

He watched the water lap against the side of the floating dock. He thought of the hospital in Gibraltar, the authorities telling him they had no idea what had happened to the ship his parents were on during the three days it had apparently vanished from the Mediterranean Sea.

"People think it's all been found," Gabriel said, "that we live in a world that has no secrets anymore. The modern world, with every inch catalogued and mapped and photographed and recorded. They don't know how wrong they are. There are still things in the world that no one's seen in thousands of years or that no one's ever seen, things no one can explain. Things that could have an enormous impact on people's lives, for good or bad. Someone's got to find them. And preferably not men like Grissom."

Joyce nodded.

"You know," Gabriel said, "your uncle wanted me to try to talk you out of pursuing a life like mine. He'd like to see you in a safe, comfortable university position, not running around in a jungle getting shot at."

"He said that to you?" Gabriel nodded. "Sorry, but my uncle doesn't get to make my decisions for me. Neither do you."

"Good," Gabriel said. "Because you're going to be great at this someday." And he leaned over to kiss her.

20

THE CRUISE SHIP *AFRICAN PRINCESS* STRETCHED SIX hundred feet from bow to stern, with three balconied levels rising above the main deck, all filled with restaurants, ballrooms, shops, two casinos, and luxury staterooms for nearly one thousand passengers. These luxury staterooms had all been booked months in advance; what Michael had managed to reserve was a pair of small cabins below deck where the white noise hum of the engines was ever-present.

"Before this, I would've guessed you traveled everywhere first class," Joyce said.

"Actually, I prefer not to," Gabriel said. "Especially when I'm trying to stay out of sight." He leaned against the closed connecting door between the cabin he and Joyce were sharing and the one they'd put Daniel in; Gabriel had told him he was confined to quarters for the duration, and he'd accepted this without complaint. He'd seemed to be glad for a way to do penance.

Gabriel watched through the porthole as they made slow progress through the rolling whitecaps. The sun dipped low in the sky, silhouetting the African coastline in the distance. They'd been sailing for two days. Madagascar wouldn't be far now, he thought. And from there, Botswana.

Behind him, Joyce gathered the rumpled sheets around her on the bunk and propped herself up on one elbow. "You look a thousand miles away."

"Just thinking about what we're going to find when we get to the desert," Gabriel said. "We've been chasing after the gemstones so much we haven't even thought about the Spearhead itself. What it is, what it looks like. How we'll recognize it. We don't even know *where* it is."

"I doubt Grissom knows either," Joyce said. "That's something, at least."

"It is," Gabriel said, "but it's not enough."

"He also doesn't know the third Eye is at World's End."

"We hope," Gabriel said. "He found ways to follow us the first two times."

"Well, even if he has again—hell, even if he's somehow figured it out for himself and gotten there first—we still have one of the Eyes ourselves. He can't do anything without it, right?"

Gabriel turned to look out the window again. Could the Spearhead be activated or used with only two of the three Eyes? It seemed unlikely. But if Grissom did find his way to the last Eye before them, all he'd have to do would be wait for them to show up carrying the one they had. They could be walking into an ambush.

"Well, there's nothing we can do about it from

aboard this ship," Joyce said. "We may as well enjoy ourselves while we're here."

"Low profile, remember?"

"I'm not talking about dancing naked on deck," Joyce said, "I'm thinking we could have a nice dinner. The three of us."

"Daniel's under house arrest," Gabriel said. "No leaving his cabin." They'd been bringing him three meals a day and paperbacks from the ship's convenience store to keep him occupied. He'd asked for nothing more.

"We can let him out for just one night, can't we?" Joyce asked. "Hasn't he been punished enough?"

"This isn't about punishment," Gabriel said. "This is about keeping us safe. He almost got us killed, for heaven's sake."

She nodded. "I know, but he hasn't tried to contact Grissom again, right?"

"He hasn't had the opportunity."

"That's not true, he could have done it anytime at Veda's house. She had a phone in every room, and a computer too, but he didn't."

"Because one of us was with him at all times," Gabriel said.

"Maybe that's why," Joyce said, "but I think he wouldn't have anyway." Gabriel looked unconvinced. "Besides, we won't be able to keep him locked up when we get to wherever we're going. We're going to have to take a chance on him again at some point. We may as well start now."

Gabriel sighed. "If anything happens, if he tries to get away…"

"We're on a boat. Where's he going to go?" She climbed off the bed and started picking through the pile of clothing on the floor, no doubt looking for something appropriate to wear among all her field gear. Good luck finding a cocktail dress in there, Gabriel thought. But it was just as well, since he only had the one outfit himself—and, just to be safe, he'd be accessorizing it his usual way, with a leather jacket just long enough to conceal his hip holster.

UNDER COVER OF NIGHT, THE THIRTY-FOOT KETCH CUT smoothly and quietly through the waters of the Indian Ocean. They'd taken down the sails so they wouldn't be seen by the *African Princess*, instead propelling themselves forward with a small, muffled motor attached to the stern. At Vassily's command, the engine was cut, and they floated up silently, small as an insect next to the hulking cruise ship. An emergency hatch in the *African Princess'* hull stood just above sea level. They tied mooring ropes to the thick bolt beside the hatch, securing the ketch in place in the shadow of the ship.

The brethren of the Cult of Ulikummis—more than a dozen men in all—stood at the ready, awaiting Vassily's orders. Arkady stood with the others in their robes and skull masks, in some cases with bows slung over one shoulder, quivers over the other, in all cases with swords through their belts. Tonight Vassily would let them spill all the blood they wanted.

Arkady reached out and pressed a square of explosives firmly against the seam of the hatch, then inserted a fuse. It took three attempts in the damp night air to get a match lit, but once he had, it took no time at all to set the fuse burning. Hastily, all the men dropped to the bottom of the ketch. The explosion, when it came, was quiet, as explosions went. Looking up, they saw that the blast had knocked the hatch off its hinges and onto the floor inside. One by one they climbed in through the opening, Vassily going last.

They found themselves in a hot, dimly lit, gray-walled hallway that ran past the engine room. A loud mechanical hum filled the corridor. At the far end, a staircase led up to the passenger decks. As they moved forward, the door of the engine room opened and two men rushed out, summoned by the noise of the explosion—it hadn't been quiet enough for no one to notice—or else the hull breach had set off some automatic monitor. Upon seeing the heavily armed cult members, the men skidded to a halt, their eyes wide with surprise.

"What the hell—" the first one sputtered. Before he'd even finished his sentence, one of the cult members had pulled the sword from his belt and slashed it mercilessly across his throat.

Vassily spun his staff and thrust its bronze blade into the second man's neck, pinning him to the wall. He made wet choking sounds as blood flowed down his shirt, and he clawed at his throat. When his grasping hands slackened and dropped to his sides, Vassily pulled the blade out. The second man's corpse fell on top of the first.

They continued silently toward the stairs.

"I APPRECIATE THIS, GABRIEL," DANIEL WINGARD SAID. The plate before him was empty except for a few decapitated asparagus stalks. "I hope this means we've come to some kind of détente."

"That depends entirely on you," Gabriel replied.

They were dining on the upper deck of the ship, the cloudless sky above them filled with bright stars and a waning gibbous moon. The open-air restaurant was called the Safari Club. It was separated it from the rest of the deck by latticed wooden walls, each decorated with spears, leopard-skin shields and large mural paintings of the African savannah and its wildlife. The waiter cleared their dishes and disappeared inside the serving station housed in a small square "hut" with a straw-thatched roof. The cruise line had spared no expense on the décor, but Gabriel couldn't help the disdain he felt for this sort of tourist's eye rendition of Africa. Whoever designed it had obviously never set foot in the real savannah, he'd just watched old Tarzan pictures or ridden the Jungle Cruise at Disneyland.

"That's certainly fair," Daniel said, sipping at his water. "So why don't I do something to make myself useful? I've had a lot of time to think, cooped up in that cabin, and something dawned on me that I don't recall any of us bringing up before."

"What's that?" Gabriel said.

"I've seen dozens of images of Teshub over the years, drawings and paintings and sculptures, I've probably read hundreds of descriptions, and every one of them is pretty much the same—oh, details vary from one to the next, but he's always portrayed as looking like a man, with ordinary human features. Nowhere is there any suggestion that Teshub has three eyes, like Shiva or Mahadeva. Teshub is always shown as having the ordinary number of eyes."

Daniel looked up from his plate and met Gabriel's gaze across the table.

"You see what I'm getting at?" Daniel continued. "We're looking for the *three* Eyes of Teshub. The number three keeps showing up in the legend—three elements, the three armies that will determine the Spearhead's fate, even the three blades on the Death's Head Key. But why three eyes when he's always shown as only having two?"

"Could it be another mistranslation?" Gabriel asked. "Maybe the word that's been translated as 'eye' also means something else…?"

Daniel shook his head. "Unlikely. The Nesili symbol for 'eye' isn't one that has multiple meanings, and the one meaning it does have is amply documented."

Gabriel took one last sip of wine, emptying his glass. More riddles. That was how Daniel chose to make himself useful? If he wanted to be useful, he'd supply some answers, not more questions.

He watched a waiter walk out of the restaurant and onto the deck with a tray of drinks, disappearing past the serving station. When he came back, maybe Gabriel would ask him for a refill…

The sudden noise of shattering glass made Gabriel spring to his feet.

He saw the crowd of white-robed cultists flooding onto the deck. "Get down!"

Joyce and Daniel threw themselves to the floor. Gabriel pulled his Colt from its holster. The other passengers in the restaurant screamed and backed away from their tables.

Three cult members nocked arrows into their bows on the run.

Gabriel kicked the table onto its side, sending their wineglasses, the empty bottle and the floral centerpiece smashing to the floor, then ducked behind it with Joyce and Daniel. The hiss of multiple arrows cut the air, and the table jolted and thumped as they struck it.

"I thought we'd seen the last of them," Joyce said.

"They must have followed us from Borneo."

"Is this the Cult of Ulikummis?" Daniel asked. His eyebrows lifted and he peeked around the side of the table. "Fascinating! Look at those masks! Twelfth century B.C. design, I'd say."

"Very helpful, professor," Gabriel said, pulling him back behind the table. More arrows flew past, embedding in the polished wooden floor around them. "But you're not watching a slide show in a lecture hall. Stay down."

He didn't take his own advice. He leapt up instead, firing the Colt. His first shot struck one of the archers and sent him spinning over the deck railing. His second and third, carefully placed, took down the other two. The remaining cult members rushed forward with their swords drawn.

"Get him out of here," Gabriel shouted to Joyce. "I'll hold them off as long as I can."

"We can't leave," Joyce shouted back.

"Don't be a hero, Joyce, just go," Gabriel said, but glancing back he saw she wasn't being a hero, she was just describing the situation. The rear wall of the restaurant blocked their escape. They were penned in.

21

GABRIEL GOT TO HIS FEET FAST AND, DUCKING UNDER
the swinging sword of the cult member closest to him,
rushed to a side wall of the restaurant where one of
the pairs of spears was held crossed in a metal bracket.
He wrenched them out of their mounting and threw
one to Joyce. She caught it in both hands and swung
it like a staff to parry another swordsman's attack.
Daniel, meanwhile, had grabbed one of the leopard-
skin shields off the wall and was hiding behind it
while another cultist battered it with his blade.

Gabriel's attention was swiftly brought back to his
own situation when the attacker whose last blow he'd
ducked came back for a second try. Gabriel made as if
to duck it again, but then stepped back and plunged the
spear downward, like a primitive fisherman spearing a
catch in a stream. The catch in this case being the cult
member's foot. The man howled in pain as the blade
plunged through his boot, pinning him to the deck, and

Gabriel breathed a silent thanks to the decorator whose taste he'd been mentally condemning earlier. It was still poor taste—but at least the man had gone as far as investing in real spears, not plastic or cast-resin fakes.

The swordsman sank to one knee, both hands going to the shaft of the spear in order to pull it out, and Gabriel snatched up the man's sword as it fell to the deck. Spinning when he heard racing footsteps behind him, Gabriel swept it upwards to meet the descending blade of one of the speared man's compatriots. The blades struck in mid-air with a clang of metal against metal. Gabriel brought his down and under for a riposte that caught the other man across his unprotected wrist. A spray of blood jetted out.

But more of them kept coming. Good god, how many were there?

Gabriel fired his Colt twice more and he saw two more men fall. But he'd be out of bullets before they'd be out of men. He looked around desperately. Where could he get away from them…?

The hut. There had to be an exit there, leading to a below-decks galley if nothing else. He ran for it, hooking a chair with one foot as he sprinted and kicking it backwards into the knees of the man closest behind him. The man went over in a tangle of robes.

Gabriel plunged into the hut—and found his way blocked by a figure he had hoped never to see again. The high priest of the Cult of Ulikummis, wearing his red and gold tunic and tall, rectangular headdress, whirled the bronze-bladed staff in his hands. Gabriel fell back as the blade sliced past his face. He blocked the next blow with his sword, though just barely—the man was attacking fiercely and with more strength than Gabriel found himself able to muster. And probably without a glass of Montepulciano in him, either.

Gabriel raised his gun and fired—only to hear the hammer land on an empty chamber. He saw a vicious smile blossom on the high priest's face at the sound.

Holstering his gun, Gabriel swung the sword in his other hand in a huge arc, not expecting to hit the high priest, just buying himself room to back out of the hut. The high priest shrank back, then came after him as he retreated.

Out in the open again, Gabriel shot a glance over at Joyce. She and Daniel were surrounded by the remaining cultists. Joyce had pulled a second shield off the wall and together with Daniel had formed an approximation of a phalanx, shield to shield, as a barrier against the swords crashing down on them.

The high priest advanced on Gabriel once more.

A loud crack followed by a clatter of wooden boards drew both men's attention. Joyce, apparently having decided they were hopelessly outnumbered, had kicked a hole in the latticed wooden wall at the back of the restaurant and she and Daniel were backing out through it, still blocking incoming blows with their shields. The shields were too large to fit through the hole, but they were perfect for covering it, and Joyce wedged them into place in front of the hole as they made their escape along the deck behind it.

But the shields didn't hold the swordsmen for long. One of them kicked them out of the way and plunged through the hole in pursuit while two others retrieved the bows and half-full quivers from their fallen comrades and let fly with new shots that carried over the lattice wall in deadly arcs.

Gabriel and the high priest watched all this in the handful of instants it took and then looked back at each other. "It's just you and me now," Gabriel said. The high priest howled in rage and swung his staff at Gabriel's head.

Gabriel watched the point race toward him through the air. Timing his movement carefully—carefully!—he grabbed at the shaft as it neared, managing to get a grip just below the blade. He pivoted swiftly, drawing the high priest along with the staff. But the man was too savvy to be caught by the same trick twice. He let go of the staff before Gabriel could use it to drag him to the edge of the deck and over the railing. Gabriel had expected this. He punched backwards with the butt end of the staff, knocking the man's wind out of him with a firm blow to the belly. The high priest dropped to his knees gasping.

It was tempting to finish him off. But some distance away Gabriel heard Joyce shouting as she continued fighting off the attackers. She needed help—that had to come first. Gabriel ran toward the hole in the lattice wall, crawled through, and then took stock of the scene before him. Some fifty feet away, Joyce and Daniel were huddled behind a couple of upended lounge chairs and the bowmen, who had somehow gotten to the other side of them, were letting fly with arrows. Gabriel lifted the high priest's staff like a javelin and heaved it in the direction of the larger of the two bowmen. The man didn't spot it sailing toward him until the instant before it buried itself in his chest. But as soon as he fell, one of the remaining swordsmen ran to take up his bow.

At that moment, the aft stairwell door burst open, and three of the ship's security guards ran out onto the deck, their guns drawn, shouting for everyone to freeze. The new bowman turned and reached for an arrow. The guards yelled at the cult members to drop their weapons. A pair of arrows shrieked through the air, piercing the torso of one guard and the neck of another. The third dropped to one knee and opened fire. Two white-robed men fell, and the others—few in number at last—pulled back. But one aimed and fired an arrow, and it found its mark. The third guard joined the first two in death.

In the distance, Gabriel saw Joyce and Daniel duck down behind the lounge chairs again. Gabriel sprinted across the deck toward them, the Death's Head Key bouncing heavily against his chest under his shirt. An arrow zipped past him, striking the wall behind the sundeck. He darted over, dodging with one arm up to protect his head, and dropped to the ground beside Joyce. He glanced over the top of the lounge chair. The high priest was on his feet again and striding toward the three remaining cult members, two of whom were loading their bows with fresh arrows. He had his staff in hand once more, its blade red with the blood of the man from whose chest he'd drawn it.

"Something you need to know," Gabriel said. "I'm out of bullets."

"I figured," Joyce said, "from how little shooting you were doing."

The door leading to the stairwell was only forty feet behind them. Gabriel nodded toward it. "Think you can make it?" he whispered.

"I think I can," Joyce said. "I'm just not sure about Daniel."

"I'll try," Daniel said.

They spun and ran for the door. Gabriel heard the twang of bowstrings, arrows cutting the air toward them. Gabriel pushed himself hard. They were almost there. Another bowstring twanged.

"Gabriel, look out!" Daniel yelled. He rammed into Gabriel from behind, knocking him to one side. The arrow that had been headed squarely at Gabriel's back stabbed into Daniel's shoulder instead. His face instantly went pale. "I'm hit," he said softly and fell to the deck.

Joyce, almost at the door, skidded to a halt. She ran back.

Gabriel looked around for some way to draw the cult members' attention away from them. His gaze fell on the bodies of the security guards slumped by the wall. Their guns lay on the floor beside them. Gabriel ran for them. As he'd hoped, the bowmen turned to follow him, taking their aim off Joyce and Daniel. Arrows pursued him across the deck. One slashed his back, slicing his shirt and drawing a hot line of pain across his shoulder blades, but he kept moving. He dropped to the deck and slid across it like he was sliding into home plate. As he fetched up against the dead guards' bodies, he grabbed one of their guns in each hand. Turning back, he squeezed the triggers repeatedly, blasting bullet after bullet at the cultists. White robes burst into red, skull masks cracked and shattered, bows dropped from their hands. When the smoke cleared, only the high priest was left standing— and he broke and made a run for it.

Gabriel fired at him but the man was already too far and the shot went wide. Gabriel considered giving chase—but Daniel needed help. He ran over to Joyce instead.

"Don't worry about us," she shouted. "Get that bastard!"

At the far end of the deck, Gabriel saw the high

priest spiraling down a metal staircase between decks. Gabriel grabbed the railing at the edge of the top deck and jumped over it, dropping twenty feet to the deck below. He landed on his feet, rolled off the impact, then sprang up and sprinted for the stairwell. The high priest was already on the next level down. Gabriel chased him down two more flights before the high priest burst through the door to the main deck. Gabriel followed a moment later, only to find the deck empty. He looked both ways, saw the door to the ballroom swinging shut, and ran for it. He grabbed it just before it closed and slipped inside.

The enormous room was dark except for flickering pinpoints of light thrown along the walls by the mirrored ball rotating on the ceiling. The stage, the dance floor and the small tables surrounding it were all empty. Everyone must have been sent back to their rooms after word spread of the attack. He looked around, but there was no sign of the high priest. Gabriel stepped deeper into the ballroom, chilled equally by the strong air conditioning and the utter silence. The high priest could be anywhere. He could be directly behind Gabriel, getting ready to launch an attack...

Movement caught his eye, the flutter of a dark curtain draped over the wall. Gabriel ran toward it, threw back the curtain. No one was there, only an emergency exit. He hit the panic bar and shoved the door open. Beyond it was a long hallway that extended to either side. He ran down both directions to the end before finally admitting to himself that he'd lost the man. The high priest was probably off the ship by now.

He returned to the stairwell and encountered Joyce helping Daniel down the stairs.

"What happened?" Joyce asked.

Gabriel shook his head. "He got away." Daniel was still pale and had a gloss of sweat on his forehead, but the arrow was gone from his shoulder, replaced with a wide circle of blood on his shirt. "How's he doing?"

"I'm okay," Daniel said, though his unsteady voice suggested otherwise. "The arrow didn't go in very deep… Joyce was able to pull it out."

"Arrows like this hurt like hell coming out," Gabriel said. "I know from experience."

"Yes, hell's a fair approximation," Daniel said, wincing, "of what it feels like to have a… a sharp piece of metal torn out of your flesh."

Gabriel took the bulk of Daniel's weight off Joyce's shoulder and helped him down the rest of the stairs and out into the hallway that led to their cabins. "It was a foolish thing to do, jumping in front of an arrow like that."

"Trust me, I have no intention of ever doing it again," Daniel said.

"But it probably did save my life," Gabriel said. "I owe you one."

"How about you pay me back by declaring house arrest over?" Daniel said.

Gabriel exchanged a glance with Joyce.

"Done," Gabriel said. "But let's make one more stop in your cabin. There's a first aid kit in the bathroom. I know a thing or two about treating arrow wounds."

"Why am I not surprised?" Daniel shook his head. "I can't believe I actually got shot with an *arrow*. By a millennia-old death cult!"

"That'll pack them in at your next lecture," Joyce said.

Daniel looked up at Gabriel. "Is it always like this for you?"

"No," he said. "Sometimes the death cults are only centuries-old."

They turned the corner and Gabriel froze as they saw the cabin doors. The door to Daniel's cabin was shut tight, but the door to his and Joyce's was slightly ajar, its edge chipped and bent near the lock. He handed Daniel back off to Joyce and whispered, "Stay here."

He pushed the door open slowly, switched on the light. The room had been tossed: the closet door was open, the drawers pulled out of the dresser, the sheets stripped from the bed. He saw Joyce's backpack lying open on the floor. He picked it up and looked inside.

"Damn it!"

"What's wrong?" Joyce asked, from the doorway.

"They're gone," Gabriel said, waving the empty backpack at her. "The Star, the map, the Eye, all of it." He'd been a fool. The attack had been a diversion. The cult's true objectives had been sitting unguarded in his cabin all along.

"Oh, that's not good," Daniel said. "That's not good at all."

VASSILY WATCHED AS ARKADY UNDID THE ROPES mooring their boat to the *African Princess*. The young man had done well, locating the interlopers' room and then stealing the sacred relics. But the two of them were the only ones who remained out of an attack force of more than a dozen. And if Arkady had been with them on deck, he would surely be as dead as the others. The interlopers, this Gabriel Hunt the other two (*Who was that fat old man?* Vassily wondered), had fought more bravely—and more effectively—than Vassily had anticipated. He'd expected to return not only with the

Star and one of the Eyes of Teshub, but also with their heads for proud display and subsequent flensing and use in worship. That they were still alive vexed him. Ulikummis would not be happy with him for letting them live.

Arkady started the engine, moving the ketch forward along the length of the cruise ship.

"When we reach shore, you must contact the African sect, Arkady," Vassily ordered. "Tell them we need more warriors."

"Yes, High Priest. How many will you require?"

"All of them," Vassily said.

22

THE JEEP'S TIRES KICKED UP CLOUDS OF DUST AS IT rattled and bumped over the uneven terrain of the desert. To make better time, Gabriel avoided the salt flats and the more verdant areas of the Kalahari, not wanting to be slowed down by traffic, safari tours or any of the native San villages. Massive, spider-like baobab trees rose up every few hundred yards like sentinels amid the ocean of sand. The dry brush that poked out of the dunes scratched at the underside of the jeep as they raced over it while dust-colored meerkats poked their heads curiously out of their burrows to watch them pass. In the seat next to him, Joyce was buckled in, but only loosely so she could twist around to face Daniel in back. They were reviewing the only information they had left: the notes and coordinates he'd written down back in Veda's house when they'd identified the location of the third Eye. As the jeep bounded over a low dune, the equipment in the back clattered.

The flight from Madagascar to Botswana had been quick and, compared to the events on the *African Princess*, painless. They'd managed to duck into a cab at the pier and go straight to the airport, evading the local police who wanted to keep all the passengers for questioning about the cult's attack. A few hours later, their plane had touched down at Sir Seretse Khama International Airport in Gabarone. They'd rented the jeep at the airport counter after the clerk had assured them it could handle off-road driving in the desert, though nearly bouncing out of the driver's seat each time they raced over a dune, Gabriel wasn't so sure they hadn't been sold a bill of goods. They'd also purchased a wide range of equipment from a local store that clearly catered mainly to hobbyists on holiday who liked to go digging in the desert. The salesman had been surprised to hear fluent Tswana coming from an American and, when Gabriel explained their bona fides, had shown them to the section of the store for professionals. Daniel and Joyce had picked out a haul that included shovels, a pickaxe, a pair of metal buckets, binoculars, lanterns, surveying tools, and more, while Gabriel had sought out a different aisle, the one where they sold bullets.

In the back seat of the jeep, Daniel consulted a pocket compass. "It shouldn't be much farther now," he shouted over the rattle of the vehicle. "Keep going straight."

Gabriel swerved around a wide baobab tree, then righted their course. He called back to Daniel: "Just let me know when we're—"

"Now!" Daniel shouted.

"Now?"

"Yes!"

Gabriel slammed on the brakes and swung the steering wheel hard around. A dust cloud surrounded the jeep for a moment, then settled. From his seat he saw only rolling dunes and small, brittle tufts of shrubbery. "Are you sure this is the place?" It looked utterly desolate, as empty and featureless as any of the landscape they'd been passing through for the better part of two hours.

"According to the map," Daniel replied, "yes. It should be about three meters ahead of us."

Gabriel opened the door and stepped out onto the sand. The afternoon sun beat down hard on his head and shoulders. Behind him, Daniel and Joyce got out of the jeep, shielded their eyes and looked around.

"I admit it doesn't look very promising," Daniel said.

"To be fair, the other sites didn't look promising either," Gabriel said.

Her brow beading with sweat from the oppressive heat, Joyce took off the shirt she wore over her tank-top and tossed it in the jeep. She circled to the rear, opened the hatchback and pulled out an armful of shovels. "I suppose it would've been too much to ask for the gemstone to be out in the open, just this once," she said. She put the shovels down and went back for the pickaxe and buckets.

Daniel walked out across the flat expanse of sand, rubbing at the bandage on his injured shoulder. He read the compass every few feet and checked it against his notes. "Think of it," he said. "I've studied the legend of the Three Eyes of Teshub for decades, as many others have. But unlike, say, El Dorado or Atlantis or any number of legends that aren't true—"

"Don't be so sure about El Dorado," Gabriel muttered.

"What?" Daniel asked.

"Nothing. Go on."

"I'm just thinking it's remarkable that after studying this legend for so long I've held one of the actual Eyes of Teshub in my hands. They're real. They're not a fantasy or a made-up story or the invention of some bard drunk on kumis. And now we're standing where the third and final Eye has rested for thousands of years. Buried by eons of wind and sand. It's extraordinary."

Gabriel shielded his eyes and looked up at the sun. They'd already lost half the day getting here. Grissom could be anywhere. If they were lucky, he hadn't figured out the location of the third gemstone and was still tooling around Turkey looking for them. Unfortunately, that had never been Gabriel's kind of luck.

"Did any of your studies suggest how far down it might be?" he asked. "We may not have a lot of time to dig."

Daniel shrugged. "Who can say? There's a small village of mastaba tombs in the shadow of the Pyramid of Cheops. They were buried in the desert for millennia before anyone found them. And do you know how far they had to dig? Just fifteen feet. In the desert, the wind is always changing and the sand is always shifting. What's buried hundreds of feet down one year might be so near the surface the next that a mild sandstorm could unearth it. We just have to hope this is a good year." He stopped walking and pointed at the sand at his feet. "Here." He stuffed his notes in his pocket, grabbed the pickaxe and used it to draw an X in the sand. "This is where we start."

The sun crawled across the desert sky as Gabriel and Joyce dug. Daniel, his shoulder still sore from the arrow wound, worked on maintaining the pit walls instead, using a shovel and bucket to move the sand away from the ditch so it wouldn't slide back in and fill up again.

It was backbreaking work. Rivulets of sweat flowed along Gabriel's back, chest, neck and forehead. They paused occasionally to swig from the gallon jugs of bottled water they'd picked up in town, then got back to work. All the while, the baking sun kept at them mercilessly. They'd dug ten feet down by the time the heat broke and the sun started to dip toward the horizon.

Gabriel grabbed a water bottle and lifted it to his parched lips. As he took a swallow and bent to replace the bottle on the ground, he felt the Death's Head Key twitch where it lay against his chest. He looked down and saw it pressing against his shirt. Reaching into his collar for the leather strap around his neck, he pulled the key out and held it over the pit. Instead of hanging straight down it trembled at the end of the strap, hanging at a ten degree angle. Joyce and Daniel stared at it. "We're close," he told them.

They resumed digging. The further down they got, the more the Death's Head Key strained against its strap. Up above them, Daniel rubbed his hands together, though whether it was with excitement or anxiety, Gabriel couldn't say. Probably a bit of both— Gabriel was certainly feeling both himself.

Gabriel drove the edge of his shovel into the wall of sand before him, and it struck something hard. Something the metal blade of the shovel struck with a ringing *clank.*

"My God," Daniel whispered. "That's it, isn't it?"

"Let's hope," Gabriel said.

The sky was turning red with sunset by the time they cleared the sand away from a buried door. The door itself was made of metal, though it was set into a wall composed of blocks of sandstone. Like the others they'd seen, this door was covered with ornate carvings and had no handle, only the keyhole with its three slots and the small skull design carved above it. Gabriel took the key from around his neck and lined it up with the lock. This time he was prepared—but when the key jumped from his hand and pulled itself into the lock, he still found his heart beating faster. Gabriel threw his strength into turning the key. It seemed to take more effort than the first two, but it was hard to say—after all, he hadn't been the one turning it the first time and they had been underwater the second. All he knew for sure was that the imprint of the skull would be pressed into the flesh of his palm for a good long time. But he kept straining until he heard the loud, metallic click he was waiting for. He felt the resistance give way as the internal mechanism kicked in and the door began creaking open. They stepped back to make way. Dry, fetid air blew out of the crypt, stirring the sands around them.

Daniel limped back to the jeep to get the flashlight. When he returned, he handed it down to Joyce. "This is your find, Joyce. It's your name they'll put on this before anyone else's. It should be you who has the honor of being the first to set foot inside."

Joyce took the flashlight from him and held onto his hand. "Thank you. That means a lot to me."

"I know, my dear. I know how much you wanted this. And I want you to know I'm sorry for—well, for everything, but especially for trying to stand in the way of your doing… this. I never should have treated you like you're still a little girl who needs her foolish, overprotective uncle's help." He squeezed her hand. "But most of all, I want you to know how proud of you I am. I'm frightened for you—but I couldn't be prouder."

Gabriel raised his left hand in the air. The luminous digits on the dial of his wristwatch had begun to glow as the daylight faded into darkness. "Not that I want to come between a girl and her uncle, but…"

"No, you're right," Daniel said. He released Joyce's hand, picked up a pair of electric lanterns and handed them down. Then he climbed down into the pit himself.

Joyce led the way through the door. Gabriel followed and Daniel brought up the rear. The stale air inside the crypt was stifling. They followed a stone stairway down into darkness, their footsteps echoing off the walls, the lanterns lending an orange tint to their surroundings.

At the bottom of the steps, a long corridor stretched into the blackness. The lantern beams illuminated alcoves along the walls on either side. The bodies inside them had been mummified by the dry air, their skin shrunken against their bones like a thin layer of old leather, brown and cracked; but their armor remained mostly intact, preserved by the lack of moisture. As the lantern light passed along the corpses' empty eye sockets, it almost looked like the dead soldiers were watching them pass.

Ahead, the corridor led through an archway into a small chamber where colored light shimmered against the wall. But instead of the green light they'd seen in the other two crypts, this time the light was a deep, rich crimson. Gabriel raised his lantern up over his head and Joyce did the same with hers. At the far end of the chamber, atop a pedestal and gripped in a stone hand, sat an enormous ruby.

"Well, that's different," she said. She walked to the pedestal for a closer look.

"Be careful," Gabriel said. "Don't touch it yet." He glanced up at the ceiling, wondering what trap the Hittite architects had in store for them this time.

"Look at this," Joyce said. "The inscription is different, too." She held her lantern up to the wall behind the pedestal. Nesili symbols were carved into the rock—but more of them this time than there had been in the other crypts.

"Fascinating," Daniel said, stepping forward.

"Want to do the honors?" Gabriel asked. "My Nesili's okay, but I'm not the best sight reader."

Daniel translated as Joyce moved the light slowly across the symbols. "'Three armies will determine its fate…' It's the final verse of the legend. It explains how, when the time comes, three armies will determine how the Spearhead will be used—as a force for destruction or as something that benefits mankind. And it describes Teshub's final judgment as to whether mankind is wise enough to possess the Spearhead."

"I guess the answer was no," Gabriel said.

"More like 'not yet,'" Daniel said. "Teshub didn't destroy it, after all. He hid it. And what's hidden can be found."

"We'll see about that," Gabriel said. "Why don't you two get over by the door." They went to stand by the archway while Gabriel carefully approached the ruby. "And if I say run, you run—understand? Don't even look back, just get the hell out of here."

Joyce nodded. "Be careful."

Gabriel studied the ruby in the stone hand's grasp. It was lit from within by the same natural iridescence as the emeralds had been. It had the same wide, flat octagonal cut, too, but this gem was bigger, almost twice the size of the others. As Gabriel reached for it, he heard the pitch of the electrical hum emanating from it change and felt the hairs on the back of his arm stand straight up. He took hold of the ruby with both hands and lifted it gently out of the stone fingers' grasp. The stone felt warm in his hands, and the electrical charge it gave off was much stronger than that of the second Eye.

The fingers of the stone hand began to scrape closed. Gabriel backed away, watching the ceiling for any signs of movement. There weren't any—in the ceiling. But the whole chamber began to shake, almost as if the area were in the grip of an earthquake. Daniel put one arm around Joyce and braced himself in the archway. Sand sifted down from cracks in the ceiling.

"Run," Gabriel said.

They raced out of the chamber and into the corridor, sprinting toward the steps leading up to the desert. Knocked free by the tremors, the mummified bodies tumbled out of their alcoves and smashed against the floor. In the lead, Joyce leapt over one and kept going, while Daniel, limping on his bad leg, took pains to skirt another. Behind them both, Gabriel hurtled over one only to find another falling against him. He found himself wrestling with a corpse, its shriveled head inches from his face, the mummified jaw hanging open in an eternal expression of shock. Gabriel shoved the body aside and kept running, taking the stairs two at a time while the crypt trembled and shook around him.

Outside, he pulled himself quickly out of the pit. Joyce and Daniel were already standing on the sand, looking around nervously. A deep rumbling continued to emanate from somewhere below, but none of the baobabs in the distance were swaying, no animals had run into the open. Definitely not an earthquake, Gabriel thought. Something rarer and stranger was happening.

"What's that?" Joyce shouted, pointing.

A few dozen yards away, the sand had begun to undulate, bulging upward in the shape of an enormous dome. A massive stone broke through the surface and kept rising, the sand pouring off its sides. Initially it looked like it was only a dome, a smaller version of Uluru in Australia, perhaps, an extrusion resulting from plate tectonics. But after a moment it became apparent that this was no mere dome. Because the next thing that came into view as the stone continued rising was a pair of roughly carved eyes. The eyes were followed by an enormous carved nose. It was a giant stone head—then a giant bearded head—then a head and neck—then head, neck, and shoulders—and still it came, this giant figure, displacing tons of sand as it emerged into the night air. The figure's wide shoulders appeared, then its chest, its torso. Its arms; its hips and thighs; its knees. Gabriel watched as the titanic figure emerged, until finally the statue towered seventy feet above them, silhouetted against the moonlit sky.

Daniel stepped forward, staring with awe. "Teshub."

The statue of Teshub stood silently before them, one hand at its side, the other held out, palm up, as if offering something to his followers. But the hand was empty. The Spearhead wasn't there.

"Look at the eyes," Daniel said, craning his neck to do so.

The statue's eyes were wide, blank ovals of stone, and where the iris of each eye should have been was a dark, empty socket, just about deep enough for one of the gemstones to fit inside.

"Fascinating," Daniel said. "The storm god risen

from the desert sand, awaiting the return of his eyes, and ready to give his gift to the world. Have you ever seen anything so magnificent?"

Before Gabriel could answer, they all heard the roar of engines behind them. Turning, Gabriel saw a half dozen jeeps speeding toward them across the desert, clouds of sand billowing in their wake. Gabriel cursed under his breath and drew his Colt. Even before he saw the man's face through the grimy windshield of the lead jeep, he knew it was Grissom. And Grissom had brought an army with him. With five or six men in each jeep, they were hopelessly outnumbered.

The jeeps pulled to a stop a few yards in front of them. Grissom and his men climbed out of the vehicles and raised a variety of shotguns and automatic handguns into view.

Grissom stepped forward. "Well, well. Here we are again." He reached out his free hand for the gemstone. "Hand it over."

Gabriel cocked the hammer of his Colt.

"Come now, Mr. Hunt. I know you're an excellent shot. And I know," Grissom said, his face clouding over for a moment, a twitch pounding on his temple, "that you have no qualms about taking a life. But I don't think of you as suicidal. And how long do you think you'd live after you pulled that trigger? How long would your friends live? It would be a foolish gesture."

Gabriel surveyed the crowd around them. Six jeeps, some three dozen men, all of them armed and all of them looking well trained in the use of arms. He ground his teeth. He wasn't confident they'd live a whole lot longer if he lowered his gun, but in cases like this, every minute was worth something. He tossed the Colt onto the sand.

"Now the gemstones."

Gabriel looked at the ruby in his hand. Its energy buzzed along his arm, a thousand feathers tickling on his skin.

Grissom held out his hand. "My men aren't used to having to restrain themselves, Mr. Hunt. I will not ask again."

Gabriel handed the ruby to Grissom, who slipped it into one of the large side pockets of his cargo vest. He turned to the gunman beside him, a man with a pockmarked face and an eyepatch over his right eye. He wore a bandolier filled with shells across his chest and was carrying a pump-action shotgun. "Bring me the other one, DeVoe," Grissom said. The mercenary went to the jeep, retrieved a black velvet sack and brought it back. Grissom took the sack from him, opened it, and let the emerald from Borneo slide onto his palm. He slid it into another pocket of his vest.

Grissom turned back to Gabriel. "Now, the last one. The gemstone from Turkey."

"Sorry, but I can't give you that one," Gabriel said. "We don't have it anymore."

Grissom's stare darkened. "What are you talking about?"

"It was stolen on the way over here," Gabriel said. "By the Cult of Ulikummis."

"Oh, that's rich," Grissom said, and he laughed. "It was stolen, was it? By the, what is it, by the cult of…?" He turned to his men. "It was *stolen* from them!" His men didn't move. Grissom spun, his fist connecting with Gabriel's face. Unprepared for the blow, Gabriel fell backward, landing hard on the sand. Joyce launched herself toward Grissom, her hands balled into fists, but Daniel grabbed her and held her back. Gabriel got to his feet again, wiping blood from his nose on the back of his hand.

"Enough games, Hunt," Grissom said. "Give me the other gemstone."

Gabriel spat on the sand. "I can't. It's gone. You can search us if you don't believe me."

Grissom spoke to DeVoe: "Do it. Search their jeep, and search them."

DeVoe gave instructions to several of the other men and within minutes a thorough search had been completed. DeVoe took responsibility himself for patting them down, taking rather longer in Joyce's case than would have been necessary just to confirm she didn't have a softball-sized emerald on her person. Gabriel saw her gritting her teeth as the eyepatched mercenary worked his way up and down her person.

"Nothing," DeVoe reported.

"All right, Hunt," Grissom said, stepping forward and whipping out the ivory-handled dagger. In a flash its three blades were open and glinting in the moonlight. "Where is it?"

"I told you," Gabriel said. "The Cult of Ulikummis took it."

"And where, exactly," Grissom said, raising the dagger to Gabriel's throat, "did they take it?"

Gabriel stared over Grissom's shoulder. "Apparently," he said, "right here."

Grissom turned, and his men turned with him. Several yards behind them, standing silent in the darkness, was an army of skull-masked men in white robes, at least one hundred of them, their bows loaded with arrows and ready to be fired. At the head of the army stood the high priest. The stolen emerald was lashed with rope to the top of his staff. They heard him shout a single word to his men.

The cultists released their bowstrings, and a wave of arrows sailed across the sky toward them.

23

"TAKE COVER!" GRISSOM SHOUTED. HE AND HIS MEN scattered, crouching behind the jeeps as the arrows bore down. Gabriel snatched his gun off the ground and, together with Joyce and Daniel, ran toward the statue, the only other source of cover in sight. Behind them, the arrows came down, landing in the sand or bouncing loudly off the hoods and frames of the jeeps. Gabriel heard several of Grissom's men cry out, but he didn't turn around or stop running until he reached the statue. Ducking behind one of its massive stone legs, he grabbed Joyce's arm and pulled her down next to him. Daniel dropped to the sand behind her.

Grissom's men frantically signaled each other and shifted position behind the jeeps. The cult let loose another volley of arrows and, under cover of the assault, ran forward, exchanging their bows for swords. Grissom's men opened fire as they came, the chatter of automatic weapons erupting loudly in the night. The smell of gunsmoke drifted over to where Gabriel was, that and the smell of blood.

Gabriel turned away from the battlefield. Daniel was still watching the battle, an expression of horror on his face. "The three armies," he murmured.

"I only see two," Joyce said.

Daniel turned to her. "No, there are three. The cult, Grissom's men... and us."

Gabriel raised his gun. He had six bullets. "Some army."

Cult members dropped under the avalanche of gunfire, their white-robed bodies littering the sand, but more kept coming, flooding into Grissom's men like a tidal wave, transforming the battle into hand-to-hand combat, where they had the advantage. Swords clashed against shotguns raised to block them.

Scanning across the carnage, Gabriel realized he didn't see Grissom in the thick of things—or the high priest, for that matter.

A figure suddenly rounded the statue's leg: DeVoe. "Hold it!" he said, leveling his shotgun at Gabriel.

Gabriel swung his leg out, sweeping it across DeVoe's feet and knocking the mercenary backward onto the ground. He jumped on top of him, wrestled the shotgun out of his hands, and butted DeVoe in the face with the stock. DeVoe groaned briefly and fell back, unconscious. Gabriel pocketed a handful of DeVoe's extra shells, then stood up and inspected the shotgun. Their army had just doubled its arms. He tossed his Colt to Joyce. "Here, take this. And keep an eye on this guy—if he's some sort of second in command, Grissom might actually value him, which would give us a bargaining chip."

"I don't think that man values anyone," Joyce said.

But she knelt beside the unconscious mercenary and aimed the gun at him. "What are you going to do?"

Gabriel opened the shotgun, inspected it quickly, and snapped it closed again. "I'm going to get the gemstones."

"I guess Grissom was wrong," Daniel said. "You *are* suicidal."

Joyce leaned forward and kissed him. "Don't go getting yourself killed," she said quietly. "Not now. Not after all this."

"I'll do my best," Gabriel said, and darted out from behind the statue's leg.

As he went, skirting the edge of the fray, Gabriel looked for Grissom in the chaos and darkness. He finally spotted him at the far end. Grissom had picked up a fallen sword and was using it to block someone's attack. At first Gabriel couldn't make out who Grissom was fighting, but then another figure stepped out of the way and he saw the flash of a long metal staff swinging down to batter Grissom's sword. The high priest. Grissom had gone straight for the missing gemstone himself.

Gabriel pumped a shell into the shotgun's chamber and dove into the battle. He weaved around the first jeep in his path, butting a cult member in the head with the shotgun, then pulled the trigger and blew another off his feet. He shouldered past one of Grissom's mercenaries, who spun on him with his handgun, and Gabriel blasted him aside. No favorites in this fight. Gunshots rang out all around him, the clash of swords, the cries of the wounded. He shoved his way past men locked in battle, ducked blades as they swung at him, and reloaded the shotgun as he went.

The fighting lessened as he broke through the crowd

and made it to the spot where Grissom and the high priest were facing each other. The high priest whirled his staff, knocking the sword out of Grissom's hand. Grissom backed away, out of reach of the staff's bronze blade, and drew his ivory-handled dagger again—his weapon of last resort, it seemed. The two extra blades slid into view as he thumbed the hidden button. The cult leader didn't look impressed.

Gabriel sprang forward, slamming the butt of the shotgun into Grissom's back. Grissom dropped to his hands and knees, coughing hard. The cult leader looked startled for a moment, then lunged at Gabriel, who side-stepped the blade, knocking the staff aside with his shotgun. Something wrapped around his shins, tripping him, and as he fell he saw Grissom's arms around his legs. Gabriel hit the sand hard. He swung the shotgun down toward Grissom, but the other man scrambled away, and suddenly Gabriel saw the high priest looming over him, the staff raised high over Gabriel's chest. Gabriel rolled aside, and the blade sank into the sand. He got to his feet, leveling the shotgun at Grissom and the cult leader both, moving the barrel back and forth between them.

The three of them circled, Grissom with his dagger, the cult leader with his staff, and Gabriel with the shotgun. His finger twitched on the trigger. He was tempted to try to blast them both, but buckshot was hardly a precision projectile. If he shot at either of them, there was a good chance he'd hit the gemstones. He didn't know what would happen if they shattered, but with the amount of energy they seemed barely to be containing he suspected it wouldn't be good.

"We are at impasse," the cult leader said, his words thick with a Russian accent. The emerald glowed at the top of his staff. "But not much longer. All Teshub's Eyes are to me soon. And world will burn in Ulikummis hand."

"Oh, just shoot this man already," Grissom said to Gabriel. "If I have to listen to one more minute of his gibbering…"

"Quiet, both of you," Gabriel said. "Now: give me the gemstones."

"Give you the sacred eye?" the high priest spat. "Never."

Grissom shrugged. "I'm certainly not going to give you anything. I suppose we are, as the man said, 'at impasse.'"

Gabriel heard a sound then overhead, a sound loud enough to cut through the clamor of battle and bloodshed. It sounded like… a helicopter? He risked a glance up, but could only make out a blur high above him, something dark moving across the sky. What would a helicopter be doing out in the middle of the Kalahari Desert at night? Had it been drawn by the sound of gunfire, or had someone reported the sudden twilight appearance of a colossus half the height of the Statue of Liberty?

But the shape—copter or otherwise—sped out of sight before he could properly make it out and Gabriel returned his gaze to the scene before him. It had changed meaningfully even in the fraction of a second he'd looked away. At first, he had the impression that Grissom and the high priest were wrestling, standing so close together they seemed to be grappling with each other. It was only when the staff fell to the ground that Gabriel realized Grissom had stabbed his dagger into the high priest's chest. Grissom shoved, driving the dagger deeper. The high priest dropped to his knees as Grissom tore the dagger out, then he fell forward onto the ground. Grissom grabbed the staff from where it lay in the sand and cut the emerald free from its lashings with a single swipe of the dagger's razor-sharp blades.

Gabriel swung the shotgun toward Grissom and stepped forward so the barrel was just inches from his face.

"What are you going to do, Hunt, shoot me?" Grissom said calmly. "And risk destroying three priceless historical artifacts in the process? I don't think so. I don't think you're the kind of man who—"

Gabriel pressed the muzzle against Grissom's forehead. "You don't know what kind of man I am."

Grissom's self-confident smile faded. "Listen to me," he said. "You don't want to do this."

"Not especially," Gabriel said, "but I will if you don't hand over the jewels."

"Well, then, Hunt, you'll have to shoot, because I'm not handing over a damn thing. But," he said, "before you do, you might want to consider what will happen if you accidentally hit one of the jewels. Ah—I see you *have* been thinking about this. Good. You are wise not to pull the trigger. It could be like a nuclear explosion if it went wrong." Grissom slid the third jewel—the emerald liberated from the high priest's staff—into yet another pocket on his vest. The thing was bulging around him now like a life jacket.

"You have to make a choice, Hunt. There are only two options. Shoot me—and risk blowing us all up, and the statue, too—or let me go."

"You're wrong," Gabriel told him. "There's another choice."

"Oh?"

Gabriel clubbed Grissom across the face with the shotgun's stock. Grissom fell backward, dropping unconscious to the sand, a streak of blood across his mouth.

"There's always another choice," Gabriel said.

Hanging the shotgun over his shoulder by its strap, Gabriel knelt beside Grissom to pull the vest off him. He felt the jewels inside, knocking gently against one another through the padded fabric. The Three Eyes of Teshub. Together again, for the first time in millennia. Even through the fabric, the energy passing from one to the others made his palms tremble.

He hung the vest over his other shoulder. The Cult of Ulikummis and Grissom's men, unaware that their leaders were out of commission, were continuing to struggle across the patch of desert standing between Gabriel and the statue. Which meant he had to go around. Cradling the vest under one arm, he started running, keeping to the outskirts and sprinting as fast as he could. Stray bullets zipped past him and puffed clouds out of the sand where they hit. He kept his head down. The statue loomed up ahead.

He glanced behind him as he skidded to a stop and in the distance saw Grissom climbing unsteadily back onto his feet. They wouldn't have long. He turned to Joyce, who was standing beside Daniel with her arms by her sides. His Colt, he noticed, was nowhere to be seen—and neither was DeVoe. "What hap—" Gabriel began, but the question answered itself: Joyce shook her head sadly, apologetically, as DeVoe stepped into view, training Gabriel's own weapon on him.

Gabriel ducked away, dashing around the statue's leg. He heard a gunshot and saw a chip of stone fly off the statue where DeVoe's bullet had hit.

Gabriel ran across the stretch of sand between the statue's legs and took refuge behind the farther one. He clutched the shotgun to his chest, got his finger around the trigger, made ready to bring it out—but, glancing over, he saw that DeVoe had run behind Joyce and Daniel for cover. DeVoe raised the Colt above Joyce's head and Gabriel snatched his head back—but very nearly too far back, since a gunshot rang out behind him, from the direction of the battlefield, and the bullet came within a hair's breadth of his ear. Gabriel's back was exposed—but there was no way to protect it without putting himself in DeVoe's sights. He looked up at the statue towering above him. There was only one way to get a better position.

Strapping the shotgun fully across his back, he began climbing the statue's leg, pulling his way up by hooking his fingers and toes into fissures in the stone. Another bullet struck near him. He forced himself to ignore it and keep climbing.

Moments later he heard Grissom's voice directly below. "Stop shooting, you fool! You'll damage the gemstones!" Looking down he saw that Grissom had managed to cross the battlefield and was standing beside DeVoe. Grissom had picked up a shotgun, too, and he used it now to gesture at Joyce and Daniel. "Leave them to me. You get up there and stop him— and bring me those stones!"

DeVoe stuffed the Colt into his belt and started scaling the statue's other leg. And damn it, the man was fast. Gabriel kept climbing, as quickly as he dared. He was approaching the statue's outstretched hand, which stood palm-up forty feet off the ground. If he could get to it—

He reached out for it, but it was still too far. He

climbed another few feet and tried again, straining across the gap. He could feel the stone under his fingers... but could he get a solid grip? He clamped down with one hand and prepared to bring the other over—and as he did, his left foot slipped out of the fissure he'd braced it in. Desperately he swung his other arm across, biting down on the rough stone with his fingertips. His other foot slipped from its hold as momentum carried him across, and he found himself dangling from the statue's hand, the jewel-filled vest pulling heavily on his arm. He tried to swing his legs up. His first try failed—not high enough. As he tried again, he glanced to the side and saw that DeVoe had reached the statue's hip and was starting to inch his way over toward him.

Pulling with all his might, Gabriel managed to get one leg over the edge of the giant stone palm. Breathing hard, he hauled himself the rest of the way over and lay back, panting. He unslung the shotgun and, rolling over onto his belly, pointed it at the mercenary's head. He pulled the trigger. The man flinched—but nothing else happened. Gabriel pumped the shotgun and fired it again. Nothing. DeVoe grinned ruthlessly and pulled himself nearer while Gabriel pawed through his pockets. One more shell—he had to have at least one more...

The sound of whirling blades overhead cut the air for the second time that night. The helicopter was back, making a wide circle over the battlefield. It was long and sleek, but also wide, built to carry several men—a military vehicle. Against the darkening sky, Gabriel could just make out a green and black camouflage design on its hull. The side door slid back, and standing in the doorway was a man whose face was masked by a helmet and goggles. Something was balanced on his shoulder—a cylinder like a poster tube.

Or a missile launcher.

The vapor trail of a missile shot out of the weapon. It hit at the edge of the battlefield, its explosion sending up a wave of sand and smoke. Gabriel saw bodies tumble through the air, propelled by a blast that was strong enough to make the statue shake a dozen yards away. He saw DeVoe struggle to keep his grip, clinging like a spider to the statue's belly. From the battlefield, bullets and arrows flew at the helicopter, which swerved away and disappeared into the night sky.

Gabriel finished going through his pockets—no shells.

He chanced a look down at the ground. DeVoe swung his shotgun up to fire at him, but as he pulled the trigger Joyce reached up with one arm and clocked him on the side of the head. The gunshot went wide—and Grissom went down to his knees. Gabriel saw Joyce drop the stone she'd picked up from the ground and run over to the statue's leg to begin climbing herself.

"No, Joyce—don't come up here," Gabriel called, but either she couldn't hear or wasn't listening, since she kept coming. And Gabriel had more immediate things to worry about, as DeVoe made the leap from the statue's side to the thumb of its upturned hand. Gabriel bent to pry the mercenary's fingers off the stone, but they were like steel. As he raised the stock of the shotgun to bring it down on DeVoe's fingers, DeVoe swung his legs up, dealing Gabriel a savage kick in the temple. Gabriel fell sideways, almost toppling off the hand entirely. He felt a trickle of blood well up and touched the side of his face. His hand came away sticky. Steel-toed boots. An inch or two to the left and he'd have been wearing an eyepatch like DeVoe's—assuming he'd survived at all.

DeVoe pulled himself up onto the palm. He drew Gabriel's Colt from his belt, pointed it at him, and held out his free hand. Palm up, like Teshub's. "Come on, Hunt. There's nowhere for you to go. Just hand the jewels over."

"You won't shoot," Gabriel said, panting. "You might damage the jewels. Maybe blow us all up."

"You think I can't put a bullet through your head without hitting that vest?" DeVoe said. "Does eight years as a sniper with the U.S. Army mean anything to you?"

"Bet you still had both your eyes back then," Gabriel said. "And your depth perception."

DeVoe cocked the gun and aimed it.

At that moment, the helicopter flew over them again. Another missile shot out of the open door in its side and landed in the middle of the battlefield. The explosion knocked both Gabriel and DeVoe off their feet. Gabriel managed to hold onto the statue's stone fingers, but DeVoe teetered on the edge and went over, clawing at the air. Gabriel crawled to the edge. The mercenary was forty feet off the ground clinging to a fold of Teshub's stone robe. Shaking his head to clear it, planting his feet solidly against the statue's side, DeVoe started climbing again.

A glance in the other direction showed Gabriel that the battlefield had been thoroughly decimated. Bodies lay scattered across the sand. Few of the figures were moving on either side, and those that were were moving slowly, white robes crawling back toward the desert, bloodstained khaki fatigues toward the jeeps.

The helicopter was flying off again, smoke trailing from bullet holes in its tail.

Who the hell is that? Gabriel thought. *And whose side is he on—Grissom's or the cult's?*

As Gabriel rose to his feet, he saw that, climbing swiftly, DeVoe had made it up to the statue's shoulder. He watched as the mercenary climbed up to the crown of the statue's head. Unfortunately, DeVoe had managed to hold onto the Colt, and now he had a perfect vantage point from which to use it.

"Gabriel!" Joyce shouted. He looked down. Joyce had reached the side of the statue directly across from the hand. Holding on with both knees and one hand, she flung something at him with the other—a handful of shotgun shells. One flew by well out of reach; he grabbed at the others. One landed squarely in his palm. Turning, he slammed the shell into the chamber and aimed at DeVoe, who was balanced atop the head and turning the Colt toward Gabriel. They both grabbed for their triggers—but Gabriel got to his first, the blast hitting DeVoe in the chest. The force of the buckshot knocked him backwards off the statue. He cried out as he fell, twisting in the air. The mercenary slammed into the ground seventy feet below, his cry suddenly silenced.

Gabriel helped Joyce up onto the statue's hand. She threw her arms around him and planted a kiss on his mouth.

"What was that for?" he asked.

"For not being dead," she said. "Yet. Do you have the Eyes?"

"All three of them," Gabriel said. He patted the vest, where the Three Eyes of Teshub felt like they were throbbing. He noticed they'd grown progressively warmer with their proximity to the statue.

A shotgun blast rang out, and a chunk at the end of the statue's middle finger broke off. Gabriel peered down. Below, Grissom was aiming up at them. Gabriel ducked back as Grissom fired again, the buckshot peppering the edge where he'd been kneeling. He took one of the gemstones from the vest—the ruby—and handed it to Joyce. "We've got to split up," he said. "Keep them away from Grissom."

"We're pretty far from Grissom up here," Joyce said.

"Not for long," Gabriel said, and pointed. Sure enough, Grissom had begun making the climb. Daniel tried to grab hold of his leg, but Grissom kicked him away, sending him sprawling.

Gabriel groped for another of the shotgun shells Joyce had thrown earlier; several lay scattered around the palm. He reloaded the gun, then took the vest and climbed with it precariously up Teshub's bent arm and across to the statue's massive head, balancing with both arms out like a high wire walker. He stopped beside one of the figure's ears. Looking back, he saw that Joyce was still standing on the upturned palm— and Grissom was coming closer by the second.

"Joyce, get away!" he shouted.

She stuffed the ruby under her belt, but didn't move off the hand. Grissom was started to make his move across, his shotgun strapped across his back.

"Joyce!" Gabriel cried again.

"I can take care of this bastard," she said. Standing over Grissom, she pulled back one leg to kick out at his head—but he snaked an arm around her other ankle and yanked, bringing her crashing down.

Grissom pulled himself the rest of the way onto Teshub's palm and swung the shotgun off his back. He leveled it at Joyce. "Get up," he said. "Slowly."

Grissom kept the gun on her as she did. The ruby glinted at her waist.

Sighting down the barrel of his shotgun from his perch by the statue's ear, Gabriel cursed under his breath. There was no way he could pull the trigger without spraying them both with buckshot. He thought of what Joyce said back in Borneo, that if he had to make a choice between saving her and stopping Grissom, he should forget about her and do what needed to be done. She'd meant it, and he'd promised that he would. The trigger felt cold against his fingertip. His heart hammered his ribs. Sweat trickled from his forehead.

The question was whether he could do it.

He looked down into Joyce's eyes and lowered the shotgun.

Grissom came around behind her, using her as a shield, the shotgun pointed up at her head. It was an awkward angle, but by bending over slightly he managed to keep his finger on the trigger. "If you don't want to see your lovely friend's brains spread across the desert, throw down the gun and come back here *now*. This is it, Hunt—the end of the line." He smiled, but there was nothing of pleasure in it. "World's End," he said.

24

GABRIEL AIMED THE SHOTGUN AGAIN, BUT ALL HE could see was half of Grissom's head behind Joyce's grimacing face. "I'm in no mood to repeat myself," Grissom called. He grabbed Joyce's hair, pulling her head back, and with his other hand jammed the shotgun muzzle under her jaw.

Gabriel lowered the shotgun and let it drop from his hands. It sailed down from where he stood until it was lost in darkness. They heard it land on the sand below.

"Very good," Grissom said. "Now come back here."

Gabriel walked along the statue's outstretched arm back to the hand.

Grissom's eyes narrowed as he watched Gabriel approach. "No surprises, Hunt." He pushed the muzzle harder against Joyce's jaw.

"Don't do it, Gabriel," Joyce managed to say through clenched teeth.

"I won't let him hurt you," Gabriel said.

"You've got to—" Grissom silenced her with another jab of the gun.

"Now," Grissom said. "Please take the ruby."

"*Take* it?"

"Yes," Grissom said. "Thousands of years ago, the Hittite Empire hid the Three Eyes of Teshub around the world. Now, I am going to let you have the honor of being the man who gives them back."

Gabriel lifted the ruby out from under Joyce's belt. He could see how rapidly she was breathing. She was frightened—but of what? That Grissom would pull the trigger? Or that he wouldn't, because Gabriel would do what he wanted?

"Let her go," Gabriel said. "I'll do it—but let her climb down. Her uncle can get her to safety."

"Not just yet," Grissom said. "Miss Wingard is my insurance policy... aren't you, my dear?" He stroked her cheek with the gun barrel, then turned back to Gabriel. "You'll do exactly as I say, or she dies. If you run, she dies. If you drop the gemstones, she dies. If you try anything at all, she dies. Am I being clear enough?"

"Perfectly," Gabriel said. He looked at Joyce. Her eyes pleaded with him not to do it. He looked back at Grissom. "What do you want me to do?"

"You can start by returning to the top of the head," Grissom said. "Go slowly, so I can see what you're up to at all times. I'll tell you what to do next once you're there."

Gabriel put the ruby back in the vest's largest pocket and walked carefully along the statue's arm. He climbed up onto the shoulder and from there up the slope toward the head. Halfway up, his foot slipped on some loose sand still covering the stone . He groped with his fingers for a handhold and found a seam between stones just deep enough to hold onto. His heart pounding, he looked down at the ground seventy feet below. He'd almost gone the way DeVoe had. He took a second to make sure of his footing, then pulled himself upright and moved slowly until he was standing between the shoulder and neck again.

Up close, he could see that Teshub's face had been carved from two blocks of stone. A long, narrow seam ran from the bridge of the nose down to the tip of the beard, though, oddly, he saw no mortar in the seam, nothing visibly holding the two pieces together. Using the statue's ear as a ladder, he climbed up the side of the head.

"Good," Grissom called when Gabriel reached the top. "Now, give Teshub back his eyes. Slowly! Keep your hands where I can see them."

Gabriel lay on his stomach and let his head hang down so he could inspect the statue's eyes. The two sockets looked identical, and measuring them against his hand, he saw they'd fit the emeralds—not the ruby. Gabriel pulled one of the emeralds from the vest. It seemed to hum louder as he brought it near the right eye. As he slid the gemstone into place, he felt it lock in. The glow emanating from the center of the emerald grew stronger until it became a bright green light, shining out across the desert like a lighthouse beam.

He looked over at Joyce and Grissom on the statue's palm. They were both staring at the beam, awed. Grissom collected himself enough to say, "Now do the other one."

Gabriel pulled the second emerald from the vest pocket and put it in the socket in the left eye. Another shaft of bright green light shot out from the statue's head, joining the first. A deep, throbbing rumble sounded from within the statue. It pulsed over and over, almost like a heartbeat.

"Now the last one," Grissom said.

Gabriel pulled out the ruby. He looked down at Teshub's huge face but didn't see anyplace he could put it. The openings in both eyes were filled. The mouth was closed, with no open space between the lips where the ruby could fit. There were no holes for the third gemstone at all.

"Where does it go?" Gabriel called down.

"I don't know," Grissom called back. "But you'd better figure it out quickly." He jabbed Joyce again with the gun. "Any ideas, Miss Wingard?"

"Drop dead," Joyce said.

"That's an idea, all right," Grissom said, "but I don't know that you really should be suggesting it to a man who's got a gun on you. Hunt," he called, "you've got till a count of three, then your friend here goes over the side."

The deep, pulsing rumble continued echoing across the desert. Gabriel looked down at the face again, the twin jade beams shooting out of its eyes. Teshub only had two eyes, as Daniel had pointed out. So where the hell did the third jewel go?

"One!" Grissom shouted.

A final riddle. Gabriel felt certain the answer was right in front of him. It had to have something to do with the legend. He thought back, racing through everything he'd learned: the Spearhead, a powerful device supposedly given to the Hittites by the storm god that could be used for good or evil, and then taken away because Teshub didn't trust them to make the right choice; the Three Eyes, supercharged gemstones that activated the Spearhead, scattered across the world to keep them from being found, to keep the Spearhead out of mankind's hands until…

Until what?

"Two!" Grissom shouted.

Gabriel looked at the ruby, trying to clear everything else out of his mind and focus on the legend. Teshub hid the Spearhead because mankind couldn't be trusted with its power.

Because they didn't have the judgment to keep it from being used for evil.

No, not the judgment. That wasn't the word the legend used. The legend said wisdom. The Spearhead would be hidden from mankind until they had the wisdom to use it for good.

And then he knew. Something he should have seen right away. *The third eye*. It appeared over and over again in the mythology of Eastern cultures, the eye of wisdom. How many times had he seen Buddhist sutras that illustrated the third eye, the eye that wasn't an eye, drawn right in the middle of the forehead? Hell, he suddenly realized the Death's Head Key had one on it, the diamond shape between the eyes of the skull…

"*Three!*"

"Hold on!" Gabriel shouted. "Wait! I've got it!"

Gabriel reached down and touched the smooth stone of the statue's forehead, between the eyes. That was another clue, he realized now: the visible seam between the two blocks of stone began lower down, at the bridge of the nose; there had to be a reason it didn't continue all the way up to the top of the head. Gabriel felt around for a hidden seam, one he couldn't see. He felt it a moment later, a hairline groove delineating a rectangular area above the nose. Gently at first and then more firmly, he pressed against it. Under this pressure, one half of a small slab swung inward on a hidden axle, while the other half swung out. He turned the concave slab all the way around until it was convex, a depression in the center of the forehead. And at the center of this depression he saw a socket. He didn't have to measure it to know it was the size and shape of the ruby.

He placed the last jewel into the socket and felt it lock in place. Like the emeralds, its internal glow intensified until a bright red beam shot out, riding atop the twin green ones. The pulsing thrum that emanated from the statue grew louder and Gabriel heard a grinding deep inside, like the sound of ancient gears beginning to turn.

Gabriel scrambled off the statue's head and hurried back along the shoulder and arm to the outstretched hand. Grissom still had the shotgun positioned under Joyce's chin, but he was staring at the beams of light. Gabriel was, too. The three beams intensified to an almost blinding brightness. He shielded his eyes.

And then, suddenly, the Three Eyes of Teshub went dark. Snapped off like blown lightbulbs.

"What happened?" Grissom whispered.

The statue began to shake. Gabriel had trouble keeping his footing. Behind Joyce, Grissom slipped, falling to one knee. Joyce kicked backwards, finally connecting with Grissom's head. He landed on his back, the shotgun skittering out of his grip. He started to get back to his feet, groping for the weapon, but Joyce tackled him, driving one shoulder into his chest.

"No!" Gabriel shouted and grabbed for her—but in an instant they had gone over the side. Gabriel rushed to the edge and looked down. They hit the sand, Grissom on the bottom, beneath Joyce. They hit with the terrible crack of bones breaking. Turning, he leapt across the gap separating Teshub's hand from his torso, grabbed onto the folds of the storm god's robe as DeVoe had, and began letting himself down swiftly, hand over hand. When he reached the statue's leg, he slid down it, letting himself drop the last fifteen feet. Even from that height, the impact wasn't pleasant—he could imagine what it had been like from more than twice as high. All he could hope was that Grissom had absorbed the worst of it.

He ran over to where Joyce lay. Daniel was there beside her, holding her hand. She'd rolled off Grissom but hadn't moved any further. "Can you stand?" Daniel was saying. "Can you sit up?"

Joyce nodded slowly. "I think so." But she winced terribly when she tried it and didn't make it all the way up.

Gabriel looked down at Grissom. He was moaning softly, between wracking coughs.

"My back…" he whispered. "My…"

Blood misted on his lips.

Meanwhile, the statue's tremors were accelerating, the noise of internal gears growing louder. As Gabriel looked up at it, the statue split suddenly in half, right down the middle, and bright white light spilled out from the opening seam. Each leg split separately down its own seam, though no light came out of those. But the more the seam along the face and torso widened, the more light came pouring out, flooding the entire area. The statue started coming apart as it broke open, huge pieces of stone crashing to the sand below: a thumb, a boulder-sized chunk of Teshub's robe, the top of his head containing the burned-out Eyes. Inside the collapsing outer shell another shape was being revealed: a monumental crystal obelisk on a forked stand, almost like a giant wishbone or divining rod, nearly as tall as the statue itself. Thick iron bands surrounded the crystal at intervals, connected to long metal posts on either side. The stone was pure white, like a piece of quartz. It emitted a deep, earth-shaking hum and blazed from within.

The light at World's End.

"The Spearhead," Grissom whispered, and his eyes slid shut forever.

A column of light blasted up from the obelisk into the sky like a beacon. Dark, roiling storm clouds appeared above the Spearhead and circled the column. Lightning flashed inside the clouds.

Gabriel struggled to his feet.

"It's magnificent," Daniel said. "Still operational after all these thousands of years. It must be some kind of natural generator, but how can it contain so much power?"

Gabriel knelt beside Joyce and slipped one arm under her lower back, one under her knees. He lifted her off the ground. She bent her head toward him, gave his neck a small kiss. "My hero," she said.

"Daniel," Gabriel said. "We have to go."

"We can't just leave it…"

"Watch me," Gabriel said, and turned to leave.

Only to find himself face to face with the high priest of the Cult of Ulikummis.

The man was leaning heavily on his staff. The front of his robe was soaked through with blood, and a trail of blood extended behind him. But he'd somehow made it this far, and wouldn't be stopped now. He bent the staff forward and swung it in a tight arc that would have drawn blood if Gabriel hadn't stepped back, Joyce still in his arms.

The high priest muttered something in Nesili.

"He says he has to receive Ulikummis," Daniel said. "That he is Ulikummis' vessel on earth."

The high priest dragged himself another step forward. He was nearly standing between the forks of the apparatus on which the crystal stood.

Joyce spoke softly, her voice strained. "Put me down. You've got... got to stop him."

But it was Daniel who stepped into the high priest's path. He swung Gabriel's Colt up before him, the gun held in both hands. "Not another step," he said.

The priest sneered and started swinging his staff.

Daniel pulled the trigger. Twice.

The bullets slammed into the high priest's chest and he jerked from each impact. He staggered—one step—two—and then collapsed on the ground directly beneath the crystal.

A thunderous explosion sounded overhead. Jagged bolts of lightning crackled in the air between the storm clouds and the Spearhead, each blasting the other with raw electrical energy. The light from the obelisk grew brighter, a hundred suns dawning in the middle of the Kalahari Desert. Gabriel used one hand to turn Joyce's face into his neck and squeezed his own eyes shut. He began running away from the Spearhead, Daniel running beside him as fast as his limping gait could take him. Even through his closed eyelids, Gabriel saw the bright light that washed over them, past them, extending outward into the night. It was warm, but not as hot as he'd expected. He kept running, waiting for the burning blast that would finish them.

It never arrived. When the light had dimmed and the temperature cooled, he stopped running and opened his eyes. The storm clouds had vanished as quickly as they'd appeared. The Spearhead still glowed, but with waning intensity. In a wide circle around it, the sand had turned to glass, stopping less than a yard from where Gabriel, Joyce and Daniel now stood.

And below the Spearhead, where the high priest had lain, a figure was now standing—a figure blazing with a vibrant white light, similar to the crystal's. Could this be the priest? That he was upright at all was extraordinary—he'd been stabbed and shot twice, he must have lost a gallon of blood. But the energy of the Spearhead seemed to have flowed into him and was animating him like some sort of puppet. He jerked from side to side. It was as if his body had somehow absorbed the immense power of the Spearhead and was desperately trying to contain it. He bent double, gripping his head in its hands. They heard him begin keening in a voice suffused with pain. The light pouring off of him intensified to a blinding glare. A moment later the light dimmed, then vanished altogether.

It took a moment before they could see at all. When their eyes adjusted, there were only the stars that dotted the night sky, and the moon hanging over the horizon. The obelisk was dark, its once clear crystal smoky and cracked.

"Are you all right?" Gabriel asked Joyce.

She nodded. "What happened? Where's the priest?"

Gabriel looked toward the spot where he had stood, but there was no sign of him—not his robes, not his staff, not his body. Only the trail of blood, leading up to a point beneath the forked stand.

"Killed by the Spearhead," Daniel said. "Vaporized."

"It really was a weapon," Gabriel said.

"At that moment it was, yes. Who's to say what it could have been in the right hands?"

"There are no hands I'd trust with a power like this," Gabriel said.

A loud cracking sound drew their attention back to the obelisk. Deep fissures spread across the crystal like spiderwebs. The crystal broke apart, sliding out of its iron supports and coming down with a crash amid the rubble from the statue.

"Well, it looks like you won't have to," Daniel said. He shook his head. "What a terrible loss."

Gabriel heard the approaching helicopter's rotors before he saw it overhead. He looked up. The wind blew back his hair and rustled his shirt. The helicopter descended, landing close enough for him to see the emergency foam patches sealing the bullet holes in its tail. The side door slid open, and four men in flight suits, helmets and goggles jumped out. Three of them held machine guns and stood in formation, looking out at the bodies scattered across the battlefield, watching for movement. The question Gabriel had posed earlier came back to him: Which army's side were these men on?

But he only wondered it until the fourth man pulled off his helmet and goggles.

"Noboru?" Gabriel said, amazed.

Noboru rushed over to his side. He looked down at Joyce, stroked one hand across her hair. "I couldn't just leave the two of you. Not when I still had something I could offer."

"Does Michiko know?" Joyce asked.

"Sh," Noboru said.

"You know this man?" Daniel asked.

"How did you find us?" Gabriel said.

"You can thank your brother," Noboru said. "Michael told me where you were headed from Turkey. He sounded worried, figured you might get yourself in trouble again. That seemed likely to me, too. I thought maybe you could use some backup."

"How'd you get your hands on a helicopter like this?" Gabriel asked. "Never mind the missiles."

"I called in a few favors from my Intelligence days," Noboru said. "It took a bit of finagling, but I got the team and equipment I asked for."

"I'm just… glad you found us," Joyce whispered.

Noboru looked at the bodies and wreckage all around them. "You guys are hard to miss."

Daniel stuck out his hand. "Daniel Wingard. Joyce's uncle."

Noboru shook Daniel's hand. He looked across the stretch of fused sand at the broken shards that were all that was left of the Spearhead. "We saw that thing's light miles away, when we were patching the chopper. What the hell was it?"

"A test," Daniel said. "After everything, it was just a test to see if mankind is ready to use something that powerful responsibly."

"How'd we do?" Noboru asked.

Gabriel gave a thin smile. "We survived."

Noboru nodded, then patted the side of the helicopter. "So. You guys need a lift?"

25

THE BARTENDER IN THE DISCOVERERS LEAGUE
lounge, Wade Boland, slid two bottles of beer across the
bar to Gabriel. "Women who like beer are something
special," he said. "You try to hold onto this one."

Clyde Harris, sitting on his usual stool at the end at
the bar, chuckled and ran a hand through his thinning
white hair. "Reminds me of a woman I met in the
Netherlands back in '43. She loved beer almost as
much as she loved garroting spies."

Wade shook his head. "Save it, old timer. Can't you
see he's busy?"

Gabriel took the bottles back to the table by the
fireplace and sat down in the plush red chair across
from Joyce. After dropping them off at the embassy
in Botswana, Noboru had returned to Borneo. Daniel
was back in Turkey, closing down his dig site, and had
promised to join them in New York in a few days' time.
Gabriel looked at his watch. Michael would be coming

over in a bit over an hour for a full debriefing. But until then, Gabriel and Joyce could finally relax. No bullets, no arrows, no explosions, just the two of them and some stress-free time alone.

She took one of the bottles from him with the arm that wasn't in a cast, clinked it against his bottle, and took a sip. "It's a shame about the Spearhead."

"Your uncle seems to think everything played out the way it was meant to."

"That's not what I mean, though," she said. "It's a shame we didn't get to study it, find out what it was. How it worked. How a civilization thousands of years in the past could have created something that channeled and contained so much energy. It was like some kind of reactor, built long before there should have been anything close to that kind of technology." She took another sip. "Now we'll never know. It's gone, all of it. The Spearhead, the gemstones."

"Not all of it." Gabriel reached into his shirt and pulled out the Death's Head Key dangling from the leather strap around his neck. "We still have this."

Joyce smiled. "True. What are you going to do with it?"

Gabriel pulled the strap over his head and looked at the key. "There are plenty of museums that I'm sure would love to have it for their collections. A few universities would love to study it, publish papers about it. I'm sure *National Geographic* and *Discovery* would love some photographs."

Joyce nodded. "I suppose."

"But I wasn't planning on doing any of that," Gabriel said. He held it out to her. "I was thinking you should have it."

"Me? Why?"

"You earned it," he said. "The Three Eyes of Teshub, the Spearhead, they were your finds, not mine. You should have it."

She took the Death's Head Key from him and hung it around her neck. Her eyes sparkled. "I don't know what to say." Then she laughed. "It's so silly. Some women get all choked up over jewelry, but with me it's a rusty old key."

Gabriel laughed. "Just one of your many endearing qualities. So what are you going to do now? Are you going to take Daniel's advice and apply for an academic job, or are you going to keep hitting the field to see what else is out there?"

"We'll see," she said. Then she smiled mischievously. "I like to keep people guessing."

"Like I said, what would the world do without Joyce Wingard to keep things interesting?"

She leaned across the table, pulled him close with her good arm, and kissed him. "Is that interesting enough?"

"We'll see," he said. "This may require further study."

Behind the bar, Wade turned to Clyde and said, "We had a bet, old timer. Pay up."

Muttering under his breath, Clyde slid a twenty-dollar bill across the bar.

ABOUT THE AUTHOR

Nicholas Kaufmann is the critically acclaimed author of numerous works, including the Bram Stoker Award-nominated *General Slocum's Gold*, the International Thriller Writers Award-nominated and Shirley Jackson Award-nominated *Chasing the Dragon*, and *Dying Is My Business*. His short fiction and non-fiction have appeared in numerous magazines and anthologies. He has also served on the Board of Trustees for the Horror Writers Association and is a member of the International Thriller Writers.

Read on for an extract from the next

GABRIEL HUNT ADVENTURE

HUNT BEYOND THE FROZEN FIRE

1

"I'D ASK WHAT A NICE GIRL LIKE YOU IS DOING IN A place like this," Gabriel told the brunette sitting at the bar with her back to him. "But I already know exactly what you're doing."

The brunette spun, reaching for the revolver beside her glass, but Gabriel grabbed her wrist before she could raise it to draw a bead between his eyes.

"I also know you're not a very nice girl," Gabriel said, tightening his grip and meeting her furious gaze without flinching.

The bar was a murky, nameless Moldovan hole-in-the-wall, spitting distance from the Transdniestrian border. The angry brunette was Dr. Fiona Rush, professor in Cambridge University's prestigious archeology department and partner in Gabriel Hunt's latest Eastern European expedition. She had also been Gabriel's lover, which made it all the worse when she'd double crossed him and run off with the legendary jewel-encrusted Cossack dagger they'd come here to find. There were some who claimed that the *kindjal* was cursed, that it would bring sorrow and strife to anyone who possessed it. After everything he'd been through in the past few days, Gabriel was inclined to agree.

When Gabriel grabbed Fiona's wrist, all conversation around them abruptly ceased. Several men nearby, taller even than Gabriel and twice as wide, raised weapons and cold, hostile glares and aimed both in Gabriel's direction. For a tense stretch of seconds, nothing happened. A Romanian melody fought its way through the static on a cheap transistor radio behind the bar. The ancient, toothless bartender suddenly remembered something critical that needed to be done right away in the storeroom in the back. Gabriel silently tried to decide which of the armed men posed the most serious threat and to measure where they were located in relation to both the front and back doors. He did not let go of Fiona's wrist.

Fiona shook her head, offering a few curt words in Romanian. The thugs pocketed their various weapons, some more reluctantly than others. They all continued to stare at Gabriel with undisguised hostility. It was clear it wouldn't take much for the weapons to reappear. Gabriel let Fiona go, but stayed alert and wary.

"Have a drink," Fiona said, casually, as if she'd just happened to run into an old friend. She took an extra glass from the rack above the bar and poured a generous knock of the rich Moldovan brandy known as *divin*. "You must be thirsty."

"I don't want a drink," Gabriel said, pushing the glass away. "I want the *kindjal*."

"You're not still cross about that, are you?" Fiona smiled and topped off her own glass from the dusty bottle. "Honestly, it was nothing personal."

"Did you think you could just cut me out and sell to the highest bidder?" Gabriel asked. "That dagger is a significant historical artifact. It should be on display in a museum, not locked up by some rich collector. You of all people ought to know that."

"You know what your problem is, Gabriel?" Fiona arched a dark eyebrow. "You're still laboring under this charmingly anachronistic sense of right and wrong. This is the twenty-first century. You need to be more…" She took a sip of her *divin* and looked up at Gabriel with the sultry gaze that had gotten him into this trouble in the first place. "More flexible."

"No more games, Fiona," Gabriel said. "I know you're planning on meeting your buyer in this bar, but I also know you're too smart to have the *kindjal* on hand for the negotiation. So where is it?"

"We could split the money," Fiona said, dropping a hand to Gabriel's thigh. "We can just claim the *kindjal* was stolen. That sort of thing happens all the time in this part of the world. No one will ever be the wiser."

"Where is it?" Gabriel asked again, pushing her hand away. "I'm asking nicely. Next time I ask, it won't be so nice."

"You really are going to be tedious about this, aren't you?" Fiona sighed and emptied her glass, but when she tried for another refill, she found the bottle empty. "Fine, I'll take you to it. But first let's have one more drink, shall we? For old time's sake."

She gestured to the bartender, who had tentatively crept back to his post when it appeared there would be no violence after all. Holding her glass up high, she called out something in Romanian that caused the entire bar to turn her way. Amazingly, the chilly scowls all melted into broad, gap-toothed smiles. Glasses were raised all around and suddenly Gabriel was surrounded by thick, strapping men slapping him on the back and shaking his hand.

"What the hell did you say to them?" Gabriel asked, searching for Fiona between the moving mountain range of giant shoulders and flushed, grinning faces. Romanian was one of the few Eastern European languages he didn't speak even a cursory amount of.

"I told them drinks were on you," Fiona said with a smirk as the bartender obligingly opened a bottle of vodka and began filling upraised glasses. "I also said that you were a big American movie director from Hollywood looking for Moldavans to cast in your new picture."

An enormous ox with a blond beard suddenly pulled Gabriel into an aromatic bear hug as if he were a long lost brother. Someone began singing a patriotic song loud and off key and the ox enthusiastically joined in, slapping Gabriel's back so hard it nearly knocked him off his feet. Another equally large but beardless man tapped Gabriel on the shoulder and began demonstrating a terrifyingly drunken knife trick on the bar, weaving the blade back and forth between fat sausage fingers.

Gabriel tried to keep Fiona in view, but she vanished between two of the bar's larger patrons.

Gabriel pressed far too many Moldovan *lei* into the astonished bartender's hand and bulled his way through the crowd toward the open back door. He was almost waylaid by a pair of eager Moldavians clamoring for their free drink, but he managed to break free and make it to the door. When he burst through, he found himself in a narrow alley barely wide enough to accommodate his shoulders. He heard the clatter of horses' hooves approaching. There was only one street light in this remote village and, in typical Moldovan fashion, it had been turned off to save money. The only illumination came from the large, nearly full moon behind swift-moving clouds.

As his eyes adjusted to the dark, he spotted Fiona's distinctive silhouette at the mouth of the alley and called out her name. She turned toward him just as the moon slipped out from behind the clouds, pale silvery light glinting off the steel barrel of her pistol.

Gabriel dove for cover, tasting brick dust as a bullet smashed into the wall inches from where his head had been. He unholstered his Colt Peacemaker and risked a glance at the mouth of the alley just in time to see a massive white horse thunder into view. The rider reached effortlessly down and grabbed Fiona's narrow waist, hauling her up and across the saddle. She let out a breathless shriek and before Gabriel could blink, the horse, its rider and Fiona were gone.

2

GABRIEL SWORE UNDER HIS BREATH AND RAN OUT TO the mouth of the alley. He could barely make out the ghostly white shape of the horse swiftly galloping down the muddy road. But he could hear Fiona continuing to scream, her voice dwindling with distance.

Not quite the escape she'd intended, Gabriel thought, and for a moment he was tempted to simply let Fiona go to whatever awful fate awaited. She had, after all, betrayed him. More than that—she'd just tried to kill him. But damn it, she was the only one who knew where the *kindjal* was hidden… and even after everything she'd put him through, his conscience wouldn't let him just stand by and let her be abducted, maybe tortured to reveal the *kindjal's* location. Maybe worse.

His Gypsy driver, Djordji, already had the cranky, Cold War-era Russian jeep running when Gabriel vaulted into the passenger seat without opening the door.

"Follow that horse," Gabriel muttered. Djordji reacted without comment, as poker-faced and nonchalant as if he had been asked to drive to another pub.

As the jeep accelerated along the deeply rutted, unpaved road, the fleeing horse vanished around a corner. When the jeep reached and rounded the same corner, Gabriel was surprised to see not one but several horses on the road ahead. The white stallion had the lead, its rider wearing a tall, distinctive fur hat. Gabriel could see Fiona's long pale legs kicking frantically off to one side of the saddle. The other horses looked brown or black—hard to tell in the darkness—and were being ridden by smaller men, hunched close to their horses' necks. They raced past a large, decrepit building that may once have been a stable but was now surrounded by rusted wrecks of farm equipment and the carcass of a Volkswagen bus. Another turn in the road loomed and the horses swung around it in a pack. Djordji floored the gas and moments later roared into the turn, engine screaming. But when they came out on the other side, the only thing visible down the road were the distant yellow lights of the Transdniestrian border crossing. The horses were gone.

"Stop," Gabriel said. Djordji laid on the brakes and they squealed to a halt in the middle of the road. Gabriel held up a finger for silence. The clattering of hooves came to them quietly from the left. Gabriel squinted and scanned the dark terrain off to the side of the road. It was an empty field—but near the horizon he could just make out several figures pounding desperately away.

"There," he said, pointing.

Djordji stepped on the gas and wrenched the wheel hard to the left, taking the jeep off the road and into the field. It was rocky and lined with the dry stalks of some crop that clearly hadn't fared well during the past season. The bone jarring jolts of the jeep's balding tires traveling over the furrowed field threatened to throw both of them out of the car.

As they drew closer to the fleeing riders, a volley of bullets ricocheted off the jeep's dented olive flank. Gabriel unholstered his Colt and returned fire without hesitation, but the uneven ground, the dark and the distance made accurate shooting next to impossible. Luckily this handicap went both ways.

"Try and hold her steady," he told Djordji, and he stood up in the open-topped jeep, bracing himself against the windshield and aiming at the rearmost rider, who was still twenty yards ahead of them and off to one side. Gabriel fired off a single shot but the jeep hit a rock and the shot went hopelessly wide. He swore and urged Djordji to close the distance. The taciturn Gypsy made a sour face under his thick white mustache.

"Is jeep," he said. "Not race car."

Gabriel ignored the comment and tried to steady his aim, fighting the uneven rhythm of bumps and dips. He slowly blew all the air out of his lungs and when the Jeep hit a miraculously smooth patch of ground, he squeezed the trigger. This time the last rider in the pack went down. His now riderless horse slowed from a gallop to a trot as Djordji pulled the jeep up alongside.

Most of the horses Gabriel had seen around the local villages were pretty sorry specimens. Bony, spavined and morose, seemingly as resigned to their disappointing lot in life as their gloomy Moldovan masters. But this muscular chestnut mare was absolutely stunning. Proud, sleek and obviously quite expensive. A Ferrari of a horse. It made Gabriel wonder about her owner, but he didn't have time to wonder for long. Because it turned out that the beautiful horse was not riderless after all.

Apparently the rider hadn't been shot—he'd simply dropped down on the far side of the horse to avoid Gabriel's bullet, clinging to the tack and keeping the horse's body between him and the jeep. Now he swung back up, leaping effortlessly to his feet in the saddle. In the moonlight Gabriel could see the rider's pale, angry face and shaved head with its long traditional Cossack forelock. He stood on the horse's back with a comfortable, loose-limbed stance like a surfer riding a wave.

The next thing Gabriel knew, the rider had leapt from the horse and knocked him into the back seat, a gleaming blade slashing the air inches from his face. Gabriel's Colt tumbled from his grip and onto the floor of the jeep.

Gabriel swiftly grabbed the Cossack's knife hand and smashed it as hard as he could against the frame of the front seat. The Cossack barred his teeth and refused to drop the knife, so Gabriel dug the tip of his thumb into the soft underside of the Cossack's wrist and gave his hand a few more knocks against the metal frame.

The jeep hit a rocky bump that sent it airborne for several seconds. The Cossack grunted and let go of the knife, clinging to Gabriel as they were bounced together into the air like ingredients in a chef's sauté pan. When the jeep hit the ground, the grappling men slammed back down to the floor. The Cossack's forehead smashed against Gabriel's and the passenger-side back door flipped open. It snapped off as Djordji sideswiped a sturdy tree. The Cossack's knife skittered across the floor and out of the jeep. He lunged for it, too late. Then he saw Gabriel's fallen pistol sliding along the floor and went for it instead. Gabriel swung a stiff elbow, cracking the Cossack in the jaw. The man's head snapped back and Gabriel reached for the Colt himself, but the jeep made a sharp right and the gun slid away, under the driver's seat.

Wiping a trail of blood from his split lip, the rider got up into a crouch and threw a short kick at Gabriel, his dusty boot narrowly missing Gabriel's face. Gabriel scrambled to his feet and threw a hard right, but the jeep hit another nasty bump and he found himself overbalanced, falling halfway out the broken back door, face down, hands scrambling for purchase. The rider was on top of him in an instant, belly to back, gripping a fistful of Gabriel's hair. A flood of hot, suffocating exhaust from the tailpipe blew into Gabriel's face as the rider pushed Gabriel's head towards the spinning rear wheel.

Spangles danced in the borders of Gabriel's vision and he felt his head go fuzzy from the fumes. He knew he had to act fast. His right cheek was less than an inch from the muddy wheel. Gripping one of the bars of the jeep's frame in one hand, he reached back and seized the rider's dangling forelock with the other. As the jeep swerved, Gabriel yanked downward on the braided hair while pushing up against the man's chest with his shoulders and hips. The rider went over, flipping out of the jeep—but as he went, he managed to wrap his arms tightly around Gabriel's chest. Gabriel felt himself dragged out of the speeding car. He clung desperately onto the bar he'd grabbed hold of, his arm nearly wrenching from its socket. The rider, meanwhile, clung desperately to Gabriel, sliding down along his body until he was holding tightly to Gabriel's waist. Gabriel looked back at the furious Cossack. He was being dragged along the ground but holding on.

Djordji, meanwhile, kept speeding along, either oblivious to what was going on behind him or convinced that following Gabriel's last instruction, to catch up with the other horses, was the best way he could be helpful.

Gabriel slammed his heel into the Cossack's kneecap. The Cossack grunted but would not let go. Glancing to the side, Gabriel saw they were approaching a wide, rocky stream. He called out to Djordji.

"Drive into the water!"

Djordji swung the steering wheel and seconds later they plunged headlong into the icy stream. Gabriel's face stayed barely above the surface, but the rider beneath him was completely submerged. Tough bastard that he was, he still managed to hang on, but Gabriel felt the grip around his waist loosen. Gabriel pulled his legs up and gave the man a savage kick. This finally dislodged him, and, freed of the excess weight, Gabriel was able to haul himself back up into the jeep. Behind him, he saw the rider rise to his knees, cursing, in the middle of the stream. The jeep squelched through the mud and climbed the opposite bank, leaving the Cossack in the distance.

"Is not good," Djordji said when Gabriel climbed, dripping, into the front seat.

Gabriel figured his driver could have been talking about any number of things. "What's not good?"

"They cross to Transdniestria," Djordji said, pointing to the remaining riders galloping ahead of them. As Gabriel watched, the white stallion and one of the other horses jumped across what appeared to be a deep, rocky ravine. "Jeep cannot go that way. We have to go around."

But Gabriel knew they couldn't go around—by the time they made it, all signs of the horses and riders would be gone.

"We're not going around," Gabriel said. "Speed up."

Djordji looked at him as if he had lost his mind, but kept his foot on the gas. They were just yards from the edge of the ravine.

Gabriel reached down into the footwell, groped around till he found his Colt, and reholstered it. "Get me next to one of those horses," he said, standing up again. He climbed onto the seat.

A third rider reached the ravine and leapt across. There were only two left. As Djordji poured on what additional speed remained in the jeep's overtaxed engine, they overtook the last horse. The rider looked to his side. He seemed surprised to see Gabriel there, standing beside him. Gabriel cocked a smile at him, and the man smiled back. "*Dobry vecher, gospodin*," Gabriel said, and swung a wide right into the rider's face, knocking him backwards off his horse. Gabriel looked ahead. There were only seconds left before they hit the ravine. Gabriel leapt astride the now empty saddle and swept the reins up in his hands.

Djordji slammed on the brakes, bringing the jeep to a halt in a massive cloud of dust, just inches from the lip of the ravine. Gabriel gripped the black mare's steaming flanks with his legs and pulled back on the reins, urging the animal to make the jump.

The horse let out a snort of protest against her new, unfamiliar rider but launched herself across the ravine after her fellows. There was a tense moment of shifting pebbles and slipping hooves as they landed on the far side and the horse fought to maintain her balance.

Gabriel leaned forward and spurred his anxious mount ahead. She regained her footing and took off after the other riders.

As the horse galloped across the moonlit steppe, their destination came into view. An ancient ruin of a large circular fortress, grim, brooding half-hidden by the low broken hills around it. This was no tourist attraction, no spectacular gothic castle out of a travel brochure. It was an ugly, forgotten place, nothing left but cold, unfriendly walls designed not for aesthetics but function, the function being to keep enemies out. But the defenses had been breached centuries ago, and enemies or not, the Cossacks were riding in.

As they approached the fortress, a heavy, rusted portcullis slowly cranked open, allowing the riders to pass beneath and into the dull yellow glow emanating from the interior. As the portcullis began to close, Gabriel urged his mount to top speed.

He wasn't going to be able to make it on horseback, he saw—the metal gate was dropping too quickly, and already there was no room. Yanking the reins sharply to the right, Gabriel dropped off the horse to his left, diving to the ground and rolling beneath the portcullis' descending spikes. As the ancient gate slammed closed, Gabriel could feel one leg of his pants catch and tear. He struggled to stand and pull his pant leg free from the spike that had pinned it to the ground. There was a loud rip as he freed himself, but the sound was drowned out by a louder ratcheting sound, a sound of metal sliding against metal that made his heart sink when he heard it. He spun to face the interior of the fortress and found himself staring into the business ends of over a dozen AK47s.

3

GABRIEL COULD SEE THE WHITE HORSE STANDING BY
the open doorway of a low stone building on the
opposite side of the courtyard. Steep stone steps were
visible through the doorway, leading sharply down
into the darkness beyond, but Fiona and the rider who
had grabbed her—the man with the tall fur hat—were
nowhere in sight.

However there was no time to contemplate where
Fiona might have been taken, because Gabriel was
distracted by the infinitely more pressing issue of
the hostile, rifle-wielding soldiers currently drawing
down on him.

One of their number, a handsome, dark-haired older
man with the insignia of a commanding officer, stepped
forward and ordered Gabriel, in Russian, to surrender
his gun. One of the younger soldiers helpfully clarified
the command by tapping Gabriel's shoulder holster
with the barrel of his Kalashnikov and then jamming

the muzzle into the soft spot under Gabriel's ear.

Gabriel raised his hands and slowly removed the Colt from its holster. His eyes desperately scanned his surroundings for any hope of escape. There were stacks of stenciled wooden crates, several parked military vehicles and a pair of noisy, foul-smelling generators powering the strings of weak yellow lightbulbs that illuminated the scene. The remaining riders had dismounted at the far end of the courtyard and were seeing to their horses with only the vaguest interest in Gabriel's predicament. A group of grim-faced African men in suits were standing to his left, conversing quietly in French and giving him occasional stony glares while one of their number counted the crates, jotting figures on a clipboard. The surrounding walls were over twenty feet high. There was no visible way out.

Gabriel held his pistol out at arm's length and tossed it to the ground. It slid across the mossy paving stones and came to rest against the commanding officer's spitshined shoe. The soldier pressing his rifle against Gabriel's neck backed off with a smug look. The smugness rapidly transformed to curiosity, then astonishment as the sound of an approaching vehicle became a deafening crash. Djordji's jeep rammed the rusty portcullis, knocking it loose from its ancient moorings and driving into the courtyard with the gate drunkenly balanced across the hood, steam billowing from the damaged engine.

Gabriel leapt aside, narrowly avoiding being flattened as the jeep scattered men before it like bowling pins. He dove for his Colt, rolling away with the gun in hand and ending up behind a stack of wooden crates. Gabriel ducked down and listened to the multilingual chaos, trying to discern Djordji's fate while his fingers moved on autopilot, emptying the Colt's spent brass and reloading. He'd only had time to slide two fresh slugs into the cylinder when a wiry young soldier dropped down on him from the stack of crates above, slamming a fist into the back of his neck and causing the remaining bullets in Gabriel's palm to drop and scatter.

Gabriel swore, twisting and bringing the hand holding the pistol up towards his attacker, but the Russian grabbed Gabriel's hand and pressed his thumb against the still open cylinder to keep it from snapping shut. Gabriel managed to wrench his hand free from the Russian's grip, but not before the struggle caused the two bullets to slip from the chamber and roll away under one of the crates. He let the young Russian have it in the temple with the butt of the empty gun. The Russian dropped as if suddenly boneless. Stepping over his crumpled form, Gabriel angrily holstered the empty Colt and peered around the stack of crates.

The courtyard was full of soldiers, running and shouting. The Jeep was upside down and on fire, but Djordji wasn't in it. In fact, he was nowhere in sight. Several men were battling the smoky blaze with foam extinguishers while others, under the supervision of the grim Africans, formed lines to swiftly move crates of ammo and other dangerous explosives away from the fire. It was then that Gabriel realized what was going on here. Clearly he had stumbled into the middle of some kind of arms deal. But what did this have to do with Fiona and the *kindjal*?

Gabriel eyed the open door and the stone steps down which Fiona and her captor had disappeared. He thought he had a clear shot and was about to make a run for it when one of the Africans came around the far corner of the stack of crates. His eyes widened in surprise and then narrowed to a slit as he pulled out a HK .45, drawing a bead on Gabriel's chest.

Gabriel raised his palms till they framed his face. In heavily accented French, the African told Gabriel to prepare for death. Gabriel responded in the same tongue. "You might want to do a little preparation yourself," he said.

"I? For what?" The man sneered. "I have the gun in my hand, and you have nothing."

"Yes," Gabriel said, "but my friend there, behind you, has a shovel."

The man got the beginning of a contemptuous laugh out before the shovel in Djordji's hands slammed into the back of his head with a loud crack. The man staggered and crumpled, clutching at the crates as he fell. One toppled onto him, breaking open when it struck the ground. A pair of smooth, spherical hand grenades spilled out.

Gabriel snatched one up. "Nobody move!" he shouted. He stepped out into view with his finger through the pin loop. "Drop your weapons."

There was a moment of shocked silence and then a ripple of outraged Russian murmurs.

"You wouldn't dare," replied the dark-haired officer who'd first confronted Gabriel.

"Of course I would," Gabriel replied in Russian. "Grenade or gun, I'm just as dead, but this way I get to take some of you with me." The logic seemed to sink in, and the officer took a step back. Gabriel motioned for Djordji to join him as he moved sideways towards the open door.

Every pair of eyes in the courtyard was focused on Gabriel as weapons were lowered but not dropped. The look in the officer's face was one of barely suppressed rage. Gabriel closed the last few feet between him and the door.

"Go," he said to Djordji, gesturing for the Gypsy to start down the stone steps.

While the older man descended, Gabriel stood in the open doorway, his finger on the pin of the hand grenade. Once he could no longer hear Djordji's steps, Gabriel called to the officer. "Here. Catch." He made as if to throw the grenade at the man, who ducked away in fear—but at the last instant, Gabriel spun and slung the grenade sidelong towards the nearest stack of munitions.

The hot fist of the ensuing explosion shoved Gabriel backwards into the stairway. Gabriel pulled the heavy wooden door closed, sliding a massive iron bar into place to seal it. He could hear the firecracker sound of explosions and gunshots, then a barrage of angry Russian as the soldiers beat their fists and gun butts against the door. Gabriel raced downward, following the path Djordji had taken—and Fiona before him—into the bowels of the ancient fortress.

He met up with Djordji halfway down. The Gypsy was leaning against the stone wall, the shovel still gripped in one fist. Djordji put the index finger of his other hand to his lips and gestured with his head below them, where the stone steps vanished into darkness. There were voices below, one male and one female, both furious.

"*Where?*" the man's voice thundered in heavily accented English. "*You tell, now!*"

"*I don't know where it is,*" Fiona shouted back, unconvincingly. "*I swear I don't.*"

Gabriel took the lead and walked silently, cautiously,

down the steps. As they crept around a turn, the darkness was replaced by a dim flickering light, the startlingly red glow a shade Gabriel remembered seeing only once before, in a Croatian monastery; when he'd asked what accounted for the unusual color of the flame, they'd explained it was the admixture of the tallow with a portion of ground-up human bone. The calcium, they explained. Calcium burns brick red.

Gabriel still couldn't see anything before him— there was another curve in the steps ahead—but he could make out a distinct and repetitive sound, a kind of sharp, resonant *thwack*, followed swiftly each time by a high-pitched feminine gasp.

He hastened ahead to the curve, Djordji just steps behind. When they came around it, the candlelit scene was revealed. Fiona stood in the center of a large, low-ceilinged room, bound to one of several thick wooden pillars with her hands above her head. Her dress was torn nearly to her waist and her shapely legs were scratched and bruised, but she held her small, defiant chin high, eyes blazing. The pillar to which she had been tied was bristling with throwing knives, their wicked points buried in the ancient wood all around her bound and squirming form. The rider in the fur hat stood before her, now revealed as a tall, brutish man with long gray hair, a sharp forked beard and an expression of avid hunger that might have been lust or greed or religious zeal, or perhaps a combination of all three. The man held several knives in one large hand like a deadly bouquet, the same sort of knives that currently surrounded Fiona's tense, quivering body. He transferred one to his empty hand, then smiled and licked his lips.

"I told you…" Fiona began to say.

The man in the fur hat raised his elbow to the ceiling and then brought his arm swiftly downward, letting the knife fly. It sank deep into the wood a bare millimeter from Fiona's temple. She yelped as she tried to twist away and found her head trapped, a thick lock of her hair pinned to the wood by the blade.

Gabriel's hand reflexively drew the now empty Colt. He looked to Djordji and motioned for the Gypsy to hand him the shovel. Should he charge the man with the shovel? Try to bluff with the gun? He needed to act fast, because the next strike of a blade could be fatal. Behind him, Djordji silently crossed himself. The man in the fur hat switched another knife to his empty hand. Gabriel looked from the shovel to the gun and back again.

"Ah, hell," he muttered, then raised the Colt so its barrel was aimed directly at the knife thrower's forehead. He called out: "Put the knives down and let her go."

With stunning speed, the man spun and let the blade fly in Gabriel's direction. Gabriel's reflexes were barely quick enough for him to bring the head of the shovel up into the knife's path. The blade rang loudly against the metal of the shovel, then ricocheted off, burying itself to the hilt in the dirt between two slabs of stone at the foot of the stairs.

Gabriel charged down the remaining steps as the man readied for another throw. Gabriel felt level ground beneath his feet and saw a second knife spinning towards him, end over end. He swung the shovel, deflecting it. He saw Djordji duck as the knife passed by him. The Gypsy flattened himself against the nearest wall, then darted away into the safety of the shadows.

The knife thrower stepped back to Fiona's side, one of

the remaining knives clutched in each hand. He held one up in throwing position and swung the other to a point directly below her chin. "You come," he said, "I carve."

Gabriel drew to a halt, gun raised. "You move, I shoot."

"This close," the man said softly, "blade is faster." And to demonstrate he took a nick out of Fiona's throat with a minute twitch of his wrist. A drop of blood formed, then a trail, a line of red reaching down toward her collarbone. Fiona didn't make a sound, but Gabriel could see the pain and fear in her eyes.

Was a blade faster than a bullet? It depended on circumstances and was a question tacticians could debate. But a real blade was definitely faster than a nonexistent bullet.

Gabriel lowered his gun. "All right," he said. "You win. I'll tell you where the *kindjal* is."

"You?" the man said, his eyes narrowing with disbelief.

"Me," Gabriel said. "She passed it to me in the bar. I hid it in the alleyway."

The man considered this for a moment, then shook his head. "You lie. You lie to save woman." He leered. "Because you like, no?"

"No," Gabriel said. "I don't like. I did once, very much. But that was a long time ago." He saw the change in Fiona's expression. The look of pain in her eyes was due to more now than just the blade at her throat.

"Then why," the man said, "do you try to save her?"

"Because," Gabriel said, "that's what I do."

The knife thrower turned then, at a sound beside him, but not before Djordji, who had crept along the shadows of the wall and circled around behind him, was able to lunge forward and seize the man in a crushing bear hug. They grappled, the knife thrower straining mightily to free his arms, which Djordji held pinned to his sides. Gabriel ran forward, the shovel swinging in a wide arc. The rust-stained metal caught the knife thrower full in the face, sending the fur hat flying. The man went limp in Djordji's grip. The Gypsy let him go, and he slid to the floor.

"Thank you," Gabriel said. "That was—"

"Gabriel!" Fiona cried. "Look out!"

The bone-jarring roar of a high caliber gunshot made Gabriel leap backwards. Djordji uttered a whispered Romany oath and, to Gabriel's horror, collapsed first to his knees and then onto his side, a dark stain spreading across the shoulder of his bright red shirt.

Gabriel dropped to the ground beside him. Djordji was still conscious, but his breaths were suddenly rapid and shallow and his face was pale and wet with cold sweat. Blood pooled on the stone beneath him.

A reedy voice issued from the shadows at far side of the room. "You... must be the famous Gabriel Hunt."

DON'T MISS THE NEXT EXCITING ADVENTURE OF GABRIEL HUNT!

THE GABRIEL HUNT ADVENTURES

"A pulp adventure series with classic style and modern sensibilities… Escapism at its best."
Publishers Weekly

From the towers of Manhattan to the jungles of South America, from the sands of the Sahara to the frozen crags of Antarctica, one man finds adventure everywhere he goes: Gabriel Hunt.

Backed by the resources of the $100 million Hunt Foundation and armed with his trusty Colt revolver, Gabriel Hunt has always been ready for anything—but is he prepared for the adventures that lie in wait for him?

HUNT AT THE WELL OF ETERNITY
James Reasoner

The woman carrying the bloodstained flag seemed desperate for help—and the attack that followed convinced Gabriel she had something men would kill for. And that was before he knew about the legendary secret hidden in the rain forest of Guatemala…

HUNT THROUGH THE CRADLE OF FEAR
Charles Ardai

When a secret chamber is discovered inside the Great Sphinx of Egypt, its contents will lead Gabriel to a remote Greek island, to a stone fortress in Sri Lanka… and to a confrontation that could decide the fate of the world!

HUNT BEYOND THE FROZEN FIRE
(June 2014)
Christa Faust

Dr. Lawrence Silver vanished while researching a mysterious phenomenon near the South Pole. His beautiful daughter wants to know where and why—and it's up to Gabriel Hunt to find out. But what they'll discover at the heart of nature's most brutal climate could change the world forever…

HUNT AMONG THE KILLERS OF MEN
(July 2014)
David J. Schow

The warlord's men came to New York to preserve a terrible secret—and left a dead body in their wake. Now Gabriel Hunt is on their trail, a path that will take him to the treacherous alleyways and rooftops of Shanghai and a showdown with a madman out to resurrect a deadly figure from China's past…

HUNT THROUGH NAPOLEON'S WEB
(August 2014)
Raymond Benson

Of all the priceless treasures Gabriel Hunt has sought, none means more to him than the one drawing him to the rugged terrain of Corsica and the exotic streets of Marrakesh: his own sister's life. To save her, Hunt will have to challenge the mind of a tyrant two centuries dead—the calculating, ingenious Napoleon Bonaparte…

TITANBOOKS.COM

THE LOST MIKE HAMMER SERIES
By Mickey Spillane & Max Allan Collins

LADY, GO DIE!
COMPLEX 90
KING OF THE WEEDS

Praise for Mickey Spillane & Max Allan Collins

"Mike Hammer is an icon of our culture."
The New York Times

"A superb writer. Spillane is one of the century's bestselling authors." *The Plain Dealer*

"Collins' witty, hardboiled prose would make Raymond Chandler proud." *Entertainment Weekly*

"Collins displays his mastery of Spillane's distinctive two-fisted prose." *Publishers Weekly*

"Collins knows the pistol-packing PI inside and out, and Hammer's vigilante rage (and gruff way with the ladies) reads authentically." *Booklist*

"A fun read that rings to the way the character was originally written by Spillane." *Crimespree Magazine*

"Another terrific Mike Hammer caper that moves non-stop like a flying cheetah across the reader's field of imagination." *Pulp Fiction Reviews*

HARD CASE CRIME
From the authors of GABRIEL HUNT

FIFTY-TO-ONE
Charles Ardai

After publishing a supposed non-fiction account of a
heist at a Mob-run nightclub, our hero is about to learn
that reading and writing pulp novels is a lot more fun
than living them…

GUN WORK
David J. Schow

Life isn't always cheap south of the border—the Mexican
kidnapping cartel was demanding a million dollars for
Carl's wife. It was time to call in some favors. Because some
situations call for negotiation, but some… call for gun work.

MONEY SHOT
Christa Faust

It all began with the phone call asking former porn star
Angel Dare to do one more movie. Before she knew it,
she'd been shot and left for dead. She'll get to the bottom
of what's been done to her even if she has to leave a trail of
bodies along the way…

CHOKE HOLD
Christa Faust

Angel Dare went into Witness Protection to escape her past
But when a former co-star is gunned down, it's up to Angel
to get his son safely through the Arizona desert, shady
Mexican bordertowns, and the neon mirage of Las Vegas…

TITANBOOKS.COM

HARD CASE CRIME
From Mickey Spillane & Max Allan Collins

THE CONSUMMATA
Mickey Spillane & Max Allan Collins

Compared to the $40 million the cops think he stole, $75,000 may not sound like much. But it's all the money in the world to the Cuban exiles who rescued Morgan the Raider. So when it's stolen, Morgan sets out to get it back.

DEAD STREET
Mickey Spillane

For 20 years, former NYPD cop Jack Stang has lived with the memory of his girlfriend's death. But what if she weren't actually dead? Now Jack has a second chance to save the only woman he ever loved—or to lose her for good…

DEADLY BELOVED
Max Allan Collins

Marcy Addwatter killed her husband—there's no question about that. But where the cops might see an open-and-shut case, private eye Michael Tree—*Ms.* Michael Tree—sees a conspiracy. Digging into it could mean digging her own grave… and digging up her own murdered husband's…

SEDUCTION OF THE INNOCENT
Max Allan Collins

Comics are corrupting America's youth. Or so Dr. Werner Frederick would have people believe. When the crusade provokes a murder, Jack Starr—comics syndicate troubleshooter—has no shortage of suspects.

TITANBOOKS.COM

HARD CASE CRIME
From Lawrence Block

BORDERLINE

On the border between Texas and Mexico, five lives are about to collide—with fatal results. The gambler, the divorcee, the beautiful hitchhiker, and the killer with a razor in his pocket…

GETTING OFF

A beautiful and deadly female serial killer is working her way across the country, tracking down every man she's ever slept with—the ones who got away—and ruthlessly murdering them…

GRIFTER'S GAME

Con man Joe Marlin was used to scoring easy cash off women. But that was before he met Mona Brassard and found himself facing the most dangerous con of his career, one that will leave him a killer—or a corpse.

KILLING CASTRO

There were five of them, each prepared to kill, each with his own reasons for accepting what might well be a suicide mission. The pay? $20,000 apiece. The mission? Find a way into Cuba and kill Castro.

LUCKY AT CARDS

Cardsharp Bill Maynard is hungry for action—but not nearly as hungry as the wife of Bill's latest mark. They hatch a scheme to get rid of her husband. But in life as in poker, the other player sometimes has an ace up his sleeve…

TITANBOOKS.COM